Never With You

Anie Michaels

Never With You

© Copyright Anie Michaels 2017

Edited by Lawrence Editing

Cover design © Cover Couture

To my grandfather —

You are missed.

Chapter One

Talia

"Don't forget to bring in the twins' things, Talia."

Angela, my sister-in-law, said the words as she walked past me, throwing them over her shoulder, not even stopping to look at me. I gaped at her, but wasn't surprised. Well, I suppose I was a little surprised the entitlement had started so soon into our vacation.

Once a year, during the summer, my parents, my brother, his family, and I, all went on a week-long vacation to the beach. My parents put down a decent amount of money to secure a beach house for seven days, leaving a small balance that my brother and I had to split. This tradition had been taking place for over ten years, since right after I graduated from college.

For a while we'd always rented the same house, but then my brother began dating Angela and things started changing. She didn't like the beach house we'd spent every summer in, so one year she convinced my brother to coerce my mother into switching beaches. The next winter my brother married her and every year since she'd been slowly killing my beach vacation.

This summer she had the twins.

My niece and nephew, whom I loved tremendously. It wasn't their fault who their mother was, after all.

And to be honest, when Brody started dating Angela, I'd liked her. She seemed sweet and genuine, and I could tell she really loved my brother. But then the more comfortable she got, her true colors started showing.

She expected me to carry in all the luggage for the twins because they had fallen asleep in the car on the drive over and she didn't want to disturb them by waking them up. She was going to hold them until, well, who knows when. She had little Raina and my brother was holding Beckett.

1

And since I was young, single, and childless, I was the designated work horse, apparently.

Angela had picked the perfect house—for her family. It was quiet, isolated, relatively close to the beach and nothing else.

Nothing.

Else.

There were no restaurants within twenty miles, no shopping malls, no movie theaters.

Nothing.

Angela had said she wanted a quiet getaway, a place to relax, where she could focus on the babies. And I wanted to focus on the babies too, but there were twenty-two other hours in the day that I'd have to fill in the middle of nowhere.

I lugged three suitcases, one portable crib, and a portable changing table up to the second floor of the house while Brody and Angela slept on the two recliners in the downstairs family room, their precious babies asleep on their chests.

If it wasn't so damn cute it would have pissed me off. Actually, it did piss me off.

"Dad, let me carry your bags upstairs," I said to my father, who was not as young anymore as he believed himself to be.

"I can carry my own bags, Talia," he replied grumpily.

"I think I saw Mom trying to figure out how to get the pilot light going on the furnace," I said, taking the bag from his hand as soon as he registered what I'd said.

"She's going to blow this place up while we're still inside," he grumbled, walking away.

I smiled because I'd won. I'd lied, but won regardless. I had no idea where my mother was. Probably upstairs making up beds for everyone. My mother was a pleaser. She wanted to take care of everyone. That was usually a good quality to have, and my mother meant well. My problem was that she was always trying to take care of me even though I didn't need or want her help. And when I didn't give in to her, she tried to help Angela, and that always turned into something different. It meant my mom was always giving in to Angela. Hence our boring beach house.

I walked up and down the stairs a million times until every single piece of luggage was upstairs, in the appropriate bedroom. I thought it was typical that my brother and I paid equally to make up the difference from my parents' down payment, but he and his family took up an extra room and made the ultimate decision as to where we stayed. But these were thoughts I kept in my head; speaking them aloud would do more harm than good.

My bedroom was the smallest in the house. A tiny room with a single twin bed, no closet, and no private bathroom. There was one tiny seaport window and I considered myself lucky to have an ocean view. I was pretty sure Angela didn't know I could see the ocean from my bedroom or she would have found some reason to move me. I took a few moments to unpack my things into the small dresser in my room, then made my way back downstairs.

I sat on the couch across from Angela and Brody. Both of them still had their eyes closed and, to be honest, I knew they needed the rest. Being the parents to eight-month-old twins was probably the most exhausting thing in the world, so I didn't begrudge them their nap.

Settling onto the couch, I pulled out my phone and opened my e-reader app.

"Talia."

I looked up when I heard Angela's whispering voice.

3

"We're trying really hard to keep the kids screen-free for the first two years."

She held my gaze and the silence settled between us. I must have looked confused, because I was. "Okay," I said slowly, drawing the word out. "Sounds good." When I didn't say anything else or make a move, she looked pointedly down at my phone.

"I would appreciate it if you could keep your phone turned off if you're in the same room as the babies." Her tone was polite, but cold.

"Angela," my brother chimed in, his voice sounding so tired and raspy. But it also sounded like a warning.

"They're sleeping," I argued. "Their eyes are closed."

"But, they're still *here*, Talia."

"Are you serious?" I wasn't asking to be rude. I was looking for clarification. "I think when pediatricians warn against screen time, it's a warning against putting them in front of a TV, a warning against letting their underdeveloped eyes look at a screen. I don't think there's anything that warns against kids being in the *same room* as screens… if they're sleeping."

"I don't expect you to understand. Maybe one day, if you have kids of your own, you'll see where I'm coming from." She sighed. "I'm not saying you can't look at your phone, just please don't do it in the same room as the babies."

I knew Brody could hear us and I was waiting for him to say something to his wife, to tell her she was being ridiculous, but he didn't. He just let out a large sigh. Didn't even open his eyes.

Instead of responding, I stood up and went back upstairs. And I stomped the whole way. Immature? Possibly. Warranted? I thought so.

I changed into my bathing suit, grabbed my towel and flip-flops and my hoodie—the Oregon coast wasn't known for its warm temperatures all the time—and I headed back down the stairs, stomping all the way. My mother met me halfway down.

"Where are you going?"

"To the beach. To read."

"That sounds relaxing." My mom gave me a sweet smile, as though she were relieved I was actually going to do something besides sulk all week. She probably wouldn't be surprised to learn I was actually sulking right then.

"Well, I don't want to disturb the babies."

"That's nice, dear." She continued up the stairs and I clomped down the last of them. I opened the slider door, not even glancing in Angela's or Brody's direction. I tried to slam it shut, but it was heavy, so I probably just looked as though I was struggling. There were folded lounge chairs leaning up against the back of the house, so I took one and found the path leading from the house down to the beach.

Oregon had beautiful beaches. That was my only consolation when my parents had settled on this house—it was a gorgeous beach. From the deck you passed the pool with a gate and took a walk through some grassy dunes. Once you were over the hills, it was just sand and ocean.

I stopped at the crest of the dune and took in the view. The ocean was my favorite place to be and just seeing it, taking it in, listening to it, calmed me. A part of me felt guilty about the way I'd acted toward Angela, and I would apologize to her about it, but there also had to be some way to make her see that just because I wasn't married with kids, it didn't mean I was inconsequential. I was an equal member of the family with equal say. We would all need to have a conversation sooner or later if I was expecting to make it through our vacation with my sanity intact.

I decided to leave my anger at the house and let myself enjoy the beach, even if I was sent outside for ridiculous reasons.

Walking closer to the water, I enjoyed the way the sand went from being warm and soft, to being wet and hard. When it reached the right consistency, I unfolded my chair and put it down, making sure the sun was pointed directly at me. I situated myself facing the water. Looking up and down the shore, I could count the number of people I saw on both hands. Turned out, an isolated beach wasn't that bad after all.

The sun was high and warm, and the wind was absent—a rarity on the Oregon coast. I draped my towel over my chair, took off my cover-up, kicked off my flip-flops, and sat down to read in the sunlight. I'd started this particular book weeks before, never finding the time to sit down and read, vowing I would finish it on this vacation. It seemed likely and very possible as there wasn't much else to do.

When I woke up, the sun was still high in the sky, but the beach was empty. I was never a midday napper, so falling asleep in the afternoon was rare for me. My e-reader was lying on the sand and I was slouched down on the lounge chair. I couldn't remember a moment in the last month where I felt as relaxed as I did right then. The sun had warmed my skin and the sound of the ocean had lulled me to sleep.

I was so relaxed, in fact, I decided not to move. Instead, I looked out at the ocean, watching the waves crash onto the shore. The tide was out and the waves weren't really impressive close in, but beyond the break they were mesmerizing to watch. After staring out to sea for a few minutes, a figure came into view. I watched as a person surfed, riding a wave as far as he could, then fell into the water with a decent splash.

Surfing in that part of Oregon was pretty rare. Not only was the water frigid year-round, but the surf wasn't actually that good. Very few times had I ever seen a person surfing on the Oregon coast, and when I did see someone, they were just averagely skilled. Nothing impressive, just someone who enjoyed riding mediocre waves.

But this person, this man—if I was seeing correctly—was doing more with the small waves than I'd ever seen. I watched him surf for an hour, just sitting in my lounge chair, eyes glued to him. The way his body moved, the control he had even when battling the sea, it was impressive and startling. And even though it must have taken so much strength and ability to surf that well, I was also drawn to the beauty of the movement. Watching his board dance across the water, the way I couldn't always tell if he was directing the board or if the board was directing him, was fascinating. When he finally came out of the water, I couldn't deny the disappointment that washed over me. I wanted to watch him surf all afternoon.

He made his way to where the sand was less solid, where your feet sank down into the warmth, and stabbed the end of his board into the grains. He picked up a towel he must have stashed there while I was sleeping and used it to dry off the parts of him that weren't in a wetsuit. His hair lightened once he'd run the towel over it a few times, and even though he was far away, I could see the strands of golden hair woven among the dark brown.

I felt like a total creeper just watching him, but I couldn't take my eyes off him. He was captivating. Especially when he started pulling down the zipper of his wet suit. I gawked. Openly. Operating under the possibly false impression that the dune I was next to was hiding me. The rational girl in the back of my mind told me that if I could see him, he could see me, but I was banking on the idea that he wasn't going to look in my direction; he had no reason to.

I watched as he pulled the zipper down the back, pulling on the long dangling string, and then slowly peeled the fabric down his arms, one by one. My mouth was suddenly dry and it felt as though I was swallowing sand paper. My breath caught when he continued to peel the suit down his torso, revealing his absolutely chiseled chest. He kept pulling, and I found myself saying a prayer that he'd take the wetsuit all the way off, but sadly he stopped right before the grand finale.

Then, like he knew I needed it, he dragged the towel over the newly revealed skin, making the muscles in his arms and abs flex and pull with every movement.

I might have whimpered.

Each of his muscles were perfectly and acutely defined. Even from a distance I could see the lines between each of his abs. But he wasn't bulky. It didn't look as though he built his muscles in a gym mindlessly lifting weights, but more like he'd developed them by using his body to do the things he enjoyed— like surfing. He definitely had a swimmer's body, his shoulders wide and back tapered to his waist. I wanted to take a picture, but didn't want to out myself as the creeper that I was.

He grabbed both ends of his towel and draped it over the back of his neck, then yanked his board out of the sand and walked away from the ocean. I craned my neck to watch him go, a weird and pathetic panic floating through me at the thought of never seeing him again. After his head disappeared behind another low dune, I decided I didn't give a fuck about public perception and stood to watch him wander away. I figured if he was walking away from me, he wouldn't have the opportunity to catch me stalking him.

I watched him walk up a similar path to the one I'd taken to the beach, just a little bit farther south than mine. My eyes followed him as he walked up the steps to a house, opened the sliding glass door, and disappeared inside.

The house he entered was the next house down the beach from my rental.

We were neighbors.

Chapter Two

Talia

"Sweetheart, can you grab the meat plate from your mother?"

My dad spent our summer vacations as king of the grill. If he could be outside grilling, he would be. He didn't get a lot of time to grill at home, and I sometimes thought he felt about grilling the way I felt about reading or getting a pedicure. This was why I felt badly for him in that moment. The rain had started about a half hour earlier, and even though my dad was optimistic, he was also being a little unreasonable.

"Dad, it's practically pouring. Come inside. We can broil the steaks. It's not safe to be out here." As if Mother Nature was trying to say I was right, a loud crack of thunder peeled through the sky, making me jump. It scared my father too, but it also made him decide his grilling dreams were dashed for the night. I hurried him in the house, both of us standing just inside the door, trying to shake off what rain water we could.

"Could you please close the door, Talia? I don't want the babies catching a draft."

I looked at Angela, who had both the babies in the traveling, folding high chairs I'd brought in from the car earlier that day. I didn't bother responding, but I did close the door. I didn't want the babies sick either.

"I guess we'll have to broil the steaks," my dad said with way too much sadness to be talking about meat.

"That'll be great, honey," my mother replied sweetly, knowing how much my father liked to be outside grilling. "Talia, dear, will you turn the broiler on?"

"Sure." As I was walking to the stove the lights flickered a few times and then went out completely. The sun had only been set for about an hour, but that close to the beach there were no streetlights or anything besides stars to offer any light, so the house went pretty dark fast. The babies immediately started crying and I heard Brody and Angela working to get them out of their seats.

"Just calm down, everyone. It's just a power outage. I'm sure lightning just hit a transformer. Let's find a flashlight or something."

My dad and I pulled out our cell phones and used the lights to look through the kitchen drawers, but neither of us found a flashlight.

"I'll head out to the garage and see if there's a flashlight or a lantern out there."

"Oh, honey, be careful. Talia, go with him."

"On it," I said, following behind my father. Dad was in his sixties and still pretty active and fit, but wandering around a dark and unfamiliar house was sort of a recipe for disaster. We made it to the garage and went inside. It was even darker in there because there were no windows. "Dad, just stay here. I'll go look."

There were only a few shelves and as I shone cell phone light around, I finally found a small flashlight.

"Got it," I said with excitement.

"That's my girl."

I pressed the button on the side and heard it click, but no light came out. "I think it's broken," I said, clicking the button over and over again. I walked back to my dad and handed it to him, then followed him back to the kitchen where we could see a little better. I heard him clicking it on and off too, but still no light. Once we got to the counter he unscrewed the lid and then turned it upside down.

"There aren't any batteries," he said grumpily. "For as much as we paid for this rental, there should at least be working flashlights with fresh batteries."

"Talia, are you sure you looked everywhere in the garage? Could you have missed any other flashlights?" This came from Angela.

"You're more than welcome to go look for yourself."

"I think it's best I stay here with the babies. They're frightened."

"There weren't a whole lot of shelves and they were all sparse."

"Maybe the power will come back on shortly," my mother said, her voice hopeful.

"If it's a transformer, it will probably take a few hours."

"I can drive to the convenience store we saw a few miles back," I offered. "I'm sure they sell batteries, maybe even flashlights or candles."

"I don't want you driving in this rain, especially on unfamiliar roads." My father was always protective over me. "There's a house just south of us on the other side of the dune. I'll walk over there and see if they have anything we can borrow for the night."

"Dad, no." I sighed, a little irritated that Brody had yet to chime in to help solve the problem. "You're not going to walk in the dark across the dune. I'll go."

"No, Talia, I don't want you out there in this storm," he said, his voice growing louder with his parental need to keep me safe.

"Dad, it's fine. I saw the other house this afternoon on the beach. I've seen the path to the house, and I know I can get there and back in ten minutes, tops."

"George, I think she'll be fine. Let her go. You sit and take a rest."

"I don't need to rest, Lillian."

"It'll be okay. I'll be right back." I put on my tennis shoes and my zip-up hoodie—wasn't planning to go out in a monsoon, so I hadn't packed my raincoat—and I walked out the back door. In the twenty minutes since I'd been on the porch with my father, the wind and rain had really picked up. I was drenched completely through my hoodie in about ten seconds and the rain was freezing. Summers on the Oregon coast meant nothing when it came to temperature. It could be sixty degrees one day and eighty the next, and the rain was never warm.

I jogged over the dune closest to our house. Well, I tried to jog. The sand was still hard to move through, but when I made it over the dune I turned south, looking for the break in the grass for the path leading to the next house down the beach. I found it after a few minutes of looking and worrying I'd gone too far, but when I saw it I jogged back up the beach until the same house I'd spied on earlier came into view.

It looked a lot different than it had that afternoon, though. Houses on the beach with absolutely no light looked absurdly scary. Almost as though it were abandoned. The house sat all alone, making it even creepier, with no houses around for at least one hundred yards, our rental being the closest.

As I made my way closer to the house, I did notice the shine of a flashlight moving about the windows and I was relieved that someone was home. It would have sucked to go out in that storm all for nothing.

I came upon the house, hoping no one could see me. I was sure I looked like some burglar sneaking around strange houses in the darkness of night. I didn't want to be mistaken for a criminal and shot by the homeowners. I quickly made my way to the front of the house, which sat situated away from the beach. I knocked on the door, my teeth chattering and body shaking.

13

I heard footsteps inside the house and when they sounded to be just on the other side of the door, I put on my best not-crazy-stalker-or-burglar smile.

The door swung open and sure enough, the hot surfer man was on the other side. He looked shocked to see me, or anyone I imagined, and I was sure I looked like a drowned rat.

"H-h-hi," I stuttered, my teeth chattering so badly I could hardly speak. "I'm f-f-rom the house just north of you, and w-w-we don't have a working fl-flashlight. D-do you happen to have one we can b-borrow?"

He stared at me for a moment, but then shook his head like he was trying to clear his mind and stepped back. "Come in," he said, motioning into his house with his hand. "You look like you're freezing," he said, stepping back and making room for me.

"I'm f-f-fine," I muttered.

The side of his mouth tipped up into a smile. "Sure, you sound super fine."

I gave him a smile in return, and then he led me into what I assumed to be the living room and kitchen area. There were a few candles lit and a fire going in the fireplace, but other than that, his house was in disarray. I couldn't see clearly, but there wasn't any furniture besides a few chairs, and there weren't any appliances in the kitchen either. Tools and supplies were scattered and it looked like parts of the floor were torn up too.

"I keep a spare flashlight here in my toolbox and it should still work."

I watched him walk through his torn-up house, only lit by candles, and tried very hard not to imagine the fabulous muscles I'd seen that afternoon, currently hidden beneath his T-shirt. His hair still looked dark, but I couldn't figure out if it was his true color, or if the lack of light was making it look that way.

14

I was still shivering as he bent down next to a rather large-looking box, and I tried to keep my eyes from his backside, but again, it was useless. He was ten times more handsome up close and in person than he was from across the beach, even in the dark. Perhaps proximity had something to do with it, and the candlelight. Even his voice was sexy. It was deep and sultry, almost like he sounded sleepy.

"Aha," he said with satisfaction, then stood up and walked toward me, all while flicking the flashlight in his hands on and off. "Looks like it still works." He held it out to me and when I reached for it, my hand trembled so much I could hardly grasp it.

"Th-thanks."

"You're in the house up the beach? The one just north of me?"

"Y-yeah. We're r-r-renting it for the week."

"All right, well, why don't I give you a coat to wear back and I'll walk you. I've got a big umbrella so you at least won't get soaked through again."

"That's really n-nice of you," I said as I tried not to search for the color of his eyes. "But you don't have to do that. It's not that far."

Even though it was dark, I could see him lift his eyebrows in exasperation and then run his eyes from my head to my toes.

"You're soaked. And freezing. I'll walk you." His tone was commanding and kind all at the same time, and even though I thought it was silly for us both to go out, I didn't want to tell him no again.

"All right," I whispered.

He walked past me and went up the stairs by the door. I heard his loud footsteps moving around the second floor and after a minute he made his way back downstairs.

"Here," he said, holding open a jacket for me.

I turned and threaded my arms through the sleeves.

"Thank you." I faced him again, noticing he was also wearing a jacket. Immediately the extra dry layer started to warm me up. All I could think about, though, was a nice warm shower.

"Ready?" he asked, his voice so rough and scratchy. Something about it made goosebumps pop up on my already pebbled flesh.

"Sure."

He opened the door for me and followed me out. I noticed he didn't bother locking the door, which struck me as small-town. Where I lived, there was no way you'd leave your door unlocked, even for five minutes. The umbrella popped open, startling me back to the present, and we moved forward together off his porch. We headed toward the ocean, walking closer to each other than I normally would have with a stranger, but it was a necessity if we were both going to stay out of the rain.

"This isn't a very good way to spend a vacation," he said, practically yelling over the noise of the storm.

"No, I guess not. But it's typical Oregon, right?"

"So, you're not from out-of-state, then?" He laughed when he asked the question and I knew why. Only an Oregonian would understand the weather and roll with the proverbial punches.

"No. My parents live in Portland, but I'm in Bend right now."

"Bend is a really beautiful town."

"Yeah, I love it there."

We'd made it out past the dune and we turned north, walking in sync, until we met with the path to my rental.

"Do you like living on the coast... oh my gosh! I'm sorry. I never even asked your name." My hand covered my face in embarrassment. "I'm Talia," I said, reaching my hand out the very small distance to him.

He took my hand, laughing, and then said with his wonderfully gravelly voice, "I'm Briggs. It's nice to meet you, although I'm sorry about the circumstances."

"Well, you know, vacation can't be all smooth sailing. There must be some strife, I suppose."

"I guess you're right."

We came up to the back porch and Briggs stopped walking. "You're not staying here alone, are you?" He asked the question with concern, and the thought of him worrying over me made my chest tighten.

"Um, no. Quite the opposite, in fact. My mother, father, brother, sister-in-law, and twin baby niece and nephew are all inside." Even in the dark I could see the surprise come over his face. "I appreciate the concern, but I'm not alone. Even though I sort of wish I were sometimes." We both laughed, but neither of us moved away. "Well, thank you for the flashlight and the coat. Oh, here. Take it back with you." I moved to take the coat off, but he grabbed both sides of the jacket by the zipper and pulled it closed over my body. It also made my body sway closer to his and the proximity made my heart beat faster.

"It's okay. You keep it for now."

"Okay, thanks again."

He smiled and it was impossible not to smile back. I turned and ran up the stairs, onto the porch, and up to the sliding glass door.

"Oh, good, you got a flashlight," my mother said, taking it from me. "You're soaked, Talia. And whose coat is that?"

"Um, Briggs. The man who lives in the house next door. He lent it to me." I peeled it off and set it on the back of a chair, then made my way to the stairs. "I'm going to take a shower and try to warm up."

"Tal, you can't take a shower without electricity. The water will be cold."

"Not if the water heater runs on gas," my father chimed in.

"Why would there be a gas water heater when the stove is electric?" argued Brody.

"The heat is gas," my mother offered.

I rolled my eyes and walked up the stairs, leaving them to argue about it. If anything, I just wanted to get the cold, soaked clothes off my body. I could still hear my family debating as I closed the door to my room. I flipped the light switch, but then laughed at myself when the light didn't come on. The room was very dark and my little port hole window didn't let much light in.

Peeling the wet clothes off surprisingly only made me colder. I left the clothes in a pile on the bathroom floor, put on the warmest pajamas I brought—which weren't very warm at all, just a T-shirt and leggings—and climbed into my bed, wrapping all the blankets around me as tight as I could.

I lay in bed, listening to the storm rage and the waves break, thinking too much about Briggs and how our brief interaction only made me even more curious about him. He seemed to be in that house alone. He certainly didn't tell anyone he was leaving with me. And the house was definitely under construction. Was he renovating? Did he even live there? Was it someone else's house? And even though all those questions were running through my mind, the image of him slipping out of his wetsuit was definitely what I fell asleep thinking about.

Chapter Three

Talia

Sunlight and the sound of seagulls woke me the next morning. I rolled toward the window to see a cloudless and bright blue sky.

"Typical," I murmured as I pushed the covers off. I was warm, but I still felt like I'd been running through a rain storm. The bedroom light was on and I wondered when the power had come back on. It didn't really matter. All that mattered was the warm water raining down on my hand after I'd turned on the shower.

Usually, I was more of a conservationist, but that morning I took the longest shower I'd had in a while. In fact, I stayed in there until the water ran cold and I didn't even feel badly about everyone else in the house possibly having to wait for theirs. I'd earned that shower.

After consulting my weather app and making sure we weren't expecting another surprise monsoon, I slipped into my favorite pair of white shorts and paired it with a green flowy tank. Green was a staple color in my wardrobe because there weren't many colors that didn't clash with my red hair.

Bouncing down the stairs, the smell of bacon cooking made my stomach grumble.

"Morning," I called to my mother, who was manning the stove.

"Morning, sweetie. I'm glad to see you didn't catch a death of a cold."

"No cold. I feel great."

I heard what sounded like a heard of elephants clomping down the stairs and looked to see Brody and Angela, both holding a baby.

"Oh, give me one of those babies," I said, holding my hands out in their general direction. "I don't care which one. Surprise me."

"Here," Angela said as she handed me whichever child she had with a smile.

Situating the baby so I could see its face, I gave a big smile. "Raina, my little princess," I said, showering her chubby face with kisses. Raina giggled and my ovaries melted a little on the inside. "You smell so good," I said, my face smooshed against her hair.

I looked up and saw my mom watching me with sad eyes. As soon as she caught my eye, she turned back around to cook her bacon, but I'd already seen the pitying look she wore on her face. If asked, I could have recited exactly what she was thinking too. She was probably all upset because she thought my opportunity to have children had passed. I wasn't sure which made me angrier—the fact that she felt that way or the fact that part of me agreed with her.

"After the enormous breakdowns they had last night when the power went out, the only thing that would calm them down was a warm bath," Angela said, sounding exhausted.

"Did it take a long time for the power to come back on?" I asked, still making silly faces at my niece.

"Only about an hour," Brody said, bouncing Beckett on his knees while sitting on the couch. "By the way, Mom, Angela and I were hoping that you and Dad could watch the twins tonight so we could go out to dinner."

"Oh, that's a good idea, sweetheart. We'd love to."

"You're going to have to drive at least forty-five minutes to find any decent restaurants," I said mostly to myself, but loud enough so everyone could hear me.

"We don't mind the drive. It'll be relaxing. In fact, an hour in a car without a baby almost sounds like a vacation in itself."

"I don't know how you two do it," my mother mused, again focused on the stove. "Having one at a time was hard enough."

Angela and Brody exchanged a look, and then Angela turned back to me and motioned toward the staircase with her head.

"Talia, do you think you could help me with something upstairs?" Her eyes were too wide and eyebrows too high, and I knew there was something she wanted to talk to me about in private.

"Uh, sure," I replied, trying to sound cooler than she had, which wasn't very hard. Keeping Raina pressed close to me, I stood and followed Angela up the stairs and into the room she was sharing with my brother. "What's up?" I asked, keeping my voice low. I knew by her tone downstairs whatever we were discussing wasn't to be shared with my mother.

"Brody and I were talking, and we were hoping you could be here tonight while we go out to dinner."

My eyebrows pressed together in confusion. "You want me to help watch the babies?"

Raina took that opportunity to put her entire baby fist in my mouth. I had to giggle a little because it was so stupidly cute, but then I kissed her chubby little fist and placed it in her lap, hoping it would stay out of my mouth.

"Well, yes. We don't want to overwhelm your parents, but we also don't want them to feel as though we think they're incapable."

"But you do?" This was the first I'd heard of Brody and Angela worrying about my parents watching the kids.

21

"Well, when they were tiny it was easy to watch them. They didn't do much. It was mainly just feeding and changing. But now, they're starting to crawl and getting into things. They could choke on their food. They could fall off a couch or something if they're left alone. There are just so many things that could go wrong and they've been out of the baby game for a long time. Your mother just said she didn't know how we do it!" Angela was getting upset and that was the last thing I wanted.

"Hey, it's all right. Mom and Dad aren't, like, ancient yet. It hasn't been too long since they had babies. I'm sure it's like riding a bicycle."

The stern glare Angela gave me indicated she didn't agree with my assessment of parenting.

"Listen, I just know I won't be able to enjoy myself if I'm worried one of the babies has rolled down the stairs."

I pulled Raina close to me as that terrible image popped into my mind.

"Okay, well, I'm not sure why we're even discussing this. It's not like there's a plethora of places for me to go."

"Don't be a Negative Nancy, Talia. Just because we didn't stay at the most touristy city on the coast doesn't mean you get to be bitchy all week."

There were a million things I wanted to say to her. A million responses I'd carefully planned and said over and over again in my mind. But I was forever a people-pleaser. A peacekeeper. A pushover.

"You're right." I said the words as I brushed my hand over the soft downy hairs on little Raina's head. "I'll be here."

"Thank you," she gushed, leaning over to hug me. Angela wasn't really a hugger, unless it was my brother she was hugging, so I knew she was truly grateful. And I knew deep down that she and my brother deserved a night away.

"No problem."

When we made it downstairs, the table was set and it was time for breakfast. Angela and Brody spent the meal talking about all the places they could go that night, and my father only spoke enough to mention he'd had to take a cold shower that morning because someone had used all the hot water. My mother calmly pointed out that perhaps it was just a glitch from the power outage. I didn't offer any other explanation.

"Talia," my mother said as we cleared the table. "Help me make some cookies to bring to the nice man next door who lent us that flashlight."

Briggs immediately flashed through my brain, but it wasn't the Briggs from last night, it was the Briggs from the beach yesterday afternoon. My eyes automatically wandered to the ocean, wondering if he was going to be surfing at all that day.

"We need to get that flashlight back to him."

"And his coat," I said absentmindedly.

Brody's head snapped up and he looked at me. "You have his coat?"

"By the time I made it to his house last night I was drenched. He loaned me a coat." I shrugged, hoping he'd drop it.

"That was very sweet of him," my mother said innocently. "I hope he likes chocolate chip cookies."

Only my mother would bring everything you would need to make cookies on vacation. My mother's cookies were knockouts. Any kind of cookie she made was delicious, but her chocolate chip cookies were the best. I had never tasted a chocolate chip cookie that beat my mother's. She never made just one batch either because she knew they'd never last. She had it down to a science and we managed to make one hundred cookies in just a few hours. I knew my mother's recipe by heart, but could never replicate the taste no matter how hard I tried, but she did take the opportunity to teach Angela the recipe. It actually ended up being kind of fun. Who knew?

Luckily, the storm had passed and the bad weather seemed to be behind us. The sun was warm on my skin as I walked back over to Briggs's house, but the wind was blowing and since I had the tray of cookie in my hands I opted to put his jacket on for the walk over. As I walked over the dune in front of his house the sound of the ocean was replaced with the loud rock music coming from inside. As I got closer one song faded out and Bon Jovi's "Living on a Prayer" started. That song brought back so many high school memories, the smile that spread across my face was unavoidable.

The song was accompanied by the ominous sounds of various power tools. There was obviously a lot of work going on inside the house. When I knocked and no one answered, I wasn't surprised. There was no way he could hear me knocking over all the noise coming from his house. But, I knocked louder, hoping there'd be a lull in music or construction noise. No dice.

I considered my options. I could just leave the cookies and the coat on his front step, but that didn't seem like a very friendly way to say thank you. I could walk around the house and hope to grab someone's attention through a window, but that seemed a little stalkery.

I remembered the way he hadn't locked the door the night before and my hand instantly reached for the doorknob and gave it a slight twist. Unlocked. With just a little push the door was opened a smidge and I took a deep breath. I edged the door open a little bit more, just far enough to get my head through.

"Hello," I called out tentatively. I knew there was no way anyone could hear me over the loud music and the sounds of what I thought was an electric saw. I debated with myself for a moment, but then decided to go in, hoping I wasn't making a mistake. "Briggs?" I called his name out as I walked toward the living room. When I turned the corner I stopped and let my mouth hang open.

Briggs has his back to me, his *shirtless* back, and was definitely operating a saw. He was bent forward a little, but that didn't obstruct any view of his muscles. His right arm was moving back and forth while his left was pushing a piece of wood over, and the repetitive motions made every muscle of his back ripple in time. My eyes took their time wandering over his upper body, but then they dropped low and it was possible a groan slipped out of me.

Not only was Briggs shirtless, he was also wearing a tool belt. Now, up until that point in my life, I don't think I'd been within ten feet of anyone wearing a tool belt. Therefore, I had absolutely no idea how incredibly sexy they were. The belt rested on his trim hips, which were covered in denim, and the view of his ass in that moment made everything in me heat up and turn on. If I'd had a physical switch, Briggs had just flipped it.

I told myself I wasn't making myself known because I didn't want to startle him while he was using that saw. I couldn't have him losing a finger over my mother's chocolate chip cookies. But the truth was, I was grateful for those thirty seconds where I could openly gawk at him. It was twice in two days I'd been able to admire him without him knowing, and each day I was getting closer to him. It was thrilling.

Suddenly the loud screeching of the saw died down and I was only left with the sounds of Jon Bon Jovi. Briggs stood tall and picked up the last piece of wood he'd cut, and I knew I had to make myself known or else I was simply an intruder. A creepy intruder at that.

"Um, Briggs?" I called out loudly, still competing with an '80s rock anthem. "Briggs!" I yelled when he clearly hadn't heard me.

He spun around and wide, chocolate brown eyes landed on me, then softened when he realized who I was. He grabbed what looked like a little remote out of his tool belt, held it in the air, and Bon Jovi slowly faded away.

"Talia?" he asked, pushing the safety goggles up on his head.

"Hi. I'm sorry. The door was unlocked and you couldn't hear me…"

I couldn't think of anything else to say in the moment because my brain backfired. Completely went haywire on me. If the view of shirtless Briggs was good from the back, then, holy freaking cow, the view from the front was debilitating. He had lean muscle everywhere. Also, a tattoo on his left arm I hadn't noticed during my spying session the day before. The black tribal ink encompassed his shoulder and looked delectable against his tanned skin.

I finally managed to tear my eyes away from his body, only to turn them to the floor. I cleared my throat, hoping I looked a little less psycho than I felt, but then put a smile on and met his gaze.

"My mom sent me over with some thank-you cookies." I held the plate up as evidence.

It took him a few seconds to realize what in the hell I was talking about, but eventually I saw realization crash over him, and he gave me a polite smile.

"Oh, uh, thanks." He reached up and scratched the valley between his pectoral muscles, and then must have remembered he wasn't wearing a shirt because he immediately blushed and then quickly walked over to a chair, picked up the shirt that lay over the back, and pulled it on.

I was both saddened and relieved. It was a lot of pressure to be in the same room as him with no shirt on and keep my eyes above his neck.

"I brought your coat and flashlight back too."

"Wow, thanks. Your mom didn't have to go to all this trouble." Taking the plate from me, he gave me a polite smile.

"While she really is grateful for the help last night, she actually just appreciates any reason to bake cookies."

"Well, I'm more than happy to be the lucky recipient." Turning away from me and walking back into the kitchen, he spoke over his shoulder. "Sorry for the mess. I'm in the middle of a tiny remodel."

"Tiny?" I asked, looking around at a bottom floor that was practically torn apart. "This looks anything but tiny."

Hands on his waist, he looked around the house. "You're right. I'm in way over my head." He said the words on a sigh and I instantly panicked, fearing I'd offended him.

"It looks like you've got it under control, though," I rambled, trying to save the moment.

"No, seriously, I'm in way over my head. But I'm just trying to get some of the beginning steps out of the way. I've got an actual contractor coming out in a couple days to do the real work."

"Oh, are you flipping it?"

"Um, no." The words were heavy and suddenly it was clear I'd brought up something uncomfortable, and that made me uncomfortable. "I got this house in my divorce settlement, but I can't afford it on my own, so I have to sell it."

Shit.

"I'm sorry," I stammered immediately. "It's none of my business."

"No, it's fine."

We stood there, just staring at each other for a moment, the low sounds of another Bon Jovi song coming through his speakers, the air surrounding us so totally filled with awkwardness.

"Well, I should probably get back." I started to slip the coat off my shoulders and Briggs stepped forward to take it from me.

"You sure you don't want to stay and help me eat a few of these cookies? If you leave them all here I *will* eat them all myself and that's diabetes waiting to happen."

I had every reason to politely decline and go back to my own house and spend the rest of my vacation peeking through the blinds to steal glances at Briggs, but I couldn't make myself leave. Even knowing there were eighty more cookies waiting to be eaten at our rental house, I couldn't say no to him.

"I'd feel guilty for the rest of my life if I was responsible for your diagnosis."

He laughed, which was great because I wanted him to think I was funny, but not great because the sound of his laughter echoing through the mostly empty house sent shockwaves through me. It wasn't fair that his laugh and his shirtless body were both sexy. I needed some sort of equalizer. Something to make the blood stop rushing to my face and other various parts of my body.

"I don't have any milk, unfortunately. Will root beer do?" He pulled his fridge open and waved a can of Barq's in the air as if he were trying to tempt me.

As if I need to be tempted.

Stepping farther into the kitchen, I said, "Root beer's great. Milk is overrated as a beverage pairing with cookies."

He laughed again and my heart rate soared.

"I'm sorry I don't have any place for us to sit at the moment," he said, placing the plate of cookies between us on the counter covered in saw dust. He handed me the cold can with a smile and I couldn't help but reciprocate.

"How long have you lived here?" My mother's cookies were delicious, but the moment I picked one up and took a bite, I wasn't paying attention to the familiar taste, I was waiting to hear any tidbit I could about his life. It was sad, really, how badly I wanted to know anything about him.

"My ex-wife and I bought it about eight years ago. It was a vacation home, but we spent a lot of time here. Most of the summers, sporadic weekends throughout the spring and fall."

He said the words methodically, but there was a twinge of sadness there.

"It looks beautiful from the outside."

Again, he laughed. "The inside isn't as impressive?"

"Well, I mean, not everyone is partial to floors, but I sort of am."

"The floors are coming." He brought a cookie to his mouth and I tried not to watch as he took a bite, but my willpower was zapped to practically nothing at that point. "Wow," he said around the bite. "These are amazing."

"My mom loves baking. That cookie is probably fifteen years' worth of recipe experimentation and tweaking."

"Well, if she's looking for any feedback, tell her they were perfect." He took another bite and let out a tiny groan, making my breath catch in my lungs. "So, how long are you all staying next door?"

"Just the week. We leave Saturday. We take a family vacation every year, but this is our first summer here."

"You vacation every year with your family? You said you were with your mother and father, right?"

"Yeah, and my brother and his family. I know it sounds weird, but my parents pay for most of the trip and they kind of insist on it every summer." I gave a tiny, one-shouldered shrug. "I don't usually mind."

"But this time is different?"

I definitely didn't want to explain my family drama, and I also didn't want to paint myself as the spinster I sometimes identified as.

"I'm just used to being in bigger towns with more to do."

"You're bored?"

"A little," I replied honestly. "I mean, the beach is nice, but there's only so much time I can spend sitting in the sun."

"Well, if you've got a steady hand, I could always use some help over here." He uttered the words and then took another bite of cookie.

Was he inviting me to hang out? To help him work on his house? The offer would have seemed strange in any other context, but the fact of the matter was, ten years ago people met in bars and then went out on dates. Was it strange to be in a man's house whom I'd only ever spoken to for about ten minutes combined? Yes. But it wasn't any different, or better really, than getting a message from a complete stranger on a dating app and meeting that person for a drink, right? My whole family knew I was next door. Plus, Briggs gave off absolutely no creepy-murderer vibes.

"I don't think I'm qualified to do any kind of home improvement projects."

"Me neither. But here I am." His tone was a little more morose than I'd heard from him, and I wondered what had happened in his marriage to leave him with a beach house. I'd never been married, but I did know what all went into a committed relationship, and I wondered whether it had been Briggs's fault, his wife's, or a combination of both scenarios. Either way, it was none of my business. "A friend of mine, Patrick, his brother-in-law is a contractor and I've hired him to do most of the work. What I'm doing is mostly stuff anyone could do with a little YouTube and ambition. For instance, I was just cutting those pieces of molding and then I was going to take them outside and paint them."

"Just painting?"

"Well, today I'm just painting. Tomorrow there're other things on the agenda. Have to prep the floors. But the contractor will be here for that." He popped the rest of the cookie in his mouth and I tried not to watch his jaw move as he chewed. "Want to help?"

I shrugged. "I can paint."

Chapter Four

Briggs

The house next door, or down the beach anyway, was rented out often during the summer months. For years I'd watched people move in and out, coming and going, and I'd never paid them much mind. But when I'd seen a redhead in an even redder bikini lounging on the beach, well, that was impossible to ignore.

I'd been out surfing, trying to keep my mind off Cecily and the divorce, attempting to numb my mind with the motion poetry of surfing, when the red flair had caught my eye. Sitting atop my board, moving with the rhythm of the ocean, she was like an exploding firework against the tan-colored sand.

When she'd shown up at my door last night, drenched and asking for a flashlight, I hadn't thought much about it. I'd given her what she'd been looking for, but I hadn't connected the dots. Hadn't pieced together that the sopping wet woman at my door was the firecracker from the beach.

Now, as I watched her slowly drag a paintbrush over the crown molding I'd been cutting all morning, I tried to keep my cool. I'd seen her from afar in the bikini, but up close—and not drenched—it was all I could do to keep myself from imagining her in it again.

When it was obviously time to either tell her goodbye or invite her to stay, I surprised myself by extending the offer. Personable wasn't a word a lot of people would have used to describe me in the past months. A nasty divorce will do that to a man. It wasn't that I didn't want to interact with other people, I just wasn't sure how to go about it. For so long I was consumed with every emotion imaginable. Hurt, anger, rage, sadness—they all filtered through me at any given moment, and it was hard to be around others because everyone else all seemed so stable. I'd ostracized myself, licking my wounds, cursing women in general.

Talia was hard to curse, though. It was difficult to think anything but good things about her. My eyes kept wandering to her arm, toned and freckled, as she dragged the paintbrush back and forth. She was to my left and just a foot or so in front of me, and I was trying my damnedest to keep my eyes off her ass. The white shorts she was wearing kept creeping up every time she leaned closer to examine her work, then slink back down when she stood up straight. It was the best kind of torture.

The part that struck me the most was that I hadn't even noticed a woman since I walked in on Cecily fucking her co-writer. There hadn't been one woman who'd caught my eye. Not that I hadn't seen beautiful women in the last six months, I just wasn't interested.

And I wasn't interested in Talia, either. Well, I suppose I was, but not in a serious way. Something urged me to ask her to stay, but it wasn't necessarily attraction. I wasn't hoping to get to know her because I was interested in her. She seemed cool and Lord knew I'd been solitary for so long. It wouldn't kill me to socialize with anyone, even if it was over home renovations.

"So, these will go along the bottom of the walls? Like baseboards?" she asked, pulling me out of my blatant staring. I quickly moved my eyes off her ass and back to my own moldings and paintbrush.

"And the tops of the walls too. Kind of like a frame."

"That will look nice." She ran her paintbrush back and forth a few times, but then she spoke again. "So you're selling this house and then where will you live? Do you have a second house somewhere?"

"Nope. No second house. Well, Cecily and I had a second house, but she got that one in the divorce."

"Cecily is your ex?"

"Yeah. She got the house in Portland."

She must have heard the underlying anger in my voice because her question followed soon after.

"Pretty nasty divorce?"

I looked up and noticed she'd stopped painting and was turned toward me. Her eyes were soft and concerned, which seemed unusual seeing as how we hardly knew each other. What her eyes didn't convey, however, was pity or even curiosity, which was what I was usually met with. I couldn't stand gossipers, which was ironic seeing as how that was exactly what Cecily was. Talia didn't come across to me as someone who was digging for information. She seemed to be genuinely concerned, which was probably why my mouth opened up and words fell out.

"I'm not sure the divorce was any nastier than the separation. I walked in on Cecily and her colleague. Turns out, as I learned, she's been sleeping with him for a while."

"Ugh, that's horrible. I'm sorry. It really sucks when people you put your trust in take it and stab you in the back with it."

She sounded as though she was speaking from experience.

"The most ironic part of this whole situation is that Jeff— the guy she slept with—was her writing partner. They'd been coming here for a few years to work, or so I thought. But I walked in on them back in that room." I hooked a thumb over my shoulder, signaling to the room we'd just been in. "She fucked him in the house we bought together with the money from their books, and in the end she made me keep it."

Talia's mouth was gaping open in what I assumed was shock or exasperation. After a moment she snapped her mouth shut and turned back to the molding she was painting. After a few moments of running the paintbrush back and forth with much more force than before, she turned suddenly and pointed the paintbrush at me.

"You know what? That's really shitty. I know it's none of my business, and we don't even actually know each other at all, but you're better off."

She turned back around and continued to angrily paint my moldings. It occurred to me that since Cecily had ruined our marriage, no one had told me I was better off without her. Everyone, even my parents, were completely shocked and couldn't understand why it had happened. Our friends, who had been mostly hers, tried to comfort me for a little while, but eventually picked their sides and went back the same way they came: with Cecily. Not one person had looked me in the eye and said, "That's really shitty."

And it *was* shitty. Our marriage hadn't been perfect, but I'd done my best. Even when I'd had little suspicions that Cess was messing around with Jeff, I'd talked myself out of it, convinced myself she'd never do that to me. She wrote fucking romance novels, for Christ's sake.

"Wanna know the most ironic part?" I said, now completely willing to open up to Talia, finding my usual filter gone. Talia turned back around, angry scowl on her face. "Cecily and Jeff wrote romance novels together. They probably are up at the house in Portland thinking they've lived the most romantic fairy tale. Meanwhile, Jeff's wife and I are royally fucked. I lost everything that was important to me in that divorce. Not the house and not my pride, but my wife."

At my words, Talia's angry scowl subsided, and a more familiar pitying expression took its place.

"I'm sorry, Briggs. Really, I know what it feels like to be cheated on, and I remember the hurt."

Suddenly I understood the anger she'd expressed. She'd been hurt too. Cheated on.

"I'm sorry too, then," I replied.

"We weren't married, but we were together for a really long time. We might as well have been married."

"How long?"

"Eleven years," she answered without hesitation. That was three years longer than I'd been with Cecily.

"Damn, Talia. That sucks."

"Yeah, well, at least you got a house out of it. I left with nothing. It should have been some sort of indication that we'd been together for so long but hadn't taken any of the steps normal people take when they're building a life together. We still had separate bank accounts, we rented our house, we didn't cosign for each other's cars, nothing. We might as well have been roommates."

"He sounds like an asshole. Or, uh, she? Either way. They're a dumbass."

She gave me a smile. "He. Chris."

For some reason, hearing she was into men made me happy.

"Chris? He sounds like some sort of douchebag accountant."

She laughed and it caught me off guard. It was bright and airy, her laughter. My grip on the paintbrush tightened as I watched her. "Close," she said, still giggling through her words. "He was a stock broker."

"We sound like a pretty pathetic pair."

She turned her head to look at me, green eyes sparkling over a freckled shoulder. "Nah. Their loss, remember?"

We worked for another hour, passing the time by painting and talking. Talking to Talia was easy. She asked questions in a way that made me feel as though she was really interested in the answer, not just filling time or forcing awkward conversation. She asked the questions and she listened to the answers. My responses only made me curious about her, so I asked about her life too. Before I could even think much about it, it was after lunch time and my stomach was complaining.

A knock sounded at the door, drawing my attention away from Talia. I put my paintbrush down and walked through the house to open the door. I wasn't expecting anyone, so I was surprised to see who was on the other side.

"Briggs, good to see you, man."

"Patrick?" I said on a laugh as he pulled me into a manly hug. "What are you doing here?"

"Megan and I took a few days off work and decided to come to the beach. I knew you were here, so it didn't take much convincing. Plus, Meg's sister and her family are here too."

I took a step back, welcoming him into the house.

"Man, this place is torn up. You've got Porter coming to help you out?"

"Yeah, he'll be here tomorrow. I'm just doing what I can to keep costs down."

Patrick's gaze moved around the room, taking in the demolition I'd managed. His eyes stopped when they reached the sliding glass door and I watched his face move from observant to intrigued.

"Got yourself a little helper?" He nodded toward the door and my eyes followed. We had a great view of Talia from the back. I'd already noticed how attractive she was, but seeing her through Patrick's eyes gave me a new view.

Talia was hot. She had a fantastic body, emphasized all too well by those damn white shorts. Patrick was a happily married man, but something inside me didn't like his eyes on Talia.

"She's staying next door. Borrowed a flashlight last night and returned it a little while ago. Seemed like she needed a break from her family." My eyes slid back to Patrick. "Where's Megan?"

"She's with her sister, visiting the niece and nephew. We're meeting for lunch. I stopped by to see if you wanted to come. Called you a few times, but you didn't answer." Patrick stepped farther into the house, so I shut the door behind him.

"Uh, yeah, that'd be great." My gaze drifted back to Talia and I caught her eye. She gave me a smile and put her paintbrush down, then walked back into the house.

"Patrick, this is Talia. She's here on vacation. Talia, this is my best friend, Patrick."

"Hi, it's nice to meet you." Talia gave him that vibrant smile and held her hand out toward him. He took it, smiling back, charming as always.

"Same goes. I was just here to invite Briggs out to lunch. Would you like to join us? My wife will be meeting us there, so you wouldn't be a third wheel, promise. In fact, Megan would probably love another woman to talk to while he and I grunt and smash things."

She laughed, which was good. Patrick was always making jokes, and it was always clear when people didn't get that about him. Cecily, for instance, hardly ever laughed at his jokes. She laughed at him plenty, but not in a friendly way. There was no love lost between the two of them.

"That's okay," she said with a smile. "I don't want to intrude."

I was surprised by the disappointment I felt at her words.

"Come on, don't be silly. You won't be intruding," Patrick said pleasantly.

Talia's gaze drifted to mine, her eyes asking me to say something to appease my friend.

"He's right," I found myself adding. "You are more than welcome. It'll be fun." Fun? I sounded like a fifteen-year-old asking a girl out on a date. "Unless you already have plans." I had to give her an out.

"My plans for the day only included the beach and a book. If I go back home I'll just be suckered into feeding the twins."

"Sounds like you're coming with us then," Patrick said with a laugh. He headed toward the front door and turned back to me. "Meet you at Tilly's in thirty?"

"Sounds good," I responded, clapping him on the shoulder.

"See you there, Talia."

"Bye," she said, smiling.

The door closed behind him and a quiet fell over the room. I looked back at Talia and as soon as our eyes met she looked away.

"It's cool if you don't want to go," I said quickly. "Patrick can be a little overbearing. But, like he said, you're more than welcome. Lunch is the least I can offer after all the painting you've done." The war she was having with herself was evident in her eyes that were darting all over the room, landing anywhere but on me.

Finally, her face tilted up, eyes meeting mine, and she said with confidence I thought she might be forcing, "It would actually be really nice to have lunch with someone other than my immediate family." She let out a breath and then continued. "I just need to go grab a jacket."

"Great. I'll meet you outside in a few minutes then? We can take my truck."

"Okay, sounds good." She gave me another shy smile and then let herself out of the house. I quickly ran upstairs to change seeing as how there was still sawdust all over my clothes and a few paint splotches.

That morning, alone was the only thing I wanted to be. I was content with my days spent by myself. But after only an hour or so with Talia, I wanted more time with her.

Chapter Five

Talia

When I flew into the house it was practically silent. I figured the babies were sleeping and knew that would work to my advantage.

"Talia?" my mother called softly from the living room. "Where've you been? We were starting to worry."

"Briggs, the man who lives next door, needed some help painting. He's invited me out to lunch." That was all the info I was willing to dispense and moved toward the stairs. If the babies truly were sleeping, there was no way my mother would risk shouting at me. I pushed the door to the bathroom open and groaned when I saw my reflection.

My red wavy hair had little splatters of paint in it, my chin sported the same flecks of paint, and I was seriously deranged to have gone over to his house without one iota of makeup on. I hastily pulled my hair up into a messy bun, thanking the hair gods that messy was the new trend, managed to pick off the flecks of paint off my face, applied some mascara and lip gloss, then gave myself another once-over in the mirror.

"Meh," I said to myself with a one-shouldered shrug. There wasn't anything wrong with the way I looked, and there wasn't any reason why I should try to impress Briggs or his friends, but there was something nagging at me, making me care about what he thought. I wanted him to like what he saw.

While we were painting I could practically feel his eyes on me, making me very self-conscious. Surprisingly, I liked the feeling of his gaze, but wanted a chance to look at him too. All I could see was the ocean, and even though it was a great view, I couldn't help but feel a little shafted that he could look all he wanted and I could only sneak a peek at him when it was socially acceptable to turn and talk to him.

Returning to the bedroom, I slipped off my flip-flops and exchanged them for a pair of gold-colored gladiator sandals. I grabbed my denim jacket and purse, then made my way back down the stairs. Not surprisingly, my mother was waiting for me at the door.

"Are you sure you want to go to lunch with him? You've only just met."

"He's not a serial killer, Mom. If he were, he would have murdered me last night when I showed up at his house in the dark, all alone. We're going to some place called Tilly's. We're meeting his best friend and his wife. He's a nice guy. Harmless. Promise." I kissed her on the cheek and then scrambled out the door before she could stop me. I'd learned a while ago that even though I was twenty-nine, my mother would never stop being a mom.

When I made it back to Briggs's house, I tried so very hard to keep my body from reacting to the vision I came upon.

Briggs was in his driveway, leaning up against the tailgate of a very large truck. His arms were laced over his chest, biceps bulging, and his ankles were crossed. He was wearing cowboy boots, which in the past had never *ever* done anything for me in the attraction department, but Briggs in boots was a sight to behold. It was strange to imagine a cowboy at the beach, but there he was and I had no complaints. Continuing toward him, I tried to keep my breaths even, but I was probably a little gaspy when I said a lame, "Hello."

"Ready?" he asked with a smile.

Unable to form any more words, I simply nodded.

He strode around to the passenger side of the truck, opened the door for me, and held out his hand. I took it and stepped onto the foot rails, then hoisted myself up and into his truck. The door closed behind me and I watched as he made his way around the front of the truck. Once his door was open, he reached up and grabbed the steering wheel, using it as leverage to effortlessly lift himself into his seat. Even as it was happening, I was telling myself to look away, that no good could come of watching, but it was no use.

His forearm rippled as he gripped the steering wheel, and then his bicep tensed as he pulled himself into the truck. I was probably gaping. You'd have to be dead not to notice the masculinity and testosterone filling the cab of the truck. I was drunk on it at that point, giving few to no fucks whether or not he caught me staring. It was too good not to look.

"I hope you like Tilly's," he remarked, completely unaware of my blatant ogling. "Porter's mom owns the place and it doesn't look like much from the outside, but the food is great and Tilly is incredible."

"Porter is Patrick's brother-in-law, right?"

"Right. Megan and Ella are sisters. Porter is Ella's husband."

"Got it," I replied, a little surprised my brain could even function after the show I'd gotten. We made it to the main road, Oregon coastal brush lining the highway, evergreen trees offering only spotty views of the ocean. The highway was right along the oceanside, but eventually turned heading east. "Can I ask you a question?"

"Sure." He took his eyes from the road for just a second, glancing at me with a smile.

"If you don't want the house, and it's the house your wife was cheating on you in, why are you fixing it up? Why not just sell it?"

43

"The truth is, if the house needs work people won't pay much for it and you'll end up selling the property to someone who will tear it down. If I fix it up, someone who wants to live in the house will buy it and I'll get more money."

"Ah, well, that makes sense."

"I don't mind doing the work. It gives me something to do, keeps my mind off things. Plus, I already missed the window for selling beach houses this year, so I have about nine months to get the work done."

"So, do you live here year-round?"

"I do now."

"And what about your job?"

"I'm a freelance graphic designer, so I can work anywhere. Portland was convenient because I could network with a lot more people, have meetings with clients if I needed to, but I can't afford to have this place and an apartment in the city. Plus, it's calm at the beach."

"And it isn't hard for you to come home to the place your wife was having an affair?"

"I walked in on them having sex on the kitchen island. Guess which part of the house I took a sledge hammer to first?" He looked over and gave me a big smile then, followed by manly laughter. I couldn't help but laugh too.

"That must have been cathartic. I kind of wish I could have destroyed something after Chris cheated."

He shrugged. "I probably would have just preferred it if she hadn't slept with someone else."

"Yeah," I said on a sigh.

It was a few minutes before we pulled into the parking lot of a decently-sized restaurant. The building had a neon sign that said Tilly's and big wooden doors with small logs as door handles. Briggs parked his truck in the far corner of the lot where all the spots were empty. His truck was big and I imagined parking it was a pain. As soon as he cut the engine I pushed my door open and looked down at the ground.

"How's a girl supposed to get outta here?" I laughed. I was ridiculously high off the ground. I heard Briggs's door close and then watched him jog around the front of the truck. He came to my door and offered his hand.

"Just put one foot on the rail there and hang on to the oh shit handle."

"Excuse me?"

"The handle there, by your head," he said, laughing.

I looked up and sure enough there was a strap hanging from the roof.

"I never knew that's what they were called." I followed his instructions and found myself ungracefully clomping my way out of his truck. I had too much momentum, though, and crashed into him on my way down. He still had my hand clasped in his, but now my chest was pressed against his front, and his other arm was wrapped around my waist, his hand settled on the small of my back, holding me steady.

"You all right?" His mouth was so close to mine, the breath of his words feathered over me.

"I'm not usually clumsy," I said, my voice a whisper. Bringing my other hand to his chest, I pushed myself off him, hovering somewhere between embarrassed to be touching him at all and not wanting to stop touching him in the slightest. "I'm sorry." His hands fell away as soon as I was stable, and I missed them instantly.

45

"It's no problem. The truck is a little tall." He said the words so nonchalantly, like it hadn't affected him at all, my body pressed up against his, and that was good. Great, even. The last thing I needed was for both of us to be getting stupid. I'd touched him accidentally, and just because my heart rate went all crazy and my palms were sweaty afterward did in no way mean things had to get complicated.

He motioned toward the front of the building and as we started walking I heard someone yell from the other side of the parking lot.

"Briggs, get your fine ass over here."

I looked up and saw a very pretty brunette standing in front of the restaurant, hand on her hip, which was jutted to the side. She was wearing a wide smile, and as she pushed her sunglasses into her dark hair, I could see her eyes were full of mischief. Patrick was standing behind her, smiling widely as well, so I figured I was looking at Megan.

"Megan," Briggs called out. "Aren't you a sight for sore eyes." As they approached each other she laughed harder and then threw herself into his arms. Briggs hugged her tightly, lifting her off the ground a little, then put her down and took a step back. "You look great, kid."

She rolled her eyes at his nickname for her and then turned to me. "Don't mind him. He's called me that since we met. He got a kick out of how short I was."

"How short you are," he corrected. Briggs was right. She was pretty short, at least compared to him and Patrick. "Megs, this is Talia, she's staying in the house next door for the week and helped me paint today, so she's letting me buy her lunch."

"Nice to meet you, Talia." Megan held her hand out to me and her handshake was firm and friendly. "I'm actually kind of glad you're here. These guys will almost definitely fall into some sort of man-lish and talk sports and I would have been bored to tears."

"Man-lish?" I asked, confused.

"You know, man talk. Sports. Trucks. Sports with trucks. Tires. Yada yada."

"Oh," I said, laughing. "How rude of them."

"Right? Come on. I'll introduce you to Tilly."

I looked back at Briggs and he winked at me, making every part of me tingle.

"We'll get a table. Go ahead."

I followed behind Megan, who walked into the restaurant like she owned the place, and I couldn't help but be jealous of the obvious self-confidence she had. She walked right past the hostess station, waving at the girl working there, and then headed for the bar.

"Oh, Megan, you get over here and give me a hug." I watched as Megan practically ran behind the bar and wrapped her arms around the woman I assumed was Tilly. She looked to be in her mid-sixties with salt and pepper hair. The color of her hair, however, was the only thing that aged her. She looked amazing and vibrant. They hugged for a long moment, rocking back and forth, until they finally pulled apart, but Tilly didn't let go of Megan fully. "How are you, sweetheart? Everything going well in Portland?"

"Everything's great. Store's great. Patrick's great. We're all just fabulous."

"That's real good," Tilly said, rubbing her hands up and down Megan's arms. Megan's eyes stole over to me and Tilly followed her gaze.

47

"Tilly, this is Talia. She's a friend of Briggs's."

At the mention of Briggs, Tilly's eyes widened, but her smile remained. "Well, any friend of Briggs's is a friend of mine." Tilly moved toward me and before I knew it I was pulled into one of the best hugs I'd ever received. Her arms were strong and wrapped around me tightly and she smelled of baby powder and Chanel Number Five—a strange combination, but surprisingly wonderful on Tilly.

"It's nice to meet you," I said as she pulled away.

"You must be visiting. I haven't seen you around here before."

"I'm here on vacation. Staying in the house next to Briggs's."

"Briggs is a nice man," she said as she patted my arm.

"So, you're Porter's mom, right?" I asked hesitantly, trying to get the relation right.

"Yes, Porter is my son. When he married Ella, he gave me the best family in the whole world." She said the words with warmth and wrapped her arm around Megan, giving her another squeeze. "You girls go ahead and sit down and I'll be around to check on you."

I followed Megan through the restaurant and took a seat next to Briggs in the booth he and Patrick had secured.

"You get your Tilly fix?" Patrick asked as he draped an arm over Megan's shoulders.

"Yes, I did. Nothing in the world is better than a hug from Tilly. Right, Talia?"

"I can't argue with you. It was a pretty incredible embrace."

Everyone laughed and a waitress appeared, taking our drink orders and handing us menus. Megan and Patrick didn't even open theirs, so that left just Briggs and me to peruse them.

"So, how long are you in town for, Talia?" Megan asked.

"Just until Sunday."

"She's here with her whole family," Briggs supplied, not looking up from his menu.

"Don't they miss you?" she asked.

Shrugging, I answered, "Not really. My brother and his wife have twin babies, so they are all pretty occupied by them."

"Ah, yes. Babies will do that," she mused with a hint of understanding.

"Do you guys have kids?" I asked.

"No, not yet." Megan's response was laced with something, and I couldn't pinpoint it exactly. Sadness, maybe? Regret? My suspicion was only solidified when Patrick's arm pulled her in closer at her words. Something was going on there, but I didn't want to pry. It wasn't my place to pick apart their personal lives.

"You should try taking them to the aquarium," she said with a new wave of friendliness. "They have a giant tank you can walk under. Lots of colorful fish to look at."

"I'll let my sister-in-law know."

"How's the house coming?" Patrick asked Briggs.

"It's a disaster at the moment. But organized chaos. Just trying to get things ready for Porter tomorrow."

"What all is he doing?" Megan asked.

The waitress returned and put our drinks in front of us, letting us know she'd be back in a few minutes. I took the opportunity to sip my water, letting my eyes stay on Briggs, watching his mouth move with his words.

"New kitchen island, cabinets, countertops, new floors throughout the downstairs, the electrical needs an update, expanding the deck."

49

"Any work on the upstairs?" Patrick asked.

"No, Cess and I did a remodel up there a few years ago."

"Well, that's good, at least," Megan supplied, her tone sour.

"I sort of just want it over with so I can sell and move on."

The irritation and hurt in his voice was evident and I fought the urge to reach out to him, to place my hand on his thigh or cover his hand with mine. I instinctively wanted to comfort him, but knew it wasn't really my place. Instead, I tried to steer the conversation to the positive.

"Where do you think you'll go once it's sold? Back to Portland?" I'd asked the question as sort of a distraction, but found myself interested in the answer. For some reason I really wanted to know where he was headed.

"I won't be going back to Portland. I know that for sure. I want something different. Something new."

"That's understandable. And you could go practically anywhere with your job, like you mentioned earlier."

"Maybe somewhere on the east coast. Boston, maybe."

I nodded, trying to look agreeable. The idea of Briggs being on the other side of the country affected me in a physical way, which was ridiculous. The idea that my stomach dropped at his words, that my first instinct was to gasp, it was embarrassing really. I wanted to grab him, hold on to him, keep him near, and I hardly knew him.

"You know you can't go that far away. Your mom would kill you," Patrick joked, making Briggs chuckle.

"That's probably true."

"You have a big family?" I found myself asking. My question prompted him to turn his big brown eyes on me.

"Not too big. Mom, Dad, and my little brother, Landon."

"They'd miss you," I offered, not letting my gaze drift from his, resisting the urge to let my eyes fall away, the intensity of his stare overwhelming.

"Perhaps," he replied softly.

"Getting any surfing in? I heard there were good waves yesterday," Patrick mentioned.

"Yeah, I was out. Waves were good. Cold, but good."

"I always thought Oregon wasn't great for surfing," I said just before taking a sip of my water.

"It's not really. There are better places." Briggs shrugged. "But sometimes you've got to work with what you've got. I'd rather surf small waves than none at all." He caught me in his gaze again, but that time it didn't fall away as quickly.

"Do you all know what you'd like?" The waitress's question brought me out of my haze and I flipped my menu open again, trying to make a split-second decision.

"Bacon cheeseburger," Patrick said.

"Turkey club," Briggs added, handing his menu over.

"I'll have the cobb salad, please," Megan said with a smile.

"That sounds good," I said as I looked up at the waitress. "I'll have the same."

The waitress scribbled on her notepad and then took our remaining menus. "I'll be back with that in just a bit."

"So, are you coming to Porter and Ella's tomorrow night?" Patrick asked Briggs as he swirled his straw around in his soda.

"I was planning on it."

"Oh, Talia, you should totally come," Megan exclaimed. "It's just a game night, nothing fancy, but it's always better to have even people. Say you'll come."

She was looking at me with wide and expectant eyes.

"Oh, um, I don't know…" I'd already intruded on their lunch, I didn't want to crash a game night too. Megan seemed really nice, but I didn't want to be the loser trailing along behind them. "My family probably has something planned."

Megan pouted. "Okay, well, you're totally welcome to come. If it turns out you can sneak away, promise you'll come with Briggs."

"Promise," I vowed with absolutely no intention of keeping that promise.

For the next hour I listened to Patrick and Briggs update each other on the events of their lives, listened to Megan talk about her job at a boutique in Portland and her plans to open another sometime in the future. They were all very friendly and tried to include me in their conversation, asking typical get-to-know-you questions.

The waitress came to clear away our plates and Tilly was right behind her.

"Everything taste okay?" she asked, resting a hand on Briggs's shoulder.

"Delicious, as always," he responded, giving her a warm smile.

"Glad to hear it." Her eyes moved to Patrick and Megan's side of the table. "I want to see you both in here again before you leave town, all right? One visit isn't enough. And stop by the house sometime. I can't sit and chat with you while I'm here."

Megan laughed. "Tilly, you're always here. You're never at your house long enough for us to stop by."

"I guess that's true enough. Just promise you'll swing by to see me before you go back to the city."

"Sure thing," Patrick said sincerely.

It was surprising to see people who weren't related by blood show each other so much affection, to openly care for one another so much. Tilly was treating Megan and Patrick like they were her own children, when clearly they were only related, and distantly at that, by marriage. Even though I'd been with Chris for so long, I'd never felt close to his family. And certainly his mother had never been interested in my brother or his well-being. I couldn't help but wonder what it must be like to quite literally join two families together by marriage. Tilly even treated Briggs like family and he had no connection whatsoever, yet she still loved him.

Either Tilly loved everybody, or Briggs was easy to love.

Or quite possibly both.

"Well, we better get going," Megan said with a sigh, then she turned to me. "We promised Ella and Porter we'd watch the babies so they could go out to a movie and dinner."

"That's so funny. I promised my sister-in-law the very same thing."

"We sound like awesome sisters," she joked.

"Do you have time for a game of pool before I take you back?" Briggs asked, catching me completely off guard. As soon as Megan and Patrick started to leave, I assumed we'd be following.

"Um, yeah, I guess." I pulled my phone out and checked the time. "I have about an hour before I should get back."

We all scooched out of our booths and I watched as Megan and Patrick said goodbye to Tilly, then Megan turned to me, pulling me into a hug as well.

"Hopefully you'll come tomorrow night," she said softly, then pulled away. "We'd really like to see you there. Ella and Kalli would really like you."

"I will definitely see what my plans are."

"Great. It was so nice meeting you." She gave a little wave and then stepped past me toward the door.

"See you later, Talia. Keep my buddy Briggs here out of trouble, okay?" With his words, Patrick's hand landed on my shoulder and he gave it a squeeze.

I laughed. "Will do."

We watched them leave for a moment, then Tilly broke the silence.

"I've got to get back to work. Don't leave without saying goodbye, honey." That was directed at Briggs, and the affection in her voice was apparent.

"I won't," he replied as she retreated behind the bar. "Are you any good at pool?"

"Nope," I replied honestly, earning me a deep laugh. I suddenly wished I were funnier so I could hear it more before we parted ways.

"Good, me neither."

Even though he claimed to be no good, he seemed to know what he was doing. He racked the balls efficiently enough, then picked out a cue for me, letting me have the first shot.

"I really suck at pool, especially breaking," I warned him, taking the appropriate stance, but feeling like an idiot. I pulled my cue back, then tried my hardest to get a good shot in. Luckily, and surprisingly, a striped ball went into a corner pocket. Walking around the table, I looked for my next best shot, but knew I'd never be able to sink any of the remaining stripes on the table as it was. I lined up my best shot but wasn't surprised when the stripe ricocheted, ending its journey in the middle of the table, nowhere near a pocket.

"You sank one, which is more than I might have." He smiled and took his position, aiming the cue at a solid ball. The cue ball knocked against its target with a clack, but the solid ball just missed the pocket. "See? Terrible."

"If you knew you were terrible, why'd you want to stay and play?"

He propped his cue on the floor, chalk end up, and wrapped both his fists around it, leaning on it for support, and met my gaze.

"I guess I wasn't ready to take you home just yet." He smiled, but it wasn't a full smile, almost sad. "Even if it was only for a few hours, it was nice to be around someone who hadn't seen me fall apart, hadn't been around to witness the last year of my life." He shrugged. "Something about you makes me feel hopeful."

It was a more truthful answer than I was expecting, but if there was one thing I could appreciate, it was honesty.

"Well, truly, going back to my family doesn't sound so appealing. This is much better."

He smiled again. That time it was bigger and it made me feel a little bit better. I didn't want Briggs to be sad. We played pool until I finally won, and normally I would think he'd let me win, but we both sucked, so I was pretty sure he'd lost fair and square.

When we went to pay our bill, Tilly kindly informed us it was on the house. We both thanked her and gave her the hugs she demanded in a way that didn't seem demanding at all. The food had been delicious, Megan and Patrick were great, and playing pool had been entertaining. But being with Briggs was what made the afternoon memorable.

Just walking beside him to his truck had me smiling.

He opened my door and held out a hand for me, likely anticipating the fact that I would need assistance. Once we were both settled and driving back, it occurred to me that not only had it been a great afternoon, it had been the best day I'd had in a while.

"Thank you for inviting me. I had a great time." I said the words and then resisted the urge to roll my eyes at myself. I sounded incredibly lame. Of course, though, Briggs was sweet and didn't make me feel more like an idiot.

"I had a great time too. Feel free to stop by whenever. You know, if you need a break from your family."

"Thanks." I knew in the days following, many times, I'd think about Briggs and imagine him over in his house working away. But I also knew I wouldn't go back. Chris had done a great job of making me feel as though I couldn't tell when a man was lying to me, and I didn't want to bother Briggs by showing up when he'd only told me I was welcome to be polite. But part of me wished I could spend my days helping him and watching him work.

It surprised me when he pulled up to my rental instead of his own house.

"Thanks for the ride and the distraction," I said, unbuckling my seatbelt.

"Anytime," he said with another smile I thought might be genuine, but wouldn't let myself hope for it. I tried to hop down from the truck as gracefully as I could, closed the door, and made my way to the house, all the while fighting the immense urge to look back at Briggs. I closed the front door behind me, the noise of Angela talking and babies crying not enough to drown out the sounds of his truck backing out of the gravel drive and then fading away.

"Did you have fun?" my mother asked, coming down the stairs.

"Yeah." For some reason, I felt as though I was stuck right where I stood. I didn't want to move forward and away from the wonderful afternoon with Briggs, didn't want to let it go.

"That's nice, sweetheart," she said as she passed me, giving my shoulder a gentle squeeze as she did.

"Oh, good, you're back," Angela said from the living room, staring at me with a baby on her hip. The blue onesie told me it was Beckett. "I was worried you'd never return." Her eyes drilled into me and I understood why; she wanted me here to help my parents with the babies.

"Don't worry. I'm here." Forcing myself farther into the house, I draped my denim jacket over a chair, let out a large sigh, and reached for the baby. "Hello, Master Beckett. How've you been today?" He answered with a gurgle and a yank on my nose. "That good, huh?"

I spent the rest of the afternoon and evening playing with babies. And while it wasn't a horrible way to spend my time, my mind wandered often to the house next door and the man who lived there.

Chapter Six

Talia

The night passed easily and quickly; taking care of two babies made time fly. While I still thought my parents would have been fine on their own, I did enjoy my time with them and the twins.

It was late and I couldn't sleep, my mind anything but restful. I'd opened the window, hoping the sound of the waves would lull me to sleep, but I still just lay there listening to the ocean.

Finally, I decided if I wasn't going to sleep, I was at least going to enjoy being close to the ocean. I pulled on some jeans and a hoodie and tiptoed downstairs. I slipped on my flip-flops and quietly let myself out the backdoor.

It was a beautiful summer night on the Oregon coast. That meant there were no clouds and no lights, but millions of stars. So many stars it was almost overwhelming. The combination of the sight of the twinkling sky and the sound of the crashing waves, and I was immediately transported to my happy place.

Nothing beat a night on the beach in Oregon.

It was dark, pitch-black even, but I could see the white of the caps of the waves and hear the ocean getting closer and I walked through the sand that was now cool to the touch.

As I neared the surf, the distinct smell of a campfire wafted over me and I looked up and down the beach until I spotted a fire with a single person sitting by it, directly down the beach from Briggs's house. I stopped, wondering if I should ignore the person sitting by the fire, or if I should continue onward and see if it was Briggs, if he wanted any company.

My curiosity propelled me forward and I headed in the direction of the fire.

The closer I got, the more sure I became that it was him. The light from the flames lit up his frame, and even though I'd only known him a day, I found myself positive that I could identify his shape. My feet kept bringing me toward him and just as surely, I began to smile.

He was terribly handsome, especially while sitting in front of a fire. He was sitting on a blanket, one knee drawn up and an elbow resting on top, the other leg folded and resting on the ground in front of him. I watched as he threw another log on the fire, silently excited that he planned to be out a while longer yet.

He must have heard my feet in the sand because eventually his head turned toward me. I saw him squint, trying to see who was approaching, and I enjoyed all too much watching his expression change from curiosity to delight when he finally realized it was me.

"What are you doing out here so late?" he asked, watching as I walked toward him, only stopping when I was a few feet away.

"Couldn't sleep. The ocean is too loud," I said, throwing a thumb over my shoulder.

"She is feisty sometimes." He was quiet for a moment, but then he patted the blanket next to him and said, "Care to join me? I didn't bring any marshmallows, but I do have this." He reached into the pocket of his jacket and pulled out a flask.

I warred with myself. I wanted to sit down next to him. Badly, in fact. But that was the very reason I kept telling myself I should just continue on my way. The wound from Chris was still raw and the more time I spent with Briggs, the more I liked him. The very last thing I needed was to get caught up in some feelings and get hurt again.

"Come on," he cajoled. "Don't leave me out here all alone."

In the end, it wouldn't be my notion of self-preservation that did me in. It would be Briggs telling me he needed me. I couldn't remember the last time I'd felt like someone needed me.

I walked behind him and took the spot on the blanket to his left. He moved so both his legs were stretched out in front of him, crossed at the ankles, and I mirrored his pose. I looked into the flames, watching them lick higher and higher as they ate away at the new log.

"What are you doing out here at this time of night?" I asked after a few quiet but content moments.

"Too loud in my house," he replied softly, only barely hearing him over the crackling of the fire.

"The ocean?"

"The memories."

I didn't really know how to respond, so I just gave him my silent company.

"Here," he said, holding his flask out to me.

Taking it from him, I asked, "What's in it?"

"Jack."

I wrinkled my nose, hoping he couldn't see. Regardless, I brought the flask to my mouth and took a dainty swig. I couldn't hide the coughing that came afterward. And he couldn't stifle his laughter.

"Not a fan of whiskey?"

"Not on its own," I sputtered, handing the flask back to him and watching him take a much bigger drink than I had.

"What are you a fan of?"

"I'm a white wine kind of girl."

"Classy," he said, not unkindly.

"When I want to be."

"Tell me something you've never told anyone before." His demand caught me off guard.

"Really?"

"Isn't there a kind of anonymity in the dark? Out here with the ocean tide to carry away your secrets?" He turned to face me and even though it was obvious he was a little tipsy, he was being very honest.

"Is that how you think the ocean works?"

"Well, the ocean isn't going to tell anyone. And neither will I."

I watched his face as he waited to hear what I would tell him. Whether I'd divulge a secret or brush off the entire idea. Something about the vulnerability I saw behind his eyes made me want to open up to him. Perhaps, I hoped, if I cracked myself open for him, he'd do the same for me. And I desperately wanted to see inside, to see the core of who he was, to know that part of him even if it was only a tiny piece of a much bigger man.

Turning away from him, looking back out at the loud and soothing sea, I told Briggs something I hadn't told anyone else.

"When Chris and I first met, we were in ninth grade. It seemed like we were meant to be together. I was a cheerleader. He was a football player. We hung around with the same friends. We had the same classes. Everything in my fourteen-year-old world seemed to be pointing me in his direction. And it was wonderful. He was a great boyfriend.

"When we decided to go to college together it was more of the same. The path was laid out for us already and there was no reason to roam, to explore. I spent so many years with him, following him, trailing along behind him, simply because I'd never thought to open my eyes and decide for myself if Chris, or the life we'd built together, was even something I wanted."

I took a deep breath, a little disappointed in myself for even having that particular story to tell, but eventually let it out because the pressure was building and I needed to release the words that were bubbling up inside of me.

"It never occurred to me that he was roaming. I never expected him to explore outside our relationship. And now, even at this very moment, as I sit here with a complete stranger, I can only blame myself for what happened. Of course he would cheat on me—there is absolutely nothing about me that would entice him to stay. I am exactly the same person I was when we met. Just older. I never found myself. Hell, I never even looked for myself. I found him instead and I latched on like a lost puppy."

I exhaled, surprised at how much of my body deflated with my breath. My shoulders crumpled forward and my head sagged, as though my body had been held up by my truth.

Briggs was quiet and I was afraid to look at him, to see in his face the disgust I felt for myself. Finally, after a few silent moments, he spoke.

"That's bullshit."

"Excuse me?" My head shot up and whipped in his direction.

"Nope. Not buying it. I mean, I get that you believe everything you just said, but it's bullshit. A real man doesn't punish a woman by cheating on her. Even if you hadn't found yourself," he said as he used his hand to make air quotation marks. "He should have helped you, held your hand through it, found himself right along with you. And if that wasn't what he wanted, then he should have ended the relationship. You aren't the reason he cheated. He cheated because he's an asshole."

Okay, I could kind of see his point. It would have been better if Chris had just broken up with me, but that didn't really change how I felt about myself.

"All right," I said slowly, not oblivious to the new fire in his eyes, the new intensity I hadn't seen before. "Regardless, the important part of what I said still remains true. I didn't bother figuring out who I was outside of our relationship and so when he left me, he kind of took me with him. I have absolutely no idea who I am, what I'm doing, or why I'm important."

"Well," he said before he took another drink from his flask. "If it's any consolation, I don't know any of that either."

I had to laugh. I'd just said, perhaps, the most devastating and important words of my adult life, and he wasn't impressed.

"The good news is," he continued, "you've got the rest of your life to figure all that out."

"Yeah, I suppose."

We were both quiet for another moment, until Briggs took one more drink from his flask and then took a deep breath.

"A few years ago, Cecily got pregnant. We hadn't planned on it and were very surprised. I was surprised in a good way, but Cess, she wasn't. She was upset. I gave her some time to get used to the idea, but she never did. Two weeks after we found out she came home and told me she'd had an abortion."

I couldn't hold in the audible gasp that left me. Of all the things Briggs could have said to me, I never expected a secret so huge and devastating.

"She cried and cried, and begged me not to tell anyone, but she'd gotten an abortion without even telling me. Not that she needed my permission, she had the right to do whatever she wanted, but she never even mentioned she was thinking about it."

"Oh, Briggs, I'm so sorry." It was all I could think of to say, but it wasn't nearly enough. "That doesn't seem fair."

"My son or daughter would've been two by now," he said after a few moments of quiet. "I wish I would have said more, spoken to her about it instead of letting her have so much time to think. I might have been able to convince her to keep it." He drew both his knees up to his chest and wrapped his elbows around, clasping his hands together in front of him. "I could have a child right now."

I had so many angry words running through my mind, but I sensed he didn't need my indignation. I could be furious, but it wouldn't change anything or make him feel any better. So, instead, I asked him an uncomfortable question, but one I thought might ease the ache I imagined burned in his heart.

"Would you have wanted a boy or a girl?" I didn't look at him as I waited for his answer, but looked through the fire at the waves instead, trying to give him the time and space he needed.

"A boy."

I let myself steal a glance at him and noticed the tiniest tug on the corner of his mouth—a grin.

"I wanted a boy first so I could teach him to respect girls and treat them like they're precious. Then I wanted a girl so I could teach her that even though a good boy will protect her, she was strong enough to take care of herself. I wanted to build that picture-perfect family." He went quiet again and the small smile fell from his lips.

"Did she ever explain why she did it?"

"She said the timing wasn't right. Her career was really taking off at that point. Her books were hitting the *New York Times* list and she was writing furiously. She said she didn't want to jeopardize her career or lose momentum. Part of me thinks, though, she knew she wasn't going to stay with me and didn't want something tying us together for the next eighteen years."

"Well, she sounds like a prize," I replied, heavy on the sarcasm. "We found ourselves some winners."

"You think we're better off?" he asked sullenly, as though he really needed confirmation.

"I hope so. I have to be. I was nothing with him. I need to be something, ya know?"

He looked over at me and I met his gaze. "You're selling yourself short, firecracker."

"Firecracker?" I asked with a laugh. My hand automatically came to my hair. Being a redhead earned me a lot of nicknames.

"It's not just the hair, although I admit that was the first thing that brought the name about. Well, your hair and that damn red bikini you were wearing the other day."

"Bikini?"

"On the beach. I was surfing and you were sitting in a chair, reading, in that damned red bikini. You looked like a fucking firecracker. I nearly wiped out at least a dozen times trying to see you from my board, trying to catch a glimpse."

Holy shit.

"You saw me?" I thought I'd been invisible that day. Or, at least, invisible to him.

"I couldn't see anything *but* you." He held my gaze, nothing but the sounds of the firewood cracking and popping between us. "It's more than the way you look," he continued. "Sometimes you just ignite."

My breath snagged in my lungs and my heart tripped, pounding away to find the normal rhythm again. "If he didn't see you, it wasn't because you weren't bright enough, Talia."

I couldn't ever remember a time when someone had said anything as sweet as those words to me. I had no idea what to say in response, but my mouth opened and I was surely going to say something stupid, but there was a loud crack from the fire as something gave a small explosion. Nothing serious, but just enough volume and surprise to cause me to shriek and jump.

"Jesus," I said on an exasperated breath, bringing my hand to my chest, trying to slow my heart. Briggs laughed and the deep rumbly sound washed over me, just like it had earlier that day, making my entire body warmer.

"I should probably walk you home," he finally said.

I didn't want him to walk me home. I didn't want to leave that beach or that sky or that man. I would have stayed out there with him until the sun came up and probably longer if he'd asked me. But instead of saying all that, I only whispered, "Okay."

I watched as he pushed sand into the fire, then kicked sand on top of it until the flames finally died, leaving us in complete darkness. Instinct had me looking at the sky to take in the stars one last time. There were even more than before, it seemed.

"Sorry I unloaded everything on you tonight. I think I drank more Jack than I should have." He didn't seem drunk to me at all, but I wasn't about to point that out to him.

"Did it make you feel better?" I couldn't see him very well, but I knew he was close because I could feel the heat from his body warming mine.

"I think so," he replied quietly, his voice fighting for volume with the waves.

"Then that's all that's important. Besides, I unloaded on you too if I remember correctly."

"Did it make you feel better?" he asked, repeating my own question back to me.

'Better' wasn't a good word to describe what I was feeling. I didn't feel worse, exactly, but I felt different. More open, more aware, maybe even a little sad, but not in a bad way. It almost felt as though I was mourning the person I was with Chris. I lost a part of myself with him, but I wasn't sad to see her go. Not really.

"You made me feel *something*, and that's a step forward." I knew if I reached my hand out, I would be touching him, he was that close, and I wanted that. Wanted to link some part of me with some part of him, even if only to ground me, to give me some sort of proof that we were here and this had happened. A man, who I hardly knew, seemed to see a part of myself I'd never shown anyone before. He saw me and that, to me, was precious.

"I guess that's all I can ask," he said, and I could feel him pull away from me. His warmth disappeared and the cool ocean air was suddenly between us.

We walked back toward the houses, the static sound of the waves becoming fainter with every step.

"Sorry if I ruined your peaceful walk on the beach," he said when my rental house came into view.

"You didn't ruin it. It was nice." Nice? Jesus.

"Hopefully you can fall asleep."

"I think I'll manage." I walked up the steps of the porch while Briggs stayed in the sand. I turned around after I'd reached the top step. "Thanks for listening to me out there. And I hope you're right, you know, about the ocean taking our secrets away. I think, or at least I hope, it might be time for both of us to let them go."

He was quiet for a moment, his eyes locked on mine, but then he said, smiling as he did, "I'll see you later, firecracker."

Chapter Seven

Briggs

I'd been up with the sun that morning. The night was practically restless, only falling asleep for a few hours. I'd lain in bed thinking about Talia, wondering if it was natural to have such strong feelings about someone I'd only known a few days. When I woke, it was to more thoughts of her, but in the bright morning light, the thoughts were more sobering.

I shouldn't have been thinking about her at all. Nothing good could come of it. Talia, after everything she'd been through, deserved a good guy who could be there for her and treat her the way her dumbass ex hadn't. And even though there was a small part of me that wanted to be that guy, I knew I was nowhere near ready to be in a relationship. Not with all the animosity that still raged inside me about Cecily.

Talia had infiltrated my mind, thoughts of her making it impossible to think of anything else, when finally, I just had to tell myself to move on. I had to accept the fact that even though I was attracted to her in a way I couldn't remember experiencing before, I was going to have to move on and try to forget her. She'd be gone in a week anyway. She had a whole life somewhere else and I was stuck there.

I threw on some old clothes that had become designated as only for the remodel with paint splotches and holes in random places, and went downstairs to assess what I could accomplish that day.

I'd just finished sweeping up the main living room area when a knock sounded. I opened the door to see Porter standing on my porch.

"Hey, man," I said, reaching my hand out to him. "Thanks for coming."

"Anytime," he said as he shook my hand. "Mind if I come in and take a look around?"

"Not at all," I replied, backing out of the way and letting him in the house. Porter and I weren't exactly friends, but we'd known each other long enough that he was more than an acquaintance. He was close with Patrick, though, so I knew he was a decent guy. "I tried to do as much prep work as I could, but I'm not a contractor and YouTube would only take me so far."

Porter laughed while his eyes wandered around my house, taking everything in.

"You ordered cabinets yet?"

"Yeah, they're sitting out in the garage, waiting to be installed. I've picked out the countertops, but haven't placed the order yet."

"And you've got flooring? Paint?"

"Yeah, also out in the garage."

"All right. Well, it looks like you got a pretty good start. My buddy Matt's going to meet me here in a few minutes and we'll get started."

"Anything I can do to help?"

"Yeah, definitely. We can show you a few things."

"Great." There was no way he knew how badly I needed a distraction.

An hour later and Porter, Matt, and I were working together to bring in all the supplies for the hardwood floor.

"You coming out to the house tonight?" Porter asked as he heaved a box of flooring up to rest on his shoulder.

"Not sure," I answered honestly.

"Patrick was looking forward to having you there. And Megan told Ella all about your new friend, and they both want to get to know her."

"Do all the women in your life meddle?" I smiled so he'd know I was joking, but it was a serious question. Lucky for me, he laughed.

"As far as I know, that's a trait all women carry."

"Hmmm." Surfing kept me fit, but I was definitely not used to lifting forty-pound boxes of wood off the ground. I was no longer astounded by Porter's massive biceps. I grunted as I lifted the last box and followed Porter into the house.

"We've got to let these rest, get acclimated to the moisture in the house, before we install. For now we can paint. With three of us here we should be able to make a pretty good dent and it can dry overnight."

"Sounds good," Matt said. "I'll start taping off the windows."

Porter and Matt were obviously professionals, and I tried to be helpful, but I really couldn't step in until the paint was ready to go on the walls. Porter handed me a roller and told me which wall to start on and I was off. Unfortunately, the work wasn't enough to take my mind off Talia. There was nothing about rolling paint onto a wall that occupied a person's brain, so it felt free to wander to her. Her hair, her smile, the shorts she was wearing the other day and the fantastic ass that certainly lay beneath.

I also thought about everything she'd told me the night before. And everything I'd told her.

The work went by quickly and before I knew it, afternoon had arrived and the walls were painted a very neutral beige color. Nothing fancy, but a good canvas so potential buyers could see the beauty of the remodel without being distracted by a paint color they'd want to replace. I wanted the house to be move-in-ready.

"We're gonna call it a day," Porter said as he used a rubber mallet to seal up a few paint cans. "Those floors should be good to go tomorrow, so we'll come by early and start laying down the subfloor." He stood up and crossed his arms over his chest and looked around the room. "The three of us might be able to get the floors done in one day, definitely two. Then we can install the cabinets."

"Thanks for all your help, man."

"It's not a problem. We had a few days between projects." Matt finished cleaning up his supplies and gave us each a handshake before he left. Porter threw some paintbrushes and folded up drop cloths into a box and then looked back at me. "So, should I tell Ella to expect you and your friend tonight?"

I knew if I sat around alone I would only think about the girl next door. Plus, an evening with Patrick would probably do me some good. "I'll be there, but I'm coming alone. I don't want to bother Talia."

Porter raised one eyebrow at me. "The way Megan was talking, it didn't sound like you'd be bothering her by spending time with her."

I laughed at his forwardness. Perhaps we were more than just acquaintances.

I ran a hand through my hair, trying to find the easiest way to explain the situation.

"I like Talia. In fact, I like her a lot. But neither of us is in a great position to start anything. I don't want to give her the wrong idea, and I think inviting her to a party with close friends might do just that."

"I understand," he said, picking up the box with all the painting supplies. "Ella will be disappointed she won't get to practice her matchmaking skills, though."

"I'm sure she'll get over it eventually."

"Probably right. Dinner's at six, okay? Just a chill barbeque, then games. The girls think we can't all get together without playing games."

"Hey, man, I'm down for whatever. Better than hanging out here alone."

"See ya then."

I sighed as the silence descended again. The past few months I hadn't minded being alone in an empty house. It wasn't until Talia showed up and reminded me what it was like to share a space with someone, even if it was only for a few minutes. Now the house felt lonely. Instead of sitting around thinking about what that could mean, I decided to throw on my swimming shorts and grab my board, hoping it would be less lonely out on the surf.

A few hours later I pulled up to Ella and Porter's house. I'd only been there once or twice before, but I was still astounded at how magnificent his house was. I knew he'd built it himself, but looking at it made that fact almost impossible to believe. The house was narrow, but tall. Three stories. Tall enough to see over the trees and have a beautiful view of the ocean.

The lights were on in the house and a few cars were parked in the front. Even from outside the house looked warm and welcoming. I parked my truck and made my way toward the house, stopping when I heard a car pulling up the gravel drive. The car emerged from behind the trees and I saw it was Talia behind the wheel. I stopped on the porch, confused as to why she was there, but excited nonetheless. Even though I said I didn't want to bring her, it didn't mean I didn't want to see her—even if I thought it was a bad idea.

She parked and then walked toward me and I knew I was in trouble. The woman was wearing a green dress that hugged her breasts in the most delicious way, and then hung loose all the way to her feet. It was a typical summertime dress with thin straps and a V-neck that showed a delectable amount of cleavage, but it was modest enough to make me want to see more, to wish there was a little less fabric. She looked incredible. And it was lucky for me and everyone else at that party that all the other men were spoken for, or else I might have kidnapped her and taken her somewhere no one else but me could see her. Like my bed.

"Hey," she said as she neared me, her voice hesitant and worried. "I hope it's okay that I came. I don't want to intrude on your life. I just couldn't handle the rest of the day with my sister-in-law and so when Megan came over and invited me—"

"Megan came to your house?"

"Yeah, she stopped by a little while ago and asked me to come."

I had to laugh. It was typical of Megan to stick her nose where it didn't belong, even if she had good intentions, which was why it was difficult to be angry with her.

73

"It's fine with me that you're here. I'm glad to see you."
And that was the truth. When I'd seen her face, there wasn't
even a twinge of irritation. I was almost relieved to see her. Part
of me had been convinced she'd leave before I saw her again,
and I was realizing, as she stood in front of me, I didn't want that
to happen.

"Did you get a lot of work done at your house today?" she
asked, seeming genuinely interested.

"Yeah, got the downstairs painted."

"That's great."

"Listen," I started, certain I wanted to make her feel
comfortable, to tell her she was welcome, that I was glad she was
there, but I wasn't sure how to say the words. However, I didn't
get the chance to string the right ones together because the door
opened behind us and Patrick hollered at us.

"I thought I heard people out here. Come on in, guys. We're
just getting food on the grill."

I gave Talia a smile and then motioned for her to proceed
me, then tried not to look at her ass in that dress as she climbed
the stairs.

"Everyone's on the back patio," he said as he closed the
door behind us.

Sure enough, through the large windows, I could see the
whole gang outside. "Come on, I'll introduce you to everyone."

She followed me to the patio and as soon as I opened the
door, all eyes were on us.

"Talia, you came," Megan squealed, clearly excited.

Talia smiled, but was obviously a little overwhelmed by the
audience.

"Porter, Ella, this is Talia. She's staying at the house next
door to mine," I said, trying to break the ice with an introduction.

74

Ella quickly approached and pulled Talia into a friendly hug. "Tilly told me she met you and said you were a total sweetheart," Ella said as she pulled away. She moved to me next, hugging me the same way she'd hugged Talia. "Briggs, it's so good to see you again."

I hugged her back, very aware of Porter coming up behind her, his hand out to Talia.

"Nice to meet you," he said with a small grin.

"You're Tilly's son, right?"

"That's correct."

"She was very nice to us the other day."

"That's her way," Ella said, still smiling, her eyes darting between Talia and me. My gaze drifted over to another woman whom I hadn't ever met. Ella noticed and moved to make the introduction. "Briggs and Talia, this is Kalli. She's visiting from California. Her fiancé, Riot, was supposed to come too, but he got caught up in some Hollywood scheduling nightmare."

Kalli walked over and gave us a friendly smile as she shook our hands.

"Hollywood?" Talia asked. "Are you in show business?"

"Kalli is engaged to Riot Bentley, you know, from television's greatest cop drama," Megan supplied, her voice high and excited, as though she enjoyed telling people.

"Oh, wow, really?" Talia asked, wide-eyed.

Kalli shrugged. "It's true. But don't let the good looks fool you. He's just like any other typical guy. He's probably sitting around in his underwear watching some sports game."

"Like that's going to stop us from fantasizing about him," Megan said, laughing. Talia laughed too. As did Ella. All the guys simultaneously rolled their eyes or let out a groan.

"True story," Ella said, a dreamy look on her face.

"Are you in the business too?" Talia asked Kalli.

"I am, but I work behind the camera. Much less exciting."

"Kalli's being modest. She's one of the most sought-after costume designers in Hollywood." This came from Megan, and her words held a lot of pride.

"What do you do?" Kalli asked Talia, a curious expression on her face.

"I'm a teacher. Fourth grade."

How had I spent so much time with Talia and didn't even take the time to ask her what she did for a living?

"That's so great," Ella said, her voice sweet. "Mattie is going to start school next year."

"Oh, no, someone get the woman a tissue. Here come the waterworks," Megan said playfully, smiling warmly at her sister.

"It's not funny, Megs. I can't believe she's old enough to go to school." Ella sniffled, and almost as if that sound alone called to him, Porter appeared, wrapped her up in a hug, and ran his hand down the back of her hair. I got the feeling he'd soothed her in that way often.

"I used to teach kindergarten, but I moved districts and fourth grade was their only opening. Elementary school is a pretty great age group. I don't think I'll ever want to teach above fifth grade."

Suddenly the image of Talia surrounded by children filled my mind. I could picture her, patient and kind, with students listening to her instructions, learning from her. Of course she was a teacher.

"Here you go, man," I heard Patrick say from beside me, holding out a bottle of beer. "Can I get you anything, Talia?"

"I'll take one of those too, if you don't mind," she said, motioning to my beer.

"We've got margaritas and cosmos in the kitchen," Ella offered.

"Oh, it's okay, beer's fine."

Shit. A beautiful schoolteacher who'd take beer over margaritas? With a fantastic body? This was torture.

"Dinner will be ready in ten minutes. Table on the deck is all ready," Porter said gruffly, kissing Ella's forehead before walking back outside to man his grill.

Patrick brought Talia a beer, she thanked him, and then he pulled Megan up from her chair and took her by the hand outside. Ella went to the kitchen, opened the refrigerator, and started removing plates and bowls filled with food.

"Is there anything I can help with?" Talia asked her.

"Oh, no, thank you. I've got it covered. Briggs can show you the back patio," Ella replied, trying to slyly sneak a wink at me, as if Talia couldn't see it.

"Way to be cool, Ella." I laughed. I nodded my head toward the sliding glass door. "Come on, Talia. Let's go outside."

I opened the door for her and we were accosted by the sound of laughter and conversation. Patrick sat in a chair around a big table, Megan on his lap. Kalli was across the table, closest to Porter, who was at his grill. Kalli and Megan seemed to be in a heated conversation about something, while Patrick seemed to be wholly entranced by Megan's hair as he kept running his fingers through one particular section.

I pulled a chair out for Talia and then took the one next to her after she sat down.

"I just don't understand how you can be such good friends with the woman after she spends her entire workday making out with your fiancé." This came from Megan and she took a healthy drink of her margarita once the words were out.

Kalli shrugged. "It's their job. Ally is a really great girl, and she's married to a great guy. They're happy. Besides, if you'd ever been on set while actors are filming steamy scenes, you'd realize it's not that sexy."

"So, it doesn't bother you that Riot simulates sex with this Ally woman all day?"

"Not when he comes home to me and fucks my brains out."

Talia practically spat out her beer.

"Sorry, Talia. These two have practically no filter," Patrick said through laughter.

"No, that's fine. I admire women who can speak their minds. And besides, if you can't speak freely around your friends, what good are they, right?"

"Right," Megan cheered, raising her glass high and Kalli following suit. I watched with a smile as Talia raised her glass and they all toasted each other.

"So, Talia," Kalli began. "How did you and Briggs meet?"

"The other night the power went out at my rental, so I went next door to borrow a flashlight, and Briggs lent me his." She looked over at me, smiled shyly, then glanced away.

"So, you don't live here at the beach?" Kalli asked.

"No, I'm from Bend. Just here on vacation."

"Alone?" Kalli continued her line of questioning.

"No. I'm here with my family. My parents and my brother's family."

"So, you two aren't…" Kalli waved her finger at us.

I put my hands in the air. "Talia is a great girl, but we just met."

"Right," Talia added, although she didn't sound convinced.

"I see," Kalli said, suspicion in her voice. "But you're both single?"

It was my turn to choke on my beer.

"It would seem we're both just recently out of bad relationships," Talia confessed rather eloquently.

"Briggs's wife was a slut bag," Megan said without apology. I watched Talia's eyes widen in shock. I, on the other hand, was used to Megan's mouth. "We're all glad it's you who's here with him, instead of her. Regardless of your relationship."

"Well, I'm glad to be here too," Talia replied with a nod.

"Talia's brother and his wife have twin babies. It's kind of ruining her vacation." I felt the need to change the subject.

"Don't get me wrong, I love my niece and nephew, but it is putting a hamper on the whole vacation aspect of vacation."

"Ella, Kalli, and I are going to go on a whale watching trip tomorrow. You should totally come with us." Megan's voice was suddenly full of excitement. "Have you ever been whale watching?"

"I can't say that I have," Talia replied with a laugh.

"We do it every summer. Well, every summer since we all met. It's kind of a girls' day. It would be incredible if you came with us." Now, Megan could be a little bitchy sometimes, even though I'd never say it to her face, and we all loved her in spite of it, but in that moment, I could have kissed her for trying to make Talia feel included. I couldn't pinpoint why, exactly, but the idea of bringing Talia into the fold of my friends made sense to me and was something I hadn't known I wanted until that exact moment.

"Oh, no, I couldn't." Talia was obviously very polite, something I really liked about her. I could see she was pleased she'd been invited, and I could almost swear she wanted to go. "I couldn't intrude on your tradition. Thank you for asking me, though."

Megan's sweetness dissipated and one of her eyebrows hiked up. "Talia, come see the whales with us. It's not like we're some band of witches whose bonds keep others out. We want you to come, right, Kalli?"

"Right. I can always use more friends." Kalli winked at Talia, but it was a sweet and sincere wink, as though she was trying to make her more comfortable. Just then, the sliding glass door opened and Ella came out carrying a tray full of condiments and bags of chips.

"Ella, tell Talia she needs to come whale watching with us tomorrow."

"Yes," Ella replied enthusiastically, placing all the food in the middle of the table with practiced ease. "It will be so much fun. Besides, all the guys will be over at Briggs's house hammering and whatnot."

"Babe." This was grunted by Porter, who turned around to look at his wife. "Hammering and whatnot? After all these years, you think I just swing a hammer?"

"No, of course not," Ella said, wrapping her arms around her husband's waist from behind.

"Okay, you know what, Talia? You've got no choice. I'm coming to pick you up at eight. Whale watching starts early."

"You should go," I said quietly to her, giving her leg a gentle pat under the table, then forcing myself to remove it instead of leaving it there and feeling her underneath my hand. "What have you got to lose?"

She smiled at me, almost like a thank you, then turned back to Megan. "Okay, I'd love to. Thanks."

"Great," Patrick said, his fingers still absently trailing through Megan's hair. "The girls are going to have a fun day on a boat, and the men will be slaving away at Briggs's house."

"Sounds great," Megan said with a chipper excitement.

Patrick responded by using the hand that was previously threaded through her hair to grip her by the back of her neck and bring her mouth to his. She laughed at first, caught off guard by his affection, but there was an obvious moment where she melted into him and their intimacy. While not inappropriate, the action made something inside me uncomfortable.

Suddenly, it was Talia's hand on my thigh under the table, giving me a squeeze as though to say she knew what I was feeling. I thought, perhaps, she was feeling it too—a longing for that connection. If I were being honest with myself, I'd admit I felt a connection to Talia. Perhaps not as strong as Megan and Patrick's, but stronger than any connection I'd had for anyone in the last nine months. Last night on the beach, I could have sworn I'd never been closer to anyone.

So when her hand lingered on my thigh a little longer than mine had on hers, well, it didn't bother me one bit.

Chapter Eight

Talia

It took a few minutes to get used to the rocking of the boat. I'd admittedly never been a boat person, but I was a whale person—if being a whale person was even a thing—so I wanted to try to stick it out. Eventually, the nausea had faded and I enjoyed looking out on the ocean.

The boat we were on went much farther out to sea than I had expected, and I began to feel very small as I looked around and could see nothing but water, imagining what was swimming around below the deck of our boat.

Kalli was with Megan, who was getting sick on the back end of the boat, and I watched with something that felt almost like jealousy as Kalli held back Megan's hair and rubbed her back. Their friendship was very apparent and it made me realize I couldn't think of one person who might hold my hair back for me as I wretched. My thoughts were turning depressing, coupled with the dark water surrounding me, so I was grateful when Ella appeared by my side.

"She's always been a little overly dramatic," Ella said, clearly speaking about her sister. "Don't get me wrong, I'm upset she's sick, but she'll milk this for all it's worth for the rest of the day." As much as I could tell Kalli was Megan's friend, I could tell Ella was her sister. That particular sometimes-love/sometimes-hate dynamic seemed apparent. It almost made me wish I didn't get so annoyed by Angela, if only just to have that sisterly bond with her.

"I have to be honest. Ten minutes ago, I was pretty sure I was going to start heaving over the side of the boat too."

"Oh, no!" Ella laughed. "Well, at least we're evenly numbered. Megan's got Kalli and you've got me. I'll make sure the barf stays out of your hair. Trust me. I've got kids. Vomit has no hold on me anymore."

All I could do was laugh.

"So, who's watching your kids if you're here and Porter is at Briggs's house?"

"Tilly. She'll take any excuse to watch the kids. I could call and tell her I needed her to take the kids so I could build a sandcastle and she'd be at my house in no time. Since we split our time between here and Salem, Tilly doesn't have easy access to the kids. She loves any opportunity to spend time with them, to take care of them. So, we let her." She shrugged and looked out at the ocean. "It always amazes me how tiny I feel out here."

"I was just thinking the same thing," I mused.

"Right? It's so vast. It looks like it could go on forever."

"Hmmm," I agreed, nodding, looking out at the same endless ocean she was.

"Stuff like this makes me wonder how everything ends up happening, ya know? Like, this world is huge. Enormous. So, how did I manage to find the one single person I was supposed to be with forever? Or how was I given the two children I know I was supposed to love to the ends of this gargantuan planet?"

I nodded again, taking in her words, but thinking something almost completely opposite. How had I managed to find the one single person who was going to screw me over? And why hadn't he been the one I could spend eternity with? Not that, in hindsight, I really wanted to spend eternity with him, but why hadn't fate thrown me a few clues along the way? Why hadn't anyone, or anything, shown me what was really happening? It took so many years of my life with him before he eventually cut me loose.

Ella's voice cut into my depressing thoughts.

"Makes me wonder what would have happened if my ex hadn't cheated on me. What would have happened if I hadn't walked in on him that night?"

"Your ex cheated on you?"

"Yeah, and I found them on my birthday. I met Porter that same night. And let me tell you, neither of us was looking for a relationship. Not even a little bit."

"So, what happened?"

"I just couldn't get him out of my mind."

I tried to keep the thought of Briggs away, tried to force myself the think about anything but him, but there he was. Hell, he might as well have been out in the ocean next to our boat on his surf board.

"He was such a lonely guy, even though he didn't know it. A bachelor, but not in the sleazy kind of way. And I didn't take no for an answer."

"Not to sound weird or anything, but last night it was really obvious how much he loves you."

She blushed and smiled, just like a woman in love, and said, "I know. It hasn't faded yet and I hope it never does."

Just as she finished her sentence, Kalli and Megan approached. Megan looked green, but better, and Kalli seemed to be finding the whole situation a little funny.

"Next time we do this, someone remind me to get the Dramamine."

"But then who would we make bets on to see how long they'd last before they lost their breakfast?" Kalli asked with a wicked grin. Turning to Ella, she said, "You owe me lunch."

"Ugh," Megan groaned with very little enthusiasm. "You guys are the worst. And no talking about food."

"Hey, don't bite the hand that holds your hair back," Kalli quipped.

Even I had to laugh at that, and eventually Megan did too.

"How's the wedding planning going, Kal?" Ella asked after a quiet moment.

"Well, we haven't completely ruled out eloping, so it's going well." Kalli groaned, but continued, "I just want to show up and have everything the way I like it and marry him. Why must I make all the decisions and plan the whole thing?"

"Have you considered hiring a wedding planner?" I asked.

"I have, but I feel as though that's still a time suck. And I'd still have to make all the decisions, I'd only be paying someone to hold up different table cloths for me." She let out a frustrated sigh. "No, I don't want a wedding planner. I just want to marry Riot."

A stupid grin crept over my face. "I still can't believe you're engaged to Riot Bentley."

"Yeah, well, me neither," she replied sweetly.

"So, elope," Megan said dismissively. "I could always use an excuse to go to Vegas."

"Oh, me too! A vacation with Porter? And no kids? Yes."

"Ugh, not Vegas. Ew. No, if we elope we'll go someplace tropical. Warm sand, drinks in pineapples, palm trees."

"That sounds amazing," I said, a little breathless at the imagery.

Megan bumped her shoulder against mine. "Speaking of weddings, what's up with you and Briggs?"

"Nothing," I said with as much nonchalance as I could muster, but I couldn't keep the traitorous blush from my cheeks.

"It didn't really seem like nothing with the way he was looking at you last night," Ella added.

"I don't think either of us is looking for a relationship at the moment," I said with confidence, hoping it would steer them toward other topics of conversation, but I was disappointed when they weren't easily deterred.

"Cecily did a number on him and I think he's more broken than he lets on," Megan said softly.

He is, I thought to myself.

"He told me about what happened between them," I stated carefully. "And I don't know Briggs better than any of you, but I do think you're right."

"He told you?" Megan asked with a shocked expression. I only nodded in response. "I gotta say, Talia." Megan leaned back a little, her hands gripping the railing of the boat as she rocked back on her heels. "He hasn't even told Patrick everything that happened. We've only gotten tiny nuggets of information out of him."

"Well, I don't know if he told me *everything*," I said in defense of myself, trying to downplay any thoughts they might have been having about Briggs and me. "I'm sure you and Patrick know more than me."

"I don't think so. I think somehow you've found a tiny crack in his armor and managed to break him open."

My eyes went wide at her words. I didn't mean to crack anyone open. I hadn't meant to pry and Briggs had offered up all the information. I didn't want those women who, for whatever reason I wanted desperately to like and accept me, to think I was forcing a relationship with Briggs.

"We were just talking. I've had a rough time too with relationships. Maybe he doesn't feel comfortable talking to you all because you're all so happy." I said the words before I could think about the effect they might have. I didn't want to isolate myself from them, didn't want to make them angry or dislike me.

"That's an excellent point," Ella said softly. "Maybe he feels like we wouldn't understand."

"You've been cheated on," Megan said to Ella.

"Yeah, but Briggs wasn't going to come to *me* to talk about his failed marriage, and he probably doesn't even know that about me. His best friend married his college sweetheart and has been head over heels in love with her for years."

"Well," Megan said with a soft smile, obviously thinking about Patrick. "That's true."

"Maybe it wouldn't be a bad thing if Briggs opened up to Talia. Even if they're both not looking for a relationship, there can't be any harm in just being friends, right?" Ella was talking to everyone except me.

I agreed with everything she was saying, except I wasn't sure I could just be friends with Briggs. I was fairly certain I could spend time with him and then go home to my old, boring, single life, but the feelings I would have for Briggs at the end of our time together wouldn't be friendly.

"Are you ladies ready to see some whales?" One of the tour guides approached us from the back of the boat, all smiles. "We've gotten a lot of reports of a pod out today, just a little farther out. Pay close attention and you might see them breaching." He pointed a finger out toward the vast ocean and we all turned our attention there.

We were silent for a few moments, as if our voices would scare the creatures away, but then, suddenly, in the distance, there seemed to be an explosion of water.

A whale shot out, almost as if it were propelled, then seemed to collapse back into the water. Then another whale appeared, and another, and soon there were at least six whales putting on a show for us, practically dancing in the water. They were enormous and as they continued to breach, our guide explained that we were looking at a pod of gray whales and that each whale could be as long as forty-nine feet and weigh as much as thirty-six tons. It was astounding to see them continue to jump out of the water.

"How many are there all together?" I asked, not able to look away from the sight, mesmerized.

"It's rare to see this many together. It's usually one or two."

"They knew we needed at least six to be impressed," Megan said with a snicker.

"Leave it to my sister to turn whale watching into something perverted," Ella said with a laugh.

The whales continued to put a on a show for about thirty minutes before disappearing into the sea again.

"That was amazing," Kalli said, a little breathless.

"Absolutely. Thank you all for inviting me." I looked around at the girls and was met with smiling faces.

"Of course. I knew the moment we met you'd fit right in," Megan replied.

The whales had departed and eventually the boat headed back to the marina. The girls had stopped talking about Briggs and me, which I was grateful for, and we decided to grab lunch before parting ways. We stopped at Molly's, which was an Oregon Coast institution, and happily waited for a table, browsing through their quaint gift shop.

The meal was simple, nothing fancy, but the food was pushed to the back of my mind. Instead, I was focused on the women around me. It had been a long time since I'd spent time with anyone socially, especially anyone I didn't work with.

My split from Chris was also a split from my friends, as I'd learned afterward where most of their loyalties lay. Sure, I mourned the loss of friendships, but I hadn't realized how much I'd missed being around other women. And these women were strong and smart. Each of them accomplished in impressive ways. More than anything, though, I loved listening to them interact. It was obvious they were close, that they had a strong bond that went deeper than friendship, and it made me long to be included, or even to be worthy of their inclusion. Even though I felt 'less than,' they never made me feel that way, which made me like them even more. I was welcomed, no questions asked, and that made me undeniably happy.

They asked me about my life and I explained the bare minimum, not wanting to turn our light and happy lunch into a pity party for four.

When the meal was over, I walked with Megan to her car. She'd picked me up that morning, telling me she had to drop Patrick off at Briggs's house anyway. Ella and Kalli gave me hugs goodbye, waving, and promising to see me again before I left. We'd all exchanged phone numbers over lunch, but I wasn't expecting to hear from them.

"That was fun," Megan said as she pulled out of the parking lot, turning toward the direction of my rental house.

"It was. I've never been that close to a whale before. It was amazing. Thanks, again, for inviting me."

"I don't think any of us got any pictures."

"Oh my gosh, you're right. I was too caught up in watching to even think about getting my phone out."

"Me too. Oh, well, there's always next time."

I didn't respond because I didn't think there would be a next time. I was just glad there was the first time.

Megan pulled up to my rental, but she didn't stop. She continued down the road and pulled up to Briggs's house. "I hope you don't mind," she said sweetly. "I thought we could check on the guys real fast. See what they're up to."

"Oh, that's okay. I can walk back to my house. Thanks for the ride." I reached for the door handle, but Megan's hand wrapped around my arm gently.

"Just come inside, Talia. Briggs won't be the one to say it, probably because he's scared, but he wants to see you."

I let out a sigh and fell back into the seat. "Listen, I know you all love Briggs and you want him to be happy, but just because I'm here and he's here, it doesn't mean something has to happen between us. He's been really nice to me, sweet even, but I'm not going to keep putting myself in his path hoping that he takes an interest."

"But you *do* want him to take an interest?"

I could tell admitting that to Megan would be like releasing the hounds. She'd hunt and fight to prove her point, to get the two of us together somehow. But denying I felt anything for Briggs felt wrong.

"I'm only here for a few more days, we're both just out of really bad relationships, and it would be a bad idea to let anything happen." Right when I'd finished saying the words, the front door opened and Patrick appeared, followed by Briggs.

"Well, you can't avoid him now," Megan said with the devilish smile I was getting to know very well, then she opened her door and left me alone in her car.

I had no choice but to get out and be social, or else I'd look like a crazy person. Letting out yet another sigh, I braced myself for the effort of keeping myself away from Briggs.

Of course, he looked incredible. He wore a blue T-shirt, made darker by the pattern of sweat he'd worked up by all the construction happening inside, I assumed. He wore a tool belt and boots, as well. And the look totally worked for him. Patrick was wearing the same carpenter look and Megan obviously approved, kissing him fiercely as soon as he was within arm's reach.

"Hey, firecracker," Briggs said in greeting, a big and bright smile on his face. Perhaps spending a day with friends did the same for his mood as it did mine.

"Hi."

He continued toward me, stopping when only a foot was left between us. "See any whales?"

"We did, in fact. A few of them. Right off the boat. It was spectacular." He nodded, still smiling, and it was beginning to make me nervous. But that didn't keep me from smiling back. "Get a lot of work done?" I nodded toward his house for emphasis.

"Cabinets are in, island is almost done, and we started the flooring."

"Sounds like you had a productive day."

"I did, in fact." He grinned at me and I felt my stomach fall away and my heart forget a few beats. "Since my kitchen is more of a mess than it's been in a while, I was thinking about going out for dinner. I thought maybe you'd want to join me."

His invitation surprised me. Surprised me enough, in fact, that I muttered something that sounded like, "Oh, erm, uh," and then paused, trying to find some real words. I could practically feel Megan's gaze on us, could imagine the sneak smile on her face. My eyes dropped to my fingers, which were fidgeting in front of my belly. I took a deep breath and managed to say the words that didn't reflect the way I felt, but instead represented what I thought was best for everyone. "I think after being gone last night and this morning and afternoon, my parents are really expecting me to be with the family this evening. But thanks for the invitation." I looked up and watched his face, trying to read his thoughts. His smile faltered, but didn't disappear completely.

"That's understandable," he remarked politely.

I wanted to stand there and look at him all day, listen to him talk, see him smile, but I knew I needed to leave. I was just torturing myself by being around him.

"Thanks, Megan, for a fun day. I had a great time." I gave her a smile and then looked at Patrick and Briggs. "Have a good rest of your day, guys." I gave a little wave and then turned toward the beach and headed back to my rental. It took every ounce of self-control I had, but I didn't look back.

When I pulled the sliding glass door open, my mom was on the couch holding a baby, and Angela was coming down the stairs with the other.

"She returns," Angela said. She was smiling, but I didn't get the friendly, welcome home vibe from her. "We were beginning to wonder why you'd come at all if you were just going to leave for days at a time."

"I'm sorry, did I miss something?"

"No, Talia, of course not," my mother replied, her tone much nicer than Angela's had been. "We were beginning to worry, that's all."

92

"Oh, I'm sorry. I would have texted, but I didn't think my going out was a big deal."

"It's not," Mom said, giving me a wink. "Did you have a good time?"

"Yeah," I said, relaxing a bit once I realized my mother wasn't upset with me. I sat down next to my mother and held my hands out for Beckett, kissing his pudgy cheek once I had him in my arms. "The whale watching was awesome. We should plan to go next year. It was incredible. Then we had lunch at Molly's."

"That sounds wonderful."

"How did you meet all these people anyway?" Angela took the chair across from the couch my mom and I were sitting on.

"Well, Briggs lives next door and his best friend is Patrick. I went out with his wife, Megan, and her sister and friend." I shrugged like it wasn't a big deal, because it wasn't. I wanted her to drop it. My day with those women felt like a gift and I didn't want Angela ruining it for me by making me feel guilty for enjoying myself. "They just kind of latched on to me. They're really nice."

"I guess it's just kind of weird that you've been spending so much time with strangers instead of your own family. It is a *family* vacation after all."

"It's okay," my mother said, almost a whisper, as she patted my knee. "But since we're all here now, let's plan to play some board games after dinner. That would be a fun family activity."

"Sounds great," I said, thankful my mother wasn't influenced by Angela.

"I guess. If we can manage to get both the babies to sleep at a decent hour. Otherwise I'll have to sit out and take care of them while the rest of you play."

Not able to take any more of her attention-seeking behavior, I stood up with Beckett and walked toward the stairs. "Let's go upstairs and read you a story. How's that sound?" I asked him, laughing when he placed a slobbery mouth on my chin. "I'll take that as a yes."

Chapter Nine

Talia

Both babies went down fine, and it almost seemed like Angela was upset about it, as though she'd missed out on a chance to complain about something. Thankfully, after my mom had made her famous margaritas and we were a few good rounds into Trivial Pursuit, crabby Angela disappeared and the fun Angela I remembered came out to play.

Angela and Brody were extremely competitive, and half the fun was watching them argue with each other. In the end, Angela won—mostly because Brody let her—and I smiled watching the two of them walk hand in hand up the stairs.

"I think having twins totally took the fun wind out of Angela's sails," I said, putting the game back in the box, not really talking to anyone in particular.

"Kids will do that to you," my dad remarked, taking glasses off the table and walking them over to the sink.

"Having one baby at a time is stressful. Two…well…I can't even imagine." My mom took the game from me and put it back in the closet. "We need to take that into consideration sometimes when she gets testy."

It was true that before Angela and Brody had the babies, they were pretty much all fun, all the time. Angela and I were closer than we are now, and I hardly ever found myself irritated with her.

"When do you think the last time Angela took off for a day with her friends without any worries?" My mom was an expert at guilt trips incognito as regular conversation.

"Probably a while," I said, my voice a little sullen. "But, in my defense, I didn't force Angela to get pregnant, so I don't think it's technically fair for her to be angry with me for having a life." Clearly, I'd had a little too much to drink. I even annoyed myself with that last statement. And I didn't really have a life. I'd had a day. Just one. And I didn't want to give in to feeling guilty about enjoying it.

"No, you didn't. But perhaps, in the future, you could have a little more understanding when it comes to Angela and her outbursts. I'm not saying she's right, but I am saying she's tired and probably missing a little bit of the life she had before the twins."

"I'll try," I agreed. And I meant it. I didn't like always having snippy thoughts about Angela, and more so, I didn't like the new dynamic of our friendship. "I think I'm going to go to bed."

"Good night, dear," my mother said, hugging me.

"Night, baby doll," my father said, kissing my cheek.

"See you tomorrow."

I walked up the stairs with a smile on my face, thinking about my brother and Angela, hoping the twins gave them a peaceful night. I went into my room, changed into some sleep shorts and a tank top, washed my face, brushed my teeth, and climbed into bed.

As soon as my head hit the pillow I was thinking about Briggs. It couldn't be helped. I'd only seen him for a few short minutes, but his image was burned into my brain. Remembering the way his dark hair was made darker by sweat, the edges of it wet and sharp, made me roll over and face the window, hoping a new position would bring sleep. It didn't, though. Now I was looking at the ocean, and the ocean, more than anything, made me think of Briggs.

A few minutes later, my thoughts of him were interrupted by the sound of my phone vibrating against the wood of my bedside table. I'd received a text.

I'm down on the beach again. If you feel like a late-night stroll, I'll be here for a while.

The number wasn't familiar, but I knew instantly who it was.

Briggs.

I also knew that Megan had somehow slipped him my phone number.

I stared at the message for a moment, then the backlight went out, letting darkness fall over me again, and I turned to stare out the window.

There was a tiny voice somewhere in my brain telling me to ignore him, to stay in bed, to let it go. But it was so very small, it absolutely couldn't compete with the other voices screaming at me to go to him.

I pushed the covers off, traded my sleep shorts for a pair of yoga pants, threw on a zip-up hoodie, and slowly made my way out of the house, hoping not to wake anyone. I made it off the porch, my bare feet hitting cold sand, and I walked in the direction of where his fire had been just a few nights before.

As soon as I made it past the dune I saw his campfire. At the sight, my belly flipped and my heart started pounding in my chest. All I could think about was that he was there and he wanted to see me. I couldn't keep the smile from my face. I kept moving toward the fire, watching as his silhouette became more detailed. He was sitting on the sand again, this time his legs stretched out in front of him crossed at the ankles, arms behind him, propping him up in the sand.

Briggs bathed in firelight was beautiful to behold. I took a moment to try and burn the image into my brain, knowing one day I would want to remember what he looked like, sitting by a campfire, hoping I'd join him.

He must have heard my footsteps in the sand because he turned to look, a smile waiting for me.

"Hey, firecracker. I was hoping you'd come."

My mouth went dry at his words and suddenly every part of my body felt alive. More than it had in months. Who was this man and why did he affect me that way?

"Here I am," I said, lifting my arms at my sides a little, almost like an offering.

He stood up, saying nothing, and kicked sand onto the fire until its light was smothered. I heard him move, no longer able to see him clearly, and then felt his hand at my elbow. His fingertips slowly slid down my arm until his palm met with mine and he took my hand in his grasp.

"Come on," he said, his voice low and gravelly.

I let him lead me by the hand toward the water while I tried to analyze exactly what it felt like to have Briggs hold my hand. His hand was rough, but not uncomfortably so. As dumb as it sounded, the only word I could think to describe it was manly. Masculine. Everything about him screamed male. And everything about him made me feel exquisitely female.

He led me to the water's edge, where the waves lapped at our feet and then disappeared into the night again. "I've been thinking a lot the last couple days," he said finally, breaking the silence that was both serene and electric. I felt completely at ease sharing the dark quiet with Briggs, but there was also that underlying feeling of anxiety, wondering what wasn't being said, or what would eventually come out.

"Oh?" I managed.

He still held my hand and I wanted to wrap my other hand around his bicep and lean my head against his arm. Whatever level of contact we were sharing, I couldn't help but want a little bit more.

"For months, I'd been trying to figure out why I was staying here. Why I couldn't bring myself to sell the property, or rent it out, and get the hell out of this place."

I didn't know how to respond, and it didn't seem like his thought was complete, so I stayed quiet.

After a few moments, he continued. "I saw you sitting on the beach and, I swear, it was the first time I'd noticed a woman in months."

There he went again, stealing my breath.

"I don't want it to sound like I'm just interested in your body, because I'm not, but that first look, Talia, you've got to know, it got my attention. I saw you, in the red bikini, and I was instantly attracted to you. You were sexy as hell, but more than that, I wondered who you were and why in the world you were sitting on the beach all by yourself." His free hand came up and I heard it run through his hair. It was so dark, the only thing I could really see was the moon and the stars. If I turned my gaze back toward the shore, to the city, I could see faint lights from houses perched up on the hills, but the darkness around us was thick. "I had this urge to go to you, talk to you, find out anything I could about you. But I pushed it away because I thought it was ridiculous. Not only was I a stranger, but surely there had to be a man in your life. I could have never fathomed you were single."

He stopped walking, his hand tugging on mine, and I found myself standing in front of him, my eyes trying desperately to see every part of his face, even though the darkness was so overpowering.

"Then you showed up on my doorstep, wet and alone, and ever since I've been fighting to keep my distance." He tugged me a little bit closer and I lost the will to stay away. I leaned into him, let him bring me closer. His hand that still held mine wrapped around my waist, resting at the small of my back, while his free hand cradled the side of my neck, his thumb brushing gently at the skin of my jaw. "Tell me I'm not alone in that battle," he whispered.

"No," I managed a ragged whisper. "You're not alone."

His face inched toward mine and instinctively my eyes drifted closed. I couldn't breathe, the anticipation taking up too much space in my chest. I had never felt more willingly out of control, had never just given myself over to someone like I did in that moment. I handed myself over to Briggs.

His lips touched mine in the slightest of brushes, gently and softly skimming his lips over the surface of mine. At the contact, his arm drew me closer and my free hand came to rest against his chest. His mouth was tentative against mine, kissing me slowly, barely touching. He pulled away slowly, but I could feel his mouth still hovering just above mine.

"Is that enough for you? Is one kiss enough? Because if I kiss you again, it's going to be bigger and deeper. I want that, but only if you do too."

"Show me."

His mouth collided with mine again, tilting at just the right angle to take all of me. His hand moved to the back of my neck, pulling me closer, all the while his tongue swept across my lips, asking for entrance.

There was nothing to do but let him in.

I opened my mouth just barely, and with a groan Briggs invaded.

His tongue licked at me, invited my tongue to dance with his, and his arms pulled me in even closer. In the distance, I could still hear the ocean, still feel the waves meeting our feet every few moments, but all I could pay attention to was Briggs and the growly sounds he made as his tongue pushed into my mouth, or the sound of his breath as he captured my bottom lip with his teeth.

Pulling his hand free from mine, it came to my hip, squeezing at first, then moving around, his fingers cleverly finding their way under the edge of my hoodie and tank top. When his fingers met my bare skin, it was my turn to moan. The sound spurred him on and almost instantly his entire masculine hand was splayed over the small of my back, inching up toward my neck.

His hand reached my shoulder blades and with a grunt his mouth tore away from mine. I heard him swallow hard as his fingers moved over my bare skin.

"You're bare under your shirt," he said a moment later.

It took a moment to realize what he meant, but finally, I understood. I hadn't put a bra on before I left the house. I nodded even though I wasn't sure he could see me. My hands were resting on his chest and I could feel the quick and steady rhythm of his breaths.

"I want to touch you."

His voice was a soft whisper, as though he were afraid to say the words too loudly that the ocean might hear. But even though his words were soft, they hit me like a tidal wave. Need rushed through me and I'd never needed anything more than I needed Briggs to touch me.

"Yes," I said with more confidence than I felt. Somewhere inside I knew Briggs's touch would eclipse all others, that his hands on me would be a pinnacle.

His forehead came to rest against mine, his breaths brushing over me as his hands moved to the front of my hoodie. He slid the zipper down and my lungs were working overtime. With each breath, my breasts pushed against the cotton of my tank top, growing heavier with every moment of anticipation. He spread the hoodie open and my eyes closed again. I couldn't take it anymore.

I felt his hands grip me just under the swell of my breasts, still over my tank top, and I nearly groaned in aggravation. I wanted his skin against mine. But his hands moved up and his thumbs took wide sweeps over my breasts, grazing my nipples, making me gasp. After that, everything happened in a blur.

One of his hands slid up and gripped the side of my neck, while the other hand slipped under my tank and cupped my bare breast, and his mouth landed under my ear. It was sensation overload. My hands fell to my sides, my knees went weak, and my eyelids fluttered. My mouth was open and I was sighing and moaning, loving everything his hands and mouth were doing to me, and I nearly forgot we were on a public beach where we could be seen by anyone else who thought to take a midnight stroll.

His teeth nipped at the skin of my neck, his tongue lashing over the same spot only a second later, and then moved on, making his way up my jaw and over to my lips. By the time his mouth was on mine, I was panting and eager for his kiss.

As soon as his tongue touched mine, I was fully engaged. My hands reached out, grasping his jacket and pulling him as close as I could manage. We kissed for what seemed like hours, standing in the sand, the sound of the waves besides us. His hands were never still—he caressed me, groped me, kneaded me, and took pleasure in all of it. I took the opportunity to let my hands wander up his chest, through his hair, which felt just as wonderful as I'd been imagining, and over the scruff of his jaw.

I started to shiver and I didn't think it was from the cold, but Briggs noticed and pulled back slightly, his hand still under my shirt but around my back, holding me to him.

"Let me take you home," he said, his voice raspy, like he hadn't spoken in years. I didn't know if he meant my home or his, but he clarified. "I want you in my bed."

"Okay," I replied before I could think about anything. I thought I saw the corners of his mouth turn up slightly, but then his mouth was on mine again.

Holy crap.

Was I going to sleep with Briggs?

Yes. Yes, I am.

His hand slid down my arm and once again he took my hand in his. He turned toward his house, away from the sound of the ocean, and led me through the sand. As we neared his house his porch light came into view, illuminating everything, and suddenly I was afraid.

What in the world were we doing? Sleeping together? A one-night stand? I had never in my life had a one-night stand. I'd never had casual sex. And even though I didn't think sex with Briggs would be casual, I was stuck between wishing it were and hoping it wouldn't be.

He held the door open for me and I walked in, still trying to sort all my feelings out. I heard the door close and then I was being led up the staircase. It was part of Briggs's home I'd never been in, and even though it was dark, I found myself straining to see anything that would give me just another tiny piece of him. I saw some pictures hanging on the wall, but I couldn't see them very well, and that was about all I gathered before he brought me into his bedroom, still holding my hand.

He walked toward his bed and then bent, turning on a small lamp on the bedside table, which cast a soft glow across the room. And for the first time that night I could see Briggs's face and it settled my nerves some.

His free hand came back up to cup my face, his thumb running gently over my bottom lip, and I waited for him to make the next move, because I was completely out of my comfort zone.

"Do you want this?" he asked softly, his brown eyes searching mine for an answer.

"I've only ever been with one person."

Oh, God.

His finger stopped tracing my face and his eyes darted back and forth between mine.

"I'm sorry. I don't know why I told you that. I guess I thought I should warn you."

"Warn me?"

"I'm just not, uh, that experienced, I guess."

His hand fell from my face and I wanted so desperately for it to return, but then I felt his fingers lace through mine, now holding both my hands, and I let out a large sigh. "I'm sorry," I whispered again, my gaze falling to my feet.

"The way I see it, Talia, there are two ways to be with someone."

I lifted my face and met his gaze, his voice soft and warm.

"You either take pleasure and perhaps the person you're with gets something out of it too, or you give pleasure and that, in and of itself, gives you pleasure. I'll admit, I've been a taker before, been with women as means to an end, but not with you. Never with you."

My breath was halted with his words, my heart absolutely stopped, waiting for whatever was coming next.

"If you tell me you want to be with me, here, now, I'll give you everything I can."

My first instinct was to agree immediately, but my heart already knew everything he could give me might not be enough. It would have to be, though, because I wasn't going to give up the opportunity to feel everything I could with Briggs. Even if it was just one night, just this one time, it was what I wanted.

"Yes," I said just before I tipped up on my toes and pressed my lips to his.

He kissed me as he peeled my hoodie down my arms, and I blindly unzipped his jacket and pulled it free from him as well. His T-shirt lifted easily and I pulled back from him just for a moment to pull it over his head, then my mouth found his again. His hands worked my pants over my ass and down my thighs. I felt them fall to the floor and kicked them away.

His arms were around my waist next, spinning me around so my legs bumped the mattress, and then he was lowering me to the bed, climbing over me, letting some of his glorious weight pin me down. My hands roamed his skin, grateful for the opportunity to touch him, for the permission to explore. He was strong everywhere, but not bulky. Toned and tight and perfect. His mouth broke away from mine and he moved lower, his hands pushing up the hem of my tank, his lips pressing against the soft skin just above my navel. The tank moved slowly up my torso, and I could tell he was going slowly for my sake, but I wanted that part over. I wanted to be naked with him, to feel his skin against mine. I reached down and pulled the tank over my head, baring myself to him, and I watched his eyes dance over my skin, taking in all of me.

105

"I've spent a lot of time picturing you topless," he said, then pressed kisses all up my torso, between my breasts, ending at my chin. "But nothing compares to seeing you in the flesh." He kissed me again, his mouth nipping at mine, as one of his hands molded to my breast, kneading the swell of it and using his fingers to tease my nipple.

His body settled into mine and he rested his hips against my core, the firmness of his erection pressing into me in the most delicious way. I wrapped my ankles around his back, bringing him closer, adding more friction. He groaned and thrust against me, and I wished his shorts and my panties would magically disappear.

"I'm in no rush," he said, his mouth leaving mine. "I intend to enjoy you for as long as I can."

I tried to take his words at face value, tried to convince myself he meant for one night, but I already knew I wanted more. He slid down my body, his hands pulling on my panties, tugging them down my legs, and then there was nothing left to protect me. I was naked and he was seeing me in my most vulnerable state.

"You're so beautiful," he said, his hands coming to rest on my thighs, gently stroking up and down, while his eyes remained locked with mine. Without permission, my hand reached out and threaded through his hair. His eyes closed and he leaned into my touch.

When his eyes opened again, the softness of them was gone, replaced by desire and need. He moved his hands farther up my thighs until they reached my core, and he used his thumbs to spread me open. Never had anyone been so intent on taking all of me in, looking at me like they were afraid I would disappear altogether. When he finally licked me, my body let out a sigh, and my fingers continued to run through his hair, silently urging him on. His tongue moved lazily through my sex, up and down, stopping to circle my clit so slowly, it was exquisite torture.

"Briggs," I whispered, needing more but not knowing how to ask for it. My hips moved up and down, seeking more friction, and his fingers pressed down with more force on my thighs, holding me to the mattress.

"Let me enjoy you, firecracker."

It was a request I couldn't deny. I relaxed as much as I could, but my hips still rocked a rhythm against his mouth. He groaned into me, and the rumbling sent shocks through my system and I could feel my body reacting to his mouth. He kissed me then, his mouth covering my sex, my pussy throbbing beneath his lips. His hands moved, one wrapping around my thigh to hold on to me from the back, while the other snaked up and found my breast. His clever thumb moved over my nipple just as his tongue found my clit, and the tightening in my belly began; the familiar build of an earth-shattering orgasm.

His tongue didn't let up, probably clued into my impending collapse by the moaning and writhing, and his hand kept toying with my breast. The final straw came, however, when his other hand moved back around my thigh and two of his fingers slid inside of me. The combination of all the sensations sent me reeling. My back arched off the bed, my heels dug into the mattress, and my head turned to the side as I cried out in release.

"Jesus," I heard him groan, his breath still hot against my sex. He pumped his fingers into me until the wave rolled over me completely, only stopping when I closed my knees, trying to stave off the sensitivity of his touch. I was on fire and couldn't take many more flames. "You're beautiful all the time, Talia. But you're fucking gorgeous when you come."

I would have acknowledged his words, or even thanked him for the compliment, had I not been rendered non-verbal. I was all panting breaths and whimpers. When I finally managed to open my eyes it was the unimaginable image of Briggs crawling up my body I saw, stealing my breath all over again.

He didn't stop until his mouth was on mine and the taste of him and me combined sent a new wave of arousal through me.

"I want to be inside of you," he groaned as he moved his lips down my throat. "Is that what you want?"

More than anything.

"Yes," I managed.

He leaned back and climbed off the bed, opening his bedside drawer and pulling out a condom. He tossed it on the bed next to my hip and then quickly pushed his shorts down, his erection springing free. There wasn't much light, but I could see all of him.

He was so incredibly *male*. His cock was thick and seemed to be the perfect length. Not too small and not so big it was intimidating. He was perfect. My gaze snapped up to his eyes and I blushed when I realized he'd been watching me ogle him. He gave me a wry smile then climbed over me until he was between my legs. He pushed my knees up and nestled his pelvis right against me, his cock lying over my mound and up my stomach.

"You're going to feel so good wrapped around me, firecracker."

He leaned down, kissing me again, but all I could feel was the hot weight of him resting against me. He sat up again and grabbed the condom, tore it open, and then expertly slid it down his shaft. It was stupidly arousing watching him handle himself. A new pulse pounded through me, concentrated on my sex, and I needed something to take the edge off. I squirmed, trying to close my thighs, anything to get a little relief, but his big, rough hands pushed my knees up and out as his eyes looked down at where I needed him most.

With a little dip of his hips he lined his cock up with my entrance and pushed in slightly, and both our gazes met with a clash. My lips parted, waiting in agony for him to fill me fully, and he looked as though he was about to burst.

He slid in slowly and completely, his eyes never leaving mine. Once he was fully seated, his eyes drifted closed on a curse.

"Fuuuuck," he groaned.

I was perfectly full. Anything more would have been too much, but he was just big enough to stretch me in the most delicious way.

"Please," I said, though my voice sounded raspy and desperate. "Please move."

"Jesus, Talia, I need a second." His head dropped down between his shoulders and he let out a breath. On instinct, I moved my hands up his arms until they cradled his face and then I leaned up and kissed him. The movement spurred him on and as our lips met he thrust into me, adding even more pressure. After a few seconds I collapsed back on the bed, but he followed me down, one of his forearms resting on the mattress beside me. He continued the kiss as he pumped in and out of me slowly.

It was probably the sloppiest kiss ever, but neither of us cared. My hands moved to his back, pulling him closer, and my legs wound around him, and we kissed.

His tongue mimicked every thrust of his hips, and I couldn't concentrate fully on either because my mind was simply overloaded with sensation. Everything he did felt incredible. The way the ridge of the head of his dick hit so many perfect spots inside of me, or how when he pushed all the way in he held himself there and then pushed just a little farther, pulling a gasp from me every single time.

I rocked my hips up to meet his thrusts, his pelvic bone hitting my clit in the most perfect way. There was nothing in the world that felt as good as Briggs inside of me. Absolutely nothing. He pushed in, then ground his hips upward, and I simply ignited.

"Oh, God," I groaned. "I'm going to come again." Disbelief fluttered in the back of my mind because previously I had never been a multiple orgasm kind of girl. But I'd never been with Briggs before and that was apparently a huge factor.

"Yes," he growled, doing exactly the same thing over and over again—thrusting and grinding. His mouth moved down my neck and when his teeth bit into my shoulder, I fell apart.

I cried out again and my whole body tensed and shuddered with the intense release. My lungs stopped working, my heart may as well have exploded in my chest, and all I could see were lights and Briggs.

He slowed his pace as I fell back down to reality, but the intensity was still there, clinging to every move he made. His mouth moved down my body and he took my nipple into his mouth, sucking hard and making me gasp. Both his hands moved down my sides and when he got to my hips, his mouth pulled away and he sat back on his ankles.

"I'm going to fuck you now, firecracker, and it's not going to be slow or sweet."

Holy. Fuck.

His hands wrapped around my thighs and he pulled my ass up his legs until my sex was fully impaled by his cock, and then he pushed both my legs to the side until they hit the mattress. I instinctively leaned up on one elbow and absolutely could not keep my eyes off Briggs. One hand gripped the meaty part of my thigh right below his navel, and the other landed a quick slap on my ass, then gripped my cheek and pushed it up, giving him what I assumed was a raw and dirty look at where we were joined. His bottom lip was pulled into his mouth by his teeth as he thrust in just once.

"It's so good," he said, not bothering to look at my eyes, but I didn't care.

I'd never seen anything hotter than Briggs taking a long and lusty look at his cock sliding in and out of me. It was too much. I couldn't watch anymore. I collapsed back down on the bed and surrendered my body to him. I was useless, but knew he'd find a way to utilize my body for his pleasure.

I wasn't wrong.

His rhythm started at a slow pace, but after a few minutes he seemed to lose control. His hips moved faster and his grunts punctuated every thrust. I was building, unbelievably, to another orgasm and he growled at me, "Get there, Talia."

"I can't," I whimpered.

"Now, baby. Come with me."

It was his words that sent me over the edge again. Well, that and the way he filled me so perfectly and how complete I felt as he bottomed out inside of me.

He groaned a long guttural sound as I gasped, and he continued to thrust slowly until he'd come down from his high. He collapsed on the bed next to me, and I felt the loss of him immediately and deeply as he left me empty and raw. He landed on his back, one arm draped over his head while the other hand rested on his chest, moving up and down with the labor of his breathing.

We both settled and our breaths slowed, but it was him who spoke first.

He raked both hands down his face and rasped, "Jesus."

I was fucked.

In every sense of the word.

Chapter Ten

Briggs

It was dark when I woke, but I could tell the sun was on its way up. The sky was no longer the inky black the night held on to, but the dark blue that said morning was oncoming fast. I knew Talia was lying on the other side of the bed, could hear her breathing, and even though I wanted to roll over and wrap my arms around her, bring her warm body close to mine, I crept slowly from the bed instead, trying not to wake her.

I went to the bathroom and turned the shower on, letting the water warm up, then I stared at myself in the mirror.

What are you doing?

It was the only question I could come up with. And the answer was that I had no idea.

Texting Talia last night was a struggle. The struggle being I'd been fighting the urge all day since she practically ran from me in the driveway. Since Megan insisted on giving me her phone number. There was a large part of me that wanted to know what she was thinking, how she was feeling, to just *know*. Anything about her I could.

I only sent the text message because I was relatively sure she wouldn't show up. But when she did, I couldn't ignore the part of me that was glad for it. It was that part, the loud part of me that yelled every time she was around, that took her hand and did everything I could to hold on to a part of her for the rest of the night.

Being with her, seeing her open up and let her walls down, watching her give herself to me, was more than I had anticipated. It made me feel more, need more, and want more. And now, standing in the bathroom as it filled with steam, it was clear I was in over my head.

I stepped into the shower and let the hot water hit my shoulders and back, taking the stinging heat and letting it force some of the tightness from my muscles.

One would think, after a night of incredible sex—mind-blowing sex—one would be less tense. And I had been, in the moment. Being with Talia, feeling her tight heat all around me, hearing her soft moans and loud cries, it had been the best medicine. It left me sated and loose. Even happy, I'd say.

But everything felt different in the morning.

Not her, not lying next to her, not hearing her breathe next to me, or feeling her warmth. No. That all felt right. I was the one in the wrong. I shouldn't have ever texted her. Shouldn't have taken her hand. Shouldn't have kissed her. Shouldn't have brought her back to my house, taken off her clothes, and sunk into her when I knew nothing could happen between us. Nothing more, anyway. I kept telling myself the day before that if she were willing, being with her once would be enough, that touching and tasting her once would be all right.

It was too right.

And I was too messed up about it.

I wanted her, that much I could admit, but she deserved better than a man still trying to get his life together after a divorce.

Taking a deep breath, I turned the water off and grabbed a towel. After drying off I wrapped the towel around my waist and steeled myself for what was waiting for me in my bed. The image of a warm, naked, sleepy Talia flashed into my mind and I knew I was in trouble.

I opened the door as quietly as I could, but was surprised to see Talia sitting up in bed, dressed, with her back to me. She heard me and turned to look over her shoulder at me, her eyes dropping to the towel at my waist. It was still quite dark, but I could see the blush come over her cheeks.

"Hey," I said quietly. "You're awake."

"Yeah," she said, standing up and running her hands down her hoodie and pants then smoothing her hand over her hair, which looked untamed and sexy. "I better go home before my family realizes I'm not there. They might worry."

"Right, of course." I tried to ignore the fact that her leaving made me twitchy.

There we stood, on opposite sides of the bed, just looking at each other. There was so much more than a bed between us.

"Good luck, you know, with the house and the renovations. I'm sure it'll look beautiful when it's done."

Was she talking to me about home improvement? My mouth dropped open and then closed promptly. I had things to say to her, but I didn't have the words. When she moved to leave, it forced me to open my mouth and let the words just land where they fell.

"Listen, about last night…" I cringed at my own word choice, but pressed on regardless. "I don't have one-night stands. I don't just sleep with women and then say goodbye and never see them again."

"It's okay, Briggs."

"No, it's not okay, that's not what this was."

"But it's okay if it is."

"I don't want it to be."

Those words shut her up. Her mouth snapped closed and she took a step back, as though my words had literally pushed her back.

"I have nothing to offer you in the way of a relationship or a future, but I care about you and would like to see you while you're here." I let out a ragged breath and pushed my hand through my hair, gripping it and tugging, frustration warring through my veins. "I know that sounds terrible, but I'm trying to be honest here. I don't want you to think I used you. Shit. Maybe I did. I don't know. All I do know is that once wasn't enough, but I can't promise any more than just this tiny piece of myself." I looked back up toward her, hating myself but hoping she didn't.

"I don't think either of us is in a good place for a relationship," she said after a few silent moments.

"I agree."

"But I wouldn't be opposed to spending time with you while I'm here."

A sigh of relief flowed out of me. A little time with her, well, it was something.

"Okay," I breathed. "We're laying the floors today, so my morning is full. But will you meet me on the beach around four?"

"Sure," she said on a breath, seemingly just as relieved to have the awkward part of our conversation over. She moved toward the door to leave, but before she got there I snagged her around the waist and pulled her against me.

"Wear your red bikini, yeah?"

The blush that covered her face made her freckles stand out more.

"Okay."

I didn't bother asking before I leaned down and kissed her. She didn't seem to mind, though. As her lips parted and she opened for me, I knew I was right; once wasn't going to be enough, and I wasn't good enough for her.

116

"I better go," she said, her voice raspy after she pulled away from my lips.

"Let me walk you."

"That's okay. I could use a little time to think on my own."

I didn't like the idea of her walking alone outside, but there really wasn't anything I could do about it.

"The beach is probably empty right now. Good time for a short walk. Get my thoughts straight before I go back to the madhouse."

My arm tightened around her, wanting her close even though I knew I had to let her go. The fact that she was still willingly wrapped in my embrace and smiling up at me went a long way to convince me that she wasn't needing alone time because she was worried she was making a bad decision, and I could understand wanting a few minutes alone to get yourself in order.

"All right. Remember, four o'clock."

"I'll be there." She slid up to her tiptoes and kissed me again, then left my room.

I stood still, listening to her footsteps down the stairs and then a few moments later the front door opened and closed, and I was alone again.

Chapter Eleven

Talia

In the few hours that had passed since the night before on the beach, a lot had happened. Not only had a lot happened between Briggs and me, less importantly, it had gotten really cold. I'm not sure what I expected at five in the morning on the Oregon coast, but it was definitely not warm enough for a contemplative stroll on the beach in just yoga pants and a hoodie.

I'd needed a minute to myself. A minute to process everything I was feeling and everything he'd said.

I'd also wanted to think about all the ways he'd worshipped my body the night before without having to worry if my mom could read the explicit thoughts on my face.

Being with Briggs had been incredible. More than incredible. Enlightening. Briggs had coaxed my body into doing things it had never done before, and I knew part of that was skill—he obviously knew what he was doing. But the other part of it, I knew, was chemistry. My body reacted to his. To him. And while that made me all kinds of happy and excited, it was also incredibly depressing. If I found this with Briggs, this amazing reaction of my body to his, something I'd never had with Chris, with someone I'd considered spending my whole life with, I dreaded the day I'd have to say goodbye to him. And I knew it would be soon. Whatever I had with Briggs was, for all intents and purposes, over before it even started. It had to be.

I hurried up the path to my rental, looking forward to slipping quietly into the house and up the stairs into my bed, hoping to catch another hour or two of sleep, but all those thoughts came to a halt when I came upon Angela sitting on the porch swing.

"Angela, hey," I said, stopping on the stairs, shocked to find her there.

She looked at me, surprise clearly written across her face, but it slowly morphed to a contemplative look, and then, eventually, her eyes went wide with recognition.

"Where have you been?" she whispered loudly.

My shoulders slumped with the weight of being caught and I walked up the stairs toward her. She flung the large fleece blanket that was draped over her lap, clearing a spot for me to sit next to her on the swing. I sat, the motion sending the swing back, and she tossed the blanket over my legs.

"Spill, woman," she said, an excited smile on her face.

"I was at Briggs's house."

"I *knew* it!" Her excitement at being right was apparent. It was also loud.

"Shhhh!" I urged. "The last thing I need is for my parents to know I snuck out of the house last night to meet a man."

"Tell me everything," she whispered excitedly.

This surprised me. Angela and I hadn't really had a meaningful conversation in a while. She was busy with babies, I was busy trying to get my life together, and so conversations had been few and far between. So, when she sat there asking me to talk to her, it struck me as sad that it was an unusual request. I wanted to talk to her, wanted to be close to her, so I figured a conversation on the porch of our rental house at five in the morning was as good a time as any to do it.

"He texted me last night and asked me to meet him on the beach. So, I did." The story was not as exciting as she was hoping it would be.

"Talia, stop it. Tell me *everything*."

"I don't know. It's complicated, I guess. But not, really. It's so irritatingly, complicatingly simple."

"What is?"

119

"Briggs. Us. Him. Everything."

"Right," she said, nodding, as though she understood.

"We had sex. Amazing sex. Then this morning he tells me he's not in a good place for a relationship—which is fine because neither am I—but tells me he wants us to see each other while I'm here."

"So, like, friends with benefits?"

"We're not friends, though. This isn't, like, a booty call."

"What is it?"

"I don't know," I whined.

"How was the sex?" she asked, her voice low and quiet, making it sound as if she was scandalized just by asking.

"Hands down, the best sex I've ever had."

"Really?"

"Absolutely. No question."

"So, there'll be more?"

"There better be."

"But just while you're here?"

"Apparently." We were both quiet for a moment, but then I added, "But that's good. He's still dealing with his ex, and I'm still trying to figure myself out. Can't find yourself if you're always with someone else." I uttered the words like a mantra. And it was. Something I'd been telling myself since Chris left and I realized I'd never developed as a person.

Angela's face pulled back like she'd tasted something sour. "What do you mean, find yourself?"

"You know, find myself. Figure out who I am all by myself. Be single for a while and just, I don't know, be."

"You don't feel like you know yourself?"

I shrugged. "I guess not. All I know for sure is that as soon as Chris was gone I felt empty. And not because I missed him, or missed us, I just felt like I didn't know what I was supposed to do next. There wasn't anything *to* do. Life had changed so dramatically, but then again, it hadn't changed at all. Chris was gone, but nothing had really changed. Isn't that weird? I mean, you're with someone for what seems like forever, but once he's gone, shouldn't it be different? Should there be a gaping hole?"

"I'd assume so," she said softly.

"Me too." I brought the blanket all the way up to my shoulders, covering as much of myself as I could, trying to block the wind. "He was gone and I was alone and while I was pissed he'd cheated, I was more upset that he hadn't taken a piece of me with him."

"Is that so bad? It would have been worse if he'd taken a piece of you."

"It might have hurt more, but it would have meant he had a piece of me to begin with. As it was, I'd never given him a part of me to hold on to." I looked up at her. "How sad is that?"

She didn't answer me and I assumed it was because it was sad, but she didn't want to say that to my face. After a moment, she finally spoke.

"Well, to be honest, I'm not sure which is worse: never giving up a piece of yourself, or giving so much of yourself up that there's nothing left." There was a definite tone of sadness to her voice, as though she were speaking from experience. "I mean, there are days I don't even remember who I was a year ago. Isn't that sad? Don't get me wrong," she hurried to say, looking at me like she was worried I was judging her. "I love the babies and I love being a mom, it's just, well, no one ever explained that once you become a mother, it almost feels like everything you were before simply falls away."

121

We both sat in silence for a while, the chair swinging gently back and forth, the sky becoming a pretty shade of light blue.

"I remember who you were a year ago," I said softly. "You were out-to-here pregnant," I said, making a wide circle in front of me with my arms. "You were happy and gorgeous and waiting very impatiently to meet your babies. You were excited about being a mom and terribly in love with my brother. You were somewhat of a shopaholic, definitely a shoe connoisseur, and an expert on '80s chick flicks."

She laughed, which made me feel as though I'd said something right, made her feel a little bit better. "Ugh," she groaned between chuckles. "My feet grew an entire size with my pregnancy. All my best shoes don't even fit anymore."

"Sounds like we need to go shoe shopping," I said, giving her a nudge with my shoulder.

"Yeah." She sighed.

"No, seriously," I said excitedly, inspiration hitting me. "Let's leave the babies here with Dad and Brody, and you, my mom, and I will go shopping. There're outlet malls about thirty minutes from here."

"Outlets?" she asked, eyes wide.

"We could stop for coffee first."

"Coffee?"

I knew I had her with coffee.

We both turned our heads toward the sliding glass door when we heard it open. My mother stepped outside and I started to panic.

"Did we wake you?" I asked, feeling guilty for being too loud.

"Sorry," Angela said, almost interrupting me. "I woke Talia up early this morning for a walk. We were just sitting here watching the sky change color and talking."

My eyes snapped to Angela, but she didn't give even one little indication of her lie. It never occurred to me that Angela would lie to my mother so I wouldn't have to explain that I'd slept with the man next door. Granted, I was an adult and could sleep with whomever I chose, but I didn't need to broadcast my sex life to my mother. I'd never felt more grateful or close to Angela than I did just then. In fact, I was going to buy her a pair of shoes.

"Oh, don't be silly. You didn't wake me up. Your father sawing logs did."

"We were talking about taking a girls' day. You know, coffee and shopping. No husbands or babies. Sound like a good idea?" I asked my mom, wanting to direct all train of thought away from why we were all up so early.

"Oh, that sounds fabulous. A girls' day!" Mom clapped her hands and then went inside, talking to herself about making breakfast and curling her hair.

"Thank you," I said softly, looking over at Angela.

She shrugged. "It's no big deal. Your mom wouldn't care. In fact, I think your mom would be pretty excited if she knew you'd let the neighbor in your pants."

"Oh my gosh," I cried, dropping my head into my hands. "You're right and it's so terrifying." I laughed, shaking my head.

"It's pretty funny, though." Her laughter trailed off with a sigh. "You know, your mom just wants you to be happy. She worries about you."

"She worries about you too," I replied.

"I know."

"We all do. You don't have to do it all on your own, you know. And don't be afraid to ask for help. Just try not to treat us all like idiots when you do." I narrowed my eyes at her, but kept the smile on my face.

"I know I can be a little overbearing." She took in a deep breath and then let it out slowly. "I'm sorry. I think I've been a little overwhelmed. It's no excuse, but it's all I've got."

"Aw, I still love ya," I said, trying to ease the tension.

Shopping had been exactly what the proverbial doctor ordered. An hour away from the responsibilities of babies and Angela was the fun, carefree woman I'd befriended so long ago. Granted, she still texted Brody every thirty minutes to check up on them, but I could tell she wasn't obsessing over it. And more importantly, she was enjoying herself. Coffee and shopping extended into lunch and cocktails, and neither me, my mother, nor Angela complained one bit.

"I'm pretty sure this means we have to stay home with the kids tomorrow so Brody and your father can go fishing in the morning."

"I can't even care," Angela said happily, taking a sip of her pink concoction. "I've had the best day. Thank you both." She gave us genuine and meaningful smiles. "I'll be happy to be on baby duty tomorrow."

"Me too," I readily agreed, clinking my glass against hers.

"What shall we do next?" Mom asked, taking a bite of her salad.

"Oh, um," I started, suddenly blushing. "I have plans this afternoon with Briggs."

"You do?" Mom asked, surprise clear in her voice. "What kind of plans?"

I shrugged. "I'm not entirely sure. He asked me to meet him at the beach at four."

"You guys sure have been spending a lot of time on the beach," Angela said with a smirk.

I narrowed my eyes at her.

"She's right," Mom added. "What's going on there?"

"Nothing. Nothing important, anyway. He's a good guy." I shrugged again. "It's no big deal."

"No big deal? He's gorgeous and single. It's most definitely a big deal." Leave it to my mother to surprise me. Angela and I let out loud laughs at her words.

"You think he's gorgeous?" I asked through my laughter.

My mother glared at me over the rim of her martini glass. "Talia, that man is sex on a stick."

That time, Angela and I couldn't contain our laughter. It peeled out of us, loud and contagious, as my mother started laughing with us as well.

"I'll make sure to pass along that little tidbit," I managed to say a few moments later, wiping tears from my face.

"If you spend the afternoon with him and only manage to tell him your mother thinks he's sexy, well, I fear I've done you wrong, my dear daughter. You should be spending your time trying to bed him."

"Bed him?" I laughed again, shocked. "Only my mother would use the terms sex on a stick and bed him within minutes of each other."

"I don't think you have to worry about Talia bedding him," Angela said quietly.

I shot her another look, only that one was much more of the What the Hell variety. My mother's mouth gaped open and her gaze landed on me, eyes wide.

125

"Have you slept with the handsome neighbor, Talia Marie?"

Oh, damn. Middle name.

"Mom, I don't think—"

"Talia, I don't need explicit details, but I think we're all adult enough to have a rational conversation about the sex you're having with the neighbor." Her words were firm and her stare was on point. I never thought I'd feel pressure to talk to my mother about my sex life, but in that moment, I had little other choice.

"Okay. Yes, I've slept with him. But just once. Last night."

Angela gave some excited claps from her chair, smiling widely.

"This is very good news," my mother stated, as though I'd just told her I had a cavity-free dental check-up.

"Please tell me you're going to sleep with him again," Angela begged.

"I, uh, well, I'm not sure. I mean, I think that's the plan."

"There is nothing wrong with a little sex *just because*," my mother added, still stabbing her salad with her fork. "You don't have to be seriously committed to every person you sleep with, Talia."

"I know," I said, a little defensively.

"I slept with a few men before I met your father, and I think that was a smart choice on my part. I never had to wonder if I was missing anything in the bedroom department."

"Mom, no," I cried, covering my ears. "I really don't want to hear about you and Dad having sex."

"Why not? I won't go into specifics. All I'm saying is that it's healthy to experience the act of sex with different men."

"I've been with five men," Angela added, obviously taking my mom's side. "Brody being the fifth." She brought her martini glass to her mouth, sipping slowly, then continued. "I agree with your mom. If I hadn't been with those other men I would have never been able to tell whether or not my connection with Brody was different, or better. I don't think we're saying you need to sleep with a bunch of men, but there's nothing wrong with having safe, consensual, casual sex with someone. Especially now."

"What do you mean, now?"

"Well, now that you're single again. The worst thing you could do would be to lock yourself away and isolate yourself."

"I don't isolate myself."

Angela glared at me. "You do."

"Okay, well, I'll make sure I have lots of sex with him while I'm here. I'll let him know you both approve."

"Oh, Lord, do not tell your father you're sleeping with the neighbor."

My eyes went crazy wide. "I wasn't planning on it."

"Your brother either," Angela added.

"I wasn't really planning on telling anyone, so unless you two open your mouths about it, the secret should be safe between us."

"Well, good. It would ruin your father's vacation if he knew you were having sex."

"Likewise," I snorted.

A few hours later I was finally walking on to the beach. My mother continued to grill me about Briggs, all the while Angela prodded for information. I tried not to give away too much—things you wouldn't want your mother knowing about your sex life—but I had to admit, their interrogation made me less nervous about meeting him. I was too focused on getting away from them and their questions that I was practically running toward the ocean.

I wore my red bikini like he'd asked, but I had my loose, white, crocheted cover-up on over it. The sand was hot against my feet, warmed by the hot afternoon sun, and the wind from that morning was gone. I absolutely couldn't stop the smile that formed on my lips when Briggs's form came into view. He was standing next to two surf boards that were sticking straight up out of the sand. His body was covered by his wetsuit, but it took no time for my mind to conjure up all the images of his naked body I'd seen from the night before.

He must have been looking for me because he turned around when I was still out of earshot, with about fifty yards between us. He rested one hand atop the surfboard closest to him and his other hand came to his hip, and he watched me as I walked toward him.

"You made it," he said as I stopped with just a foot between us.

"Here I am." I held a hand up over my brows, trying to block the bright sun as I looked up at him. "Am I here to watch you surf? 'Cause I could totally be on board with that plan." Watching him surf before had been ridiculously sexy and I hadn't even known him then.

"Sort of. I'm going to teach you how to surf."

My face pulled back and brows drew together in surprise. "Uh, I don't think so. There's very little in this world that would compel me to enter the Pacific Ocean. It's freezing, Briggs."

"That's what wet suits are for."

"I don't have a wet suit."

"Is that the only reason? The water temperature?"

"I repeat, it's *freezing*."

"Okay, well, if that's your only complaint, I'm happy to tell you that I have a wet suit for you to borrow. No need to thank me." Sure enough, Briggs reached down into a bag I hadn't noticed sitting next to his board and pulled out a wet suit.

"Oh, my word."

"That's right. We're getting you up on a board." His smile was adorable and made my belly flutter with warmth.

"Okay." I sighed, realizing I had lost the battle before it started.

Fast forward twenty minutes and Briggs unabashedly watching me shimmy myself into a wetsuit, and he had me closer to the water, which looked ridiculously cold. I watched as he drew a very rough outline of a surfboard on the sand.

"Okay, it's simple really. You lie down on the board, wait for a wave to come in, then paddle as hard as you can, and right before it breaks under you, you pop up and ride it in. Sounds easy, right?"

"Not really," I deadpan.

"It's easier to learn through trial and error, but it's smart to go through the basics on land just in case. So, lie down on your stomach."

"On the sand?"

"Yeah, firecracker, on the sand."

I rolled my eyes but did as he said. He knelt next to me and placed his hand on the small of my back, applying a small amount of pressure. Even through the thick layer of neoprene of the wetsuit, his hand against me still sent shocks of electricity through my body. I definitely remembered what his hands felt like on my skin and I was currently cursing the frigid waters of the Pacific that made the wetsuit necessary.

"So, like I said, you're just going to be waiting for a good-sized wave. They're not going to be huge here, but you'll be able to tell a good one from a bad one. Wait for a good one. Surfing takes a lot of energy and if you go after small waves you'll just tire yourself out. When a good wave comes, you're going to paddle to get in front of it, yeah? So, show me how you paddle."

I rolled my eyes again, but smiled too, and started to pantomime paddling in the ocean.

"Very good." His voice was low and husky and I held my breath as his hand slid over my ass.

"I feel like you're taking advantage of your instructor role." I tried to sound authoritative, but the words came out breathy.

"Really? I always thought positive reinforcement was a good teaching method." The smile was evident in this voice and I wanted to call him a smartass, but I refrained. "Okay, so you're paddling and now it's time to pop up. Use your hands to push yourself up, stay low, and keep your feet a little wider than shoulder width apart. Got it?"

"Okay," I said with less surety than I felt. His hand disappeared from my body. I pushed myself off the sand and attempted to pop up like he'd instructed. And I felt like an idiot. Luckily there weren't many people on the beach, but it was still a little mortifying pretending to surf on my imaginary board. My thoughts were interrupted by Briggs's hands gripping my waist on either side.

"Lower," he said, his lips suddenly right next to my ear, as he used his hands to pull my hips. "The lower your center of gravity, the easier it will be to balance." His fingers dug into me as he tugged me lower still. "Bend your knees. Arms out." I followed his instructions and felt him press closer into me from behind. "So now, I want you to practice popping up and getting into this position as fast as you can. After you've done it fifteen times to my satisfaction, we can move into the water."

Thirty minutes later I was exhausted and sweaty, but I'd managed to improve my pop up and Briggs deemed me water-worthy. I knew the water would be cold, but I was so hot from the workout, I welcomed the frigid bath.

Briggs handed me my board, took his, and we walked out to the water. When we were thigh deep, he laid his board on the water and I followed suit.

"Climb on," he said, rapping his hand on the hard surface of my board.

I gave him a hesitant look but climbed on. It was terribly ungraceful and I felt like an idiot, but I made it on and then watched as he effortlessly slid up onto his. He started paddling and then looked over his shoulder at me.

"Let's go," he said with a nod toward the water.

I sighed but paddled after him. Who was I kidding? I'd probably follow him anywhere. And it wasn't a bad view either.

When he finally stopped paddling I realized we were farther out into the ocean than I'd ever been without the protection of a boat. Suddenly the dark water was a little frightening. He pushed himself up into a sitting position and I copied him, still freaking out about my feet dangling in the water.

"Are there sharks here?"

I heard him try to stifle a chuckle.

"No sharks will get you," he said, still laughing a little.

"That's not what I asked you," I grumbled.

"You'll be fine. Okay, so, why don't you watch me go once, and then I'll come back and you'll give it a try?"

"Okay." I watched as he faced his board toward the shore and looked over his shoulder at the waves coming in. He seemed to spot one he liked because he started paddling and then it was just as he described. His arms propelled him through the water until the wave was right below him and then suddenly he was standing, using his body to maneuver the board through the water. I watched in awe, totally impressed by the show—it was even better up close. He rode the wave until it seemed to disintegrate beneath his board, then he dove into the water, popping up a few moments later and shaking the water from his hair. He grabbed his board with one hand, but his eyes found mine and he smiled.

God, he was beautiful.

He smiled the entire time he was paddling back toward me and it only grew brighter as he came to float next to me.

"That was incredible," I said, still in awe of his ability.

"Your turn." He sat up on his board again and ran a hand through his wet hair.

"I can guarantee you I won't be any good at this."

"Probably not on the first try, no. But you might surprise yourself. Look, there's a good wave coming."

I looked over my shoulder and sure enough there was a wave coming that was considerably bigger than the last few had been. I sighed but started paddling anyway. I tried looking behind me to see how close the wave was after a few strokes and was surprised to see Briggs paddling along next to me.

"In about four seconds you're gonna want to pop up, firecracker."

132

I counted to four and felt the board dip in a new way and took that as my cue. I placed my hands flat on the board and pushed up at the same time as I brought my feet forward. Fortunately, my feet hit the board at the same time and I felt relatively balanced, so I tried to stand. As soon as my hands left the board I was headed for the water. But there were about two seconds where I felt as though I was soaring.

Hitting the water was jarring, but not terrible, and when I popped through the surface, gasping for air, I could hear Briggs immediately.

"You were so close, Talia! You were almost there. Come on, try again."

His excitement was contagious and I found myself smiling at him, wanting to give it another go. I pulled myself back up onto my board and paddled after him.

Two hours passed filled with Briggs teaching me to surf. He was a good instructor, never losing his patience, even when I made the same mistake of popping up too soon what seemed like a million times. I got up on my feet a couple of times and I could understand why people surfed; it was exhilarating. I felt powerful and inconsequential at the same time. It was almost as if I owned the waves, controlled the sea, but at the same time knew I was completely at its mercy. Each time I saw a little success Briggs was clapping and hollering from atop his board, which was completely adorable.

Every once in a while, I think he could tell I needed a rest, so he'd ride a few waves, giving me the opportunity to watch him. It was incredible, the way he owned his board. The last wave he'd ridden almost all the way to the shore, only abandoning his board when the wave finally died. He stood, the water only coming to the middle of this thigh, and waved me toward him.

I paddled, catching one last wave and practically squealing with delight when I stood up and counted to eight before falling in the water.

"And you thought you wouldn't be any good," he said as I finally made it to him.

"Oh, please, that wasn't good. That was passable."

"Pretty damn passable for a first try."

I would have blushed if I wasn't so cold. Paddling and swimming kept me pretty warm for the past few hours, but now, with half my body out of the water, the cold was setting in.

"You hungry?" he asked.

I realized it was close to dinner time, almost past, in fact.

"Yeah. I could eat."

"You like pizza?" he asked, head cocked and grin on his lips.

"I do."

"Good, 'cause my kitchen is not ready for cooking. Come on," he said, nodding toward his house. "We'll go dry off and I'll order in."

I could find no good reason to argue.

We both grabbed our boards and walked back to the spot on the beach where his bag waited with my cover-up and flip-flops. He packed it all up and put the handle of the bag over his shoulder, picked up his board, and then grabbed my hand in his. We continued away from the ocean, toward his house, walking over the dune, through the path lined with tall grass, and eventually his house came into view.

When we got close to the house, I started toward the left, heading to the front door, but he gently pulled on my hand, leading me to the right. He walked me to the back of the house, the side that faced the ocean, and leaned his board against the house, then took my board from me and did the same. He left the bag by the boards, then took my hand and tugged me farther around the house. Finally, I realized where we were going when I noticed a cement slab and a shower nozzle jutting out from the house.

Without any words or explanation, he pulled on the handle to turn the water on and adjusted the temperature, using his hand to test the water. When it had apparently met his desired temperature, he turned me around until my back was facing him and I felt him tugging down the zipper on the back of my wetsuit. His hands grasped each side of the neoprene and he pulled the suit over my shoulders and down my arms. I pulled up, helping to free my arms, and with a little effort he got the suit peeled down to my waist.

He turned me slowly, pulling me into the warm spray of the water, and I leaned back out of habit, letting the water cascade through my hair. When I opened my eyes again, after smoothing my hair back from my face, Briggs's eyes were roaming over every exposed part of me. While I liked the fact that he was looking at me, I didn't think it was fair.

"Turn around," I said with more confidence than I felt.

He spun around and I gripped the zipper, pulling it down slowly, enjoying all too much watching the muscles of his back appear. I slipped my fingers under the wetsuit and moved my hand up his shoulder blades, feeling all the corded muscle in his back. I tried to push the wetsuit over his arms, but I wasn't as strong as he was and the suit snagged just over his shoulders. He took over, peeling one arm out at a time as he turned back to me. Faster than I thought possible his arms were free and he was closing the distance between us, his hands coming up to frame my face and his lips crashing down on mine.

135

Instantly his tongue pushed into my mouth and I welcomed it, groaning at the salty taste of him. He tasted like the sea and man and it was incredibly arousing. Hell, mostly everything about Briggs was arousing. He walked me backward until I was pressed up against the house, his hands moving to span my waist, his mouth still devouring mine. Slowly his hands moved up my body until his thumbs stopped just below the triangle of my bikini covering each breast.

"Ever since you walked onto the beach today I've wanted to peel this scrap of fabric off you." He breathed the words against my lips, not even pulling away far enough to speak without our lips touching. His tongue darted out and grazed my bottom lip, gently swiping across, and I heard myself moan.

Somewhere in the back of my mind I was trying to figure out if anyone from the beach could see us. The sun was setting, so it was getting darker, and the dune would block most of us from view. I simply didn't care enough to stop him.

His thumbs snuck under the edge of my bikini top, gently caressing the underside of my breasts. I gasped against his mouth then reached out and pulled him closer, one hand grabbing his bicep, while the other wound around his neck. I let my fingers thread through his wet hair and I heard him groan quietly. Slowly, his thumbs made another pass, this time passing right over both of my nipples. My pulse was thundering through my body, throbbing between my legs, and warmth flooded through me.

"Please take me upstairs," I mumbled against his mouth.

Not a moment later both his hands abandoned my breasts, the water shut off, and I was being lifted by my ass. My legs instinctively wrapped around his waist and I cursed the multiple layers of wetsuit between us. His mouth pulled away from mine as he walked around the outside of his house, but my mouth found his neck and I laved kisses all along the length of it.

136

Before I knew it, he was in the house and up the stairs, placing my feet on the floor of his bedroom. He knelt in front of me, gripping the wetsuit around my waist and pulling it down, taking my bikini bottoms with it. Then he removed his wetsuit just as quickly, revealing he'd been wearing absolutely nothing under his. I tried not to gawk at his naked form, but I only had so much self-control. He was beautiful. Everything about him was masculine, especially the way he looked right into my eyes and said, "Get on the bed."

I didn't waste any time.

I backed up until my legs hit the bed and then I crawled backward, never breaking eye contact. When I was in the center of the bed I rested back on my elbows and tilted my knees to one side, trying to hold on to some modesty. He smirked at me, then grabbed one of my ankles in each hand and yanked me down the bed back toward him. My legs spread and my arms went over my head and in an instant, he was over me, kissing his way up my body.

His mouth covered my nipple, sucking hard over my bikini top, then biting gently. At the same time his hand slid from my waist down to my core and a finger slipped between my folds, dipping in and then coming back up to circle my clit. It was a cacophony of sensations, each action warring for attention, my body absolutely writhing from the onslaught of stimulation.

"I want to make you come like this," he rasped against my breast. His free hand pushed the fabric up and over my breast, his strong and rough hand running over my nipple, then his mouth was back. All the while he worked his fingers in, out, and up, over and over again. My hips worked against his hand, trying desperately to give him exactly what he wanted—my climax.

"Yes," I breathed, my hands finding purchase on the sheets. My face turned to the side, eyes closed, solely focused on the immensity of what I was feeling, on what Briggs was doing to my body. "Don't stop."

137

"Wouldn't dream of it, firecracker." He pushed up the other side of my bikini and I felt him tug on it, the knot in the back giving way, and I was bare. It was all I could do to just take whatever he was giving me. Finally, he thrust two fingers deep, rubbing me in exactly the most glorious spot, and his thumb circled my clit. It took just a few moments and I was coming. My back arched, my jaw fell open, and I was moaning so loud I would look back later and be embarrassed about it. But right then, with my body convulsing in pleasure, feeling his mouth smile and growl around my breast, I couldn't find it in me to care what I looked or sounded like. All that mattered was he was playing my body like an instrument and I absolutely loved it.

He slowed his movements as I came down from my orgasm, his hand moving slowly through my wetness, leaving lazy kisses from one breast to the other. I finally managed to open my eyes and I found him looking at me with a smug grin on his face.

"Don't look so pleased with yourself," I said with a laugh.

"It looked like you enjoyed yourself."

I shivered—a combination of his words and the fact that his fingers were still trailing between my folds, my clit still overly sensitive. I loved how intimate it was, how he seemed to want to touch me all the time as much as he could, but it was unnerving as well. I was keyed up and his touch was almost too much. I put a hand to his shoulder and pushed as I sat up. He got the message and rolled to his back, allowing me to climb on top of him. His hands went to my hips, holding me close to him. I leaned down, pressing my lips to his, letting my messy and wet hair fall around us. He kissed me back, his tongue pushing into my mouth, his hands gripping my waist, his hips jutting up. He wanted in, and I wanted that too, but I wanted something else first.

I moved down, pressing my lips along his neck, his chest, his stomach. He figured out where I was headed and let out a gruff, "Fuck."

I settled between his thighs and took him in my hand. There hadn't been a great opportunity to take inventory before, but right then, while up close and personal with his cock, I determined it was impressive. Stupidly male, just like everything else about him.

My tongue darted out, licking the head, and I felt him jerk beneath me, his hips moving off the bed slightly. I smiled, loving the idea of him reacting to what I was doing. I moved to the base and licked from root to tip. When I reached the top, I didn't stop, just took him all the way in my mouth and slid back down. He groaned and his hand came to my head, sweeping my hair away from one side of my face and flipping it to the other side. I angled my head so he could watch, since that seemed to be his goal. I had to admit, knowing he was looking at what I was doing, taking him in my mouth while he held my hair back, it was possibly the sexiest I'd ever felt.

Blow jobs had never been something I particularly enjoyed. It did it on occasion but usually just to please a partner. However, it was a completely different experience with Briggs. When I took him deep, when I felt him all the way at the back of my throat, it wasn't annoyance I felt, or obligation. I felt powerful. His eyes were on me and he was obviously enjoying it. If the slight thrusting of his hips didn't give it away, his bottom lip between his teeth and his hand still gripping my hair told me everything I wanted to know.

I sucked him down again, hearing a groan when I'd taken him as far as I could, and I slipped my hand from his length and cupped his balls, rolling them gently.

"Damn, Tal," he said through gritted teeth.

I hummed around him, loving the way he felt in my mouth, the way I could still smell the sea on him. I pulled back, sucking hard, and I heard his gasp, then suddenly I was being hauled off him, his hands under my arms. He rolled me, putting me on my back, and I watched him reach for his bedside table, rip open a condom, slide it down his length, and then settle over me, all within a matter of seconds.

Before I could even register anything else happening, his hands were pushing my knees out and up, and he was thrusting into me. We let out matching groans and he stilled when he was buried in me, letting me stretch to accommodate him. He pulled out then pushed back in roughly, as though he was trying to reach the very end of me, to fill every part of me to the absolute hilt.

I reached out for him, my hands hitting his stomach, feeling all his muscles hardened from effort, and I slid my fingers around to the back of him, trying to pull him closer. I needed the weight of him to press down on me, for the weight of the way I was feeling at the moment to match what I was experiencing physically.

He came down to me willingly, and he rested his face in the crook of my neck, still thrusting powerfully into me. I wrapped my arms around him and took everything he was offering. Soon we were both coming apart and coming together.

Chapter Twelve

Briggs

I pulled the front door open, wanting the incessant banging to stop. The pounding woke me up from a very deep, very comfortable sleep. In fact, I'd had my arm wrapped tightly around Talia and hadn't been too happy to let her go, but I knew who was at the door as soon as I'd heard the loud knocking.

"Hey, Porter," I said, my voice groggy. I opened the door wide and stepped back, giving him the room he needed to come in.

"Briggs," he said with a knowing grin. "Did I wake you?"

"Something like that."

"Sorry, man," he apologized, but didn't sound sorry at all. "Gotta get started early."

"I know. It's cool." And it was. Hell, I was paying Porter to do a job and I wanted it done. I just wanted to lie with Talia in my arms a little more than I wanted the construction on my kitchen to start. "You need me for anything today?"

"Nah, man. You've helped enough. I got some men showing up here any minute."

Suddenly, the idea of my house being full of men and Talia upstairs without any clothes on bothered me. "We're probably gonna head out then. Stay out of your hair."

"We?" he asked, his smile stretching even wider. "You got someone up there? Anyone I know?"

"Fuck off," I said with a laugh as I headed back up the stairs. I walked into the bedroom and met Talia's eyes. She was awake, lying naked in my bed, and the sight nearly made me turn around and tell Porter to come back the next day. Or perhaps the next week. We only had a limited amount of time together, and right now it seemed like a great idea to spend it in bed.

141

"How'd you sleep?" I asked as I slid into bed next to her.

She had the covers pulled all the way up to her chin. She looked comfortable and relaxed.

"Great." Her voice was raspy and adorable. Her red hair was fanned out behind her, messy and sexy all at the same time. "Too good, actually. I kind of never want to leave your bed." She smiled as she said the words, but then she closed her eyes and seemed to burrow even deeper into the covers.

"As much as I'd love to keep you captive, in a few minutes my house is going to be full of men and it's going to get loud. Want to go get some breakfast?"

She peeped one eye open at me and seemed to contemplate my question. "I'm pretty sure any establishment that sells food has a No Shirt, No Service policy."

I laughed. "Well, I wasn't planning on letting you go naked."

Her eye closed again and she mumbled into my pillow. "I only have my swimsuit, Briggs. I might as well just go home. You probably have a lot of stuff to do today."

She was right. She should probably just go home. That would probably be best for both of us, but that wasn't what I wanted. I wanted to spend time with her. When she told me she would be there until the end of the week, when we agreed to spend time together, a few days seemed like it would be enough. It was becoming clear I was wrong about that.

"I can find something for you to wear. Where I want to take you isn't fancy and there's no dress code."

Both her eyes opened now, but she gave me a skeptical look.

"Come on, it'll be fine. Promise," I said in my most convincing tone.

142

She sighed, but I got the feeling she was more upset about getting out of bed than spending the morning with me, and I could understand that. I went to my dresser and found a pair of sweatpants with a drawstring in the waistband and an old T-shirt. When I turned back around she was sitting up, holding the blanket to her body, covered from the breasts down. Her flaming locks fell around her face and shoulders, and I took a moment to look at all the freckles along her collarbone. I walked toward her until I was just a few inches away, and she looked up at me from where she sat on the bed.

There was an overwhelming urge to reach out, to touch her, even if it wasn't sexual. I wanted to push her hair behind her ear or trail a finger down her neck. Instead, though, I held the clothes out to her.

"Feel free to take a shower if you want. There are extra towels under the sink."

"Briggs?" Her voice was soft and unsure and it made something in my stomach tighten.

"Yeah?"

"I think I left my phone in the bag outside last night." She finished and then immediately started blushing crimson. It took me a second, but then I realized she was referring to the shower we'd started to take yesterday after surfing, and how we'd abandoned everything when I carried her in the house instead of fucking her against the wall outside.

I leaned down and brushed a kiss against her flushed cheeks. "I'll go grab it."

"Thank you," she whispered.

I walked outside, passing two more men on Porter's crew as I did, and continued around to the back where I found the carnage of our evening. I chastised myself a little. Leaving two surf boards lying around wasn't the smartest idea. Anyone could have stolen them. The bag that held Talia's phone was on the ground next to the boards and it looked untouched. We were lucky it hadn't rained or else her things could have been ruined. Even though it was pretty dumb to have left everything out all night, I couldn't regret it.

Not even a little bit.

I grabbed the bag and put the straps over my shoulder, then took both boards and headed toward the garage. I stored the boards and continued back into the house, which was already loud with music and the sounds of construction. I made it all the way up the stairs before I heard the shower running and it took every ounce of self-control not to undress and join her.

Instead, I sat on the edge of my bed and dropped my head into my hands, trying to figure out how I was going to get this woman out from under my skin when we inevitably had to part ways.

When the door opened and she appeared, her wet hair up in some sort of knot, dressed in my clothes, I knew I was in over my head. I'd never seen anyone more beautiful than her at that moment. I could have spent the rest of my life seeing her in my T-shirt, beautiful flaming hair pulled into an unruly bundle, and it would never get old. She would never be more attractive or appealing than she was just then.

My pants were obviously too big on her, but the drawstring was pulled tight and the waistband was rolled up, making them fit a little better. My T-shirt hung off one of her shoulders, showing me those damn freckles again, and it took all my self-control not to just toss her back on the bed where I really wanted her.

Instead, I held out her phone to her. She smiled as she took it, but only looked at it for a short moment before her eyes were back to me. "I don't really feel comfortable going out in this, Briggs." She gave me an apologetic smile and looked down at my clothes hanging from her body.

I stood and went to her, resting my hands on her shoulders, letting my thumbs trail over the galaxy of freckles exposed by my too big shirt. "Trust me. You'll be fine. I wouldn't lead you astray."

She let out a sigh, but it was definitely a sigh that said, "Fine. Since you insist."

"Your flip-flops are downstairs." Before I could stop myself, I leaned down and pressed a kiss to her lips. It felt familiar and right, her lips against mine, and it was just one more thing I would have to miss after she was gone.

I took her hand and led her down the stairs, stopping to let her put her flip-flops on, then we continued to my truck. I opened her door and waited until she was situated to close the door, then rounded the front of the hood and climbed into the driver's side.

"Where did you learn to surf?" Talia and I had both been quiet for a few moments. I didn't feel the need to fill the silence, felt comfortable enough with her to not force conversation, but I smiled at her question. "I mean, you're probably the tenth person I'd ever seen surfing in Oregon. You couldn't have learned here."

"No, I didn't. My grandparents lived in Santa Cruz, California, when I was younger. I spent nearly a whole month there every summer until I graduated from high school. We'd walk to the beach almost every day. It was a great place to learn to surf."

"Are you serious?" she asked, disbelieving.

"Yeah. Why?"

"My great-grandma lived in Scott's Valley. She was thirty minutes from Santa Cruz."

"No shit?"

"Absolutely no shit." She was smiling widely at me, eyes twinkling. "She passed away a few years ago, but I've been to her house a few times. I got lost one summer on my sixth birthday on the boardwalk at Santa Cruz."

"That doesn't sound like a great memory."

"At the time it was petrifying, but now it's just another one of those things you look back on and laugh about. My grandmother was supposed to be watching me swim, but I was hit by a sneaker wave and then got disoriented. I wandered around crying, trying to find her, but couldn't, so I went back up to the boardwalk where the Ferris wheel was to find my mom. My mom was *pissed* at my grandma." She laughed again and I couldn't help but smile at the sound. "I remember the merry-go-round too, and how they had those old-fashioned rings you had to toss while you went around."

"And the roller coaster. Don't forget about that."

"Oh my gosh. I could never go on the roller coaster. Even when I was fourteen, it looked like it was going to fall apart at any moment and I was sure it would be the one time I rode it."

"Nah, that thing held up for years and years. I took my very first date on that roller coaster."

"You did? That's adorable. Tell me about it."

I shrugged, suddenly embarrassed, but she seemed genuinely interested. "We were fifteen and there really isn't much else to do there unless you are old enough to drive or drink, so I asked her to go to the boardwalk with me."

"What was her name?"

"Katie Miller."

"Was she pretty?" Talia's voice was full of curiosity and excitement. She seemed to really be interested in hearing about my first date. I couldn't understand the notion because if the roles were reversed, I definitely wouldn't be excited to hear about her dating anyone else, even if it was fifteen years ago. But, she was so cute looking at me with the question in her eyes and adorable smile on her lips, it wasn't within my capabilities to not answer.

"I mean, yeah. She was cute. I was a fifteen-year-old guy, though. I wanted to go on a date with practically anyone who had boobs."

Her laughter filled the cab of my truck and I wanted to listen to it as long as I could. It was light and unrestrained. She was laughing hard, her hand to her chest, and she was beautiful. We were driving down Highway 101, the ocean was big and blue in the background behind her, and she was laughing like she'd just heard the funniest thing in the world.

"Oh my gosh," she said, taking in a deep breath and then laughing some more. "That was the best thing I've heard in a while. Such a guy thing to say. And totally true, too."

"I have no shame about how my brain operated at fifteen."

"Your thirty-something brain doesn't have the same thoughts?" She was looking at me with mischief in her eyes.

"All I'll say is that breasts aren't my only requirements anymore."

She laughed again, this time softer, and said, "Glad to see you've broadened your horizons."

I pulled off the highway and up to a tiny drive-thru coffee stand. I wasn't particular about my coffee—it was all the same to me—but this particular stand was not a franchise and I liked the idea of supporting a small business, so I usually went out of my way to stop there. Plus, the woman who owned it made all the pastries by hand and they were incredible.

There was no line, so I pulled right up to the window and I was greeted by Nancy's smiling face.

"Briggs." She beamed as soon as I got my window down. "How've you been?"

"I've been good, Nancy. How about yourself?"

"Oh, can't complain. Been busy here, so that's all I can ask for. What are you and your lady friend drinking?" Nancy winked at me and it was not covert at all.

I looked over at Talia and she was smiling the warm smile I'd grown accustomed to.

"Well, what's your drink of choice?" I asked her.

She leaned forward, completely bypassing me, and said to Nancy, "Can I get a medium vanilla latte?"

"Sure thing, sweetheart," Nancy said sweetly. "You want your regular?" she asked me.

"Yeah, please. And two of your blueberry scones."

"Coming right up." She gave the windowsill two taps and then disappeared into her coffee stand.

"Come here often?" Talia asked with a smirk.

"A few times a week. Once you try the scones you'll understand."

"Baked goods are the way to my heart."

"Noted."

"What's your regular drink?"

"Just black coffee."

"Regular black coffee? No cream? No sugar?"

"Plain black coffee."

"That's so gross." She made a face but followed it with a smile. "I can't drink coffee unless it tastes like something other than coffee." She laughed and brought her foot up to rest on the seat, wrapping her arms around her knee. "But I need coffee to function."

"I like the flavor of coffee."

"Well, I won't hold that against you."

"Here you go, honey." Nancy was holding out a cardboard drink carrier filled with our drinks and pastry bags.

"Thanks," I said, handing over some cash. "Keep the change."

"You two have a great day, now."

"We will. Bye, Nancy!" This came from Talia as I handed her the drink carrier. She leaned forward and said her goodbye, waving and smiling like she and Nancy were old friends. I pulled forward and turned back onto the highway, still heading away from town and my house. "Where are we going?" Talia asked, her voice full of curiosity.

"I made a reservation." Her eyes went wide and I knew she was worried about her clothes. "Don't worry."

She narrowed her eyes at me, but then pulled her latte from the carrier and took a slow sip.

It took just a few minutes to get to our destination and when I pulled into the parking lot I glanced over at Talia and watched her face light up.

"This is perfect," she said quietly, then looked back at me, eyes shining.

I reached behind her seat and grabbed a hoodie I kept there and held it out to her. "Here, put this on. It can get pretty windy out there."

She took it from me and I hopped out of the truck, heading over to her door. When I opened it, she was pulling the hoodie over her head, still smiling. She brushed her hand over her hair, trying to tame the damage the hoodie had done, which I knew would be useless once we made it to our destination. She grabbed the carrier, which held both our drinks and scones again, and I reached out for her other hand to help her down.

I tried to ignore the way her hand felt in mine. I didn't want to think about the way it fit so perfectly, or felt as though it belonged there. Instead of focusing on those feelings, I decided to just not let it go right away. So I closed her door and threaded my fingers through hers and led the way.

Just as I suspected for mid-morning on a weekday, no one was at the coastal viewpoint and we had it all to ourselves. There was a jutting hill that ended with a sharp cliffside where one could watch waves crash against the wall of rock, but there were also a few picnic tables not so close to the edge and that was where I took Talia.

As we approached I took the carrier from her and placed it on the table. I straddled the bench and sat facing the ocean. Then I patted the bench in front of me and Talia took the hint, situating herself in the same manner as me and sitting right in between my legs. She took her coffee, sipping it as she looked out over the ocean, and I leaned one elbow on the table, letting my other hand rest on her hip.

"This is an incredible view, Briggs." She spoke the words a little loudly, talking over the breeze that was always present there. I loved the way it made the wispy hairs on the back of her neck float and swirl around. They looked like tiny little flames against her pale skin.

"Mmm. I agree." I could see the blush creep up her neck as she realized I wasn't talking about the ocean. Neither of us said anything for a few minutes and I was thoroughly enjoying doing nothing with her. All of a sudden, she spoke.

"It's weird how loudly quiet it is."

I couldn't help but laugh. "Loudly quiet?"

"Yeah. I mean, it's quiet here, right? There's no sound except the wind and the ocean, which are loud, but it still feels silent. Quiet enough to hear my thoughts, I suppose, which are louder than the wind and waves combined."

"I get that," I agreed. "Sometimes our thoughts are louder than anything."

"Yeah," she said so quietly, she probably didn't think I could hear.

After a few moments of quiet, a large gust of wind came and I watched her curl into her center, bringing her coffee close to her chest. Wrapping my arm around her shoulders, I brought her back to my chest and then wrapped my hoodie around her and held her close to me. She let me take her weight and rested against me, and then her head fell back against my shoulder and her body relaxed with a sigh. And that was how we stayed. I didn't know if two minutes or two hours had passed. All I knew was that I was content.

When we did finally move, it was because she started vibrating. Literally. She sat up and pulled her phone from her pocket, swiped her finger across the screen and said, "Hey, Mom." The phone was to her ear, and the wind was still blowing, but even I could hear the panicked cries coming from the other end of the phone. I was instantly on edge and could feel the fear pulse through Talia. "Mom, calm down, I can't understand you." She stood up, holding a finger to her ear, trying to hear her mother better. I was on my feet with her. "Oh my God," she gasped, wide eyes turned to me. I put my hand on her back and guided her toward the truck. I didn't know what was going on, but I knew we needed to go.

151

"Okay, I'm on my way. Oh my God." Her voice sounded on the verge of tears. I opened the passenger door and helped her in, then jogged to my door. When I looked over at her after climbing up, she had tears in her eyes. I moved to the middle of the bench seat and pulled her into me. I felt her crying before I heard it, but it broke some part of me just the same.

"Shhh," I said, running my hand up and down her back, then up to rest on the back of her neck. "Tell me what I need to do. Where are we going?"

"Samaritan North," she rasped against my neck.

Fuck. The hospital.

"Okay," I said gently. I pulled back and kissed her forehead. I moved back to my side of the truck and didn't complain when she moved with me. She was clinging to my arm, crying quietly. I wanted to comfort her, to just hold her and tell her everything was going to be all right, but I knew I had to get her to the hospital. So I drove.

Chapter Thirteen

Talia

Briggs never asked what had happened, he just held me and then took me where I needed to go. In fact, I had no idea where the hospital was. I just trusted him to get me there. And he did. He pulled right up to the entrance of the emergency room. All I had to do was open my door and I'd be right where I needed to be.

"Go find your family," he said.

Even in my emotionally ransacked state, I was a little disappointed he would just drop me off. But I shook the thought from my head. Of course he was just dropping me off. He didn't know my family. He didn't even really know me. It was so kind of him to have even driven me there. I looked up at him, wiped my eyes, and said a shaky, "Thank you." I scooted over to my side of the truck, opened the door, hopped down, and he immediately pulled away.

I took a deep breath and walked into the hospital. It was a tiny building, nothing compared to the hospitals in Portland, but since it was so small, it was very clear where I was headed. I followed the signs to the emergency room and walked straight to the admit desk. A friendly-looking woman smiled at me as I approached.

"Hi, I'm looking for my family. Should be Lennick. Angela or Brody. Or Beckett."

"Ah, yes. They're in room four. Through those doors, second room on the right."

"Thank you," I said quickly as I turned toward the doors. I found room four and went in, expecting the worst.

Angela was sitting on the hospital bed, cradling Beckett in her arms, and it was very obvious she'd been crying. Hard. Brody was at her bedside, one hand on her shoulder, the other on Beckett's back. My mother and father were sitting in chairs against the wall, little Raina asleep in her car seat next to my mother.

"Hey," I said quietly as I entered, my eyes sweeping over everyone, trying to figure out where the danger was. "What's going on?" In truth, I was in the dark. My mother had called, frantic, and was crying about the baby and an ambulance, but I never really got more details from her because she was out of her mind.

At my question, Angela immediately burst into tears again and a wave of guilt crashed over me. Brody leaned over and wrapped his arms around her, and Beckett stirred a little, but Angela rocked him back to sleep as she cried. I looked over at my parents and my mother was weeping, my father sporting a sad look on his face.

Finally, my brother spoke.

"Somehow, Beckett got a hold of a quarter and managed to get it to his mouth. He swallowed it and choked."

"I was changing Raina's diaper and I looked over and he was turning blue, making a weird noise."

"Oh no," I gasped, my hand coming to cover my mouth.

"I shouted for Brody to call nine-one-one, and I flipped him over and started pounding on his back, but it wouldn't come out..." Her last word trailed off with a sob and I walked over to her and Beckett, resting my hand on her leg and trying to keep my own cries in. Just picturing Beckett choking on anything made my stomach hurt and my chest feel tight. I couldn't imagine being there, being his mother, and seeing him that way. It made my heart ache.

154

"The ambulance was dispatched and he was still choking. Angela must have hit him on the back thirty times. And eventually, the quarter flew out. And he immediately started crying." Brody told me this as Angela was still sobbing, rocking her baby boy in her arms.

"Is he all right?" I asked, never more afraid to hear an answer to a question.

"They think he's probably fine," my brother said, but he didn't sound happy about it. He sounded worried and scared. "They said since he was conscious the whole time and started crying as soon as it dislodged, there probably isn't any serious damage. But if Angela hadn't gotten the quarter out..." He couldn't finish his sentence and I didn't want him to.

"But she did," I said gently, giving Angela a squeeze.

"He was blue," Angela cried, her face buried in her baby's neck. I heard my mother sniffling from her chair across the room.

"You saved him, Angela. You did so great. He needed help and you were there and you did everything right." I was trying to be strong for her. I knew she didn't need me crying too, but it was hard. "What did the doctors say?"

"They are mainly just observing right now. They say there may be some soreness in his esophagus, and his back may be sore too. But they looked him over and checked all his vitals and said he looked normal. I think they're just keeping him here for a few hours to monitor him." Brody, my annoying brother, had never sounded more like a father than he did in that moment.

"That sounds promising. This is good news." Just as I said those words the door opened and a doctor walked in, complete with stethoscope around his neck. He looked like he was my parents' age with gray hair, glasses, and a reassuring smile.

He walked to the edge of the bed and placed a friendly hand on Angela's ankle. "How's Beckett doing?"

"Still sleeping," Brody answered.

"Any changes?" he asked with a smile. Angela shook her head. "Great. I'll just examine him quickly and get out of your hair." He walked toward the head of the bed where I was standing, so I moved to stand next to my mother and watched the gentle doctor examine little Beckett without disturbing him or Angela. He listened to his breathing, checked his pulse, and generally just gave him a good looking over. "He looks perfect. We'll watch him for a bit longer, but I'm pretty confident we can get you home by dinner time."

Angela nodded, but didn't say anything in response.

The doctor placed a hand on her shoulder. "He's very lucky you were there. You did exactly the right thing."

Angela nodded again, but still said nothing.

"Thank you, Doctor," Brody said and reached over the bed to shake his hand.

"No problem. He's definitely a little fighter. Ring the nurse if anything changes or you have any questions."

"We will."

The doctor ran his hand over Beckett's soft, baby fine hair, gave Angela one last smile, and then left, giving the rest of us a practiced smile.

"That sounds promising," I said, hoping to lighten the mood a little. "Home by dinner."

"What are you wearing?" Brody asked, seeming to suddenly take a good look at me.

I looked down and my stomach dropped. I was definitely wearing Briggs's clothes. And there was no mistaking them. Men's sweatpants and shirt. Shit.

"My pajamas." I was a terrible liar.

"Those clothes are huge on you. They can't be yours." The glare I aimed at Brody rivaled all other glares.

"They're comfy," I said harshly, narrowing my eyes at him, hoping he'd get the hint.

Angela and my mom probably knew what was up, but the last thing I needed was to explain to my father that I'd slept somewhere else last night. Although, I'm sure the fact that I wasn't there that morning probably clued him in. Regardless, I didn't think the hospital room was the time or place to discuss whose clothes I was currently wearing.

Thankfully, Raina chose that exact moment to start squawking in her car seat. I turned toward her and knelt down to undo the harness and clips keeping her secured in the contraption. She smiled at me as soon as I was within her sight and my heart melted a little like it always did when the babies showed me their toothy and gummy grins.

"Hello, sweet girl, come see Auntie Tally." I lifted her and brought her to my chest, holding her close and gently swaying back and forth. She let me rock her for a minute, but then lost interest in snuggling and pulled back, twisting at the waist to see the rest of the room and probably evaluate what kind of chaos she wanted to initiate first. Her eyes were drawn to the window, so I walked over to it so she could look out, hoping that would buy us some time before she was inevitably bored and started squawking again.

The next two hours passed with my mom, my dad, and me trying to entertain Raina while Angela and Brody comforted Beckett. He was awake on and off, but Angela was worried about how much he was sleeping. The nurse who came in periodically to check on him said it was normal, that he was probably tired after such a stressful event. When Beckett was awake, he was cranky. The doctor ordered some baby pain medicine, saying it was very likely his throat and back hurt. But still, there was little concern on the medical staff's part. They seemed to think he was recovering nicely.

After a few minutes of crying, Angela gave Beckett a warm bottle and that seemed to calm him, sending him back to dreamland. Raina, on the other hand, wasn't satisfied with a bottle and we'd run out of the little baby poof things Angela had in the diaper bag.

"Do you want me to go see if there's a cafeteria here? Maybe they have some saltines or something Raina can eat."

"Thanks, sis," Brody said, giving me a weak smile.

I handed Raina back over to my mom, kissing the baby's head as I did, and walked out of the room. I headed back to the admin desk I'd stopped at before, but when I exited into the waiting room, my heart stopped.

There sat Briggs.

He was in a chair along the wall, legs splayed out in front of him, arms crossed over his chest, and head resting back against the window behind him. His eyes were closed, so he didn't see me and that meant he couldn't see the confused look on my face at his presence.

My heart lurched at the sight of him. I thought he'd dropped me off and gone home. He'd been nice enough to drive me to the hospital, and even though I didn't want to let go of the warmth he offered as he drove me, I understood when he left. My family's medical drama didn't concern him. So why was he there?

I walked up to him and gently laid my hand on his knee. He jerked at my touch, sitting up, eyes opening and his gaze moving wildly around the room before it landed on me.

"Hey," he said quickly. "Is everything okay?"

"You didn't leave."

"Huh?" he asked, running a hand over the top of his head, making his dark hair flop about.

"I thought you left."

"I just went to park the truck." He stood up then and I was forced to take a step back. He closed the distance I'd just put between us and wrapped his large, warm hand around my neck. "Is everything okay?" His eyes were so full of concern and that made my eyes fill with tears.

I leaned into him, pressing my cheek to his chest and immediately his arms circled around me, holding me, while I finally cried. He held me and I cried into his shirt, my hands gripping the fabric at his waist.

Finally, after I'd had a mini-breakdown, I took a deep breath and gave him a watered-down version of the story.

"My nephew, Beckett, got a hold of a quarter and choked on it. My sister-in-law managed to dislodge it, but not before she experienced something no mother should ever have to experience."

His hands moved to my neck, his thumbs right below my jaw, gently forcing me to look up at him. "Is he all right?" His voice was so gentle, softer than I'd ever heard it.

I nodded as a tear streamed down my cheek. "He'll be okay. I'm more worried about her at this point. She's a wreck." At my words, he pulled me back into him, holding me close. "I'm sorry. I had no idea you were out here."

"It's fine. I just wanted to make sure you were all right. I should probably go."

"No, stay," I said before I had a chance to think about it, pulling back and looking up at him again. The idea of him not being there, not being within arm's reach, for whatever reason, felt wrong. "I want you to stay."

"Then I'll stay," he replied simply.

Twenty minutes later I brought Briggs back with me to the ER room where my family was, saltines acquired.

"I come with cracker rations," I said brightly, trying again to lift the dark gloominess as much as I could. All eyes came to us as we entered, but they all stayed on Briggs. And I could have sworn I saw one side of Angela's mouth turn up, even if just for a moment. "I also brought a friend. Family, this is Briggs. Briggs, this is my mom, dad, brother Brody, and his wife Angela. That precious boy in her arms is Beckett, and this, little angel here," I said, taking Raina from my mother's lap, "is my niece, Princess Raina."

"Is my sister wearing your clothes?" Brody asked, his voice full of brotherly vibrato.

"Brody, shut up." That came from my father, which surprised me, and based on my brother's face, it surprised him as well. My father stood from his chair and held his hand out to Briggs. "You're the one who sent my little girl home in a rain storm in your coat and loaned us a flashlight?"

"Yes, sir," Briggs answered, shaking his hand.

I knew my father's handshakes, and they were notoriously firm, but by the way Briggs's forearms were bulging, it looked as though he was giving my dad a run for his money.

160

"And I take it you're the one who drove her here today."

"Yes, again, sir."

"You've been waiting out there all this time?" He was still shaking his hand, but his eyes were glued to Briggs's.

"I wanted to make sure Talia was all right. I'm not meaning to intrude."

My father watched Briggs for a quiet moment, then his other hand clapped him on the back and a smile spread across his face. "Any man who takes care of my girl is okay by me."

"Come sit down, George, stop pestering the man."

I sent my mother a silent thank you for intervening. It was sweet the way my father and brother were protective of me, but there was nothing threatening about Briggs.

"Would you like some crackers, Ray Ray?" I asked my niece, placing her in her car seat since we were missing a high chair. Usually she would have fussed at the thought of being strapped in, but she saw the crackers and knew what was up, eyes going wide with excitement and her little pudgy fists opening and closing in rapid succession. A girl's relationship with carbs started early.

"Tal?"

I looked up when I heard Angela's voice, raspy and weary.

"Be sure to break the cracker up into tiny pieces, okay?"

My heart ached at her words and I saw the panic she was trying to tamp down.

"You got it," I told her. I broke the cracker into tiny pieces and fed them to Raina one by one. She had a sippy cup with some water and I made sure to give her a sip between bites. She ate those crackers as though she'd never tasted anything so delicious and I was glad I'd grabbed a handful of packages. Soon her cup was empty and she started to whine when no water came out. I went to stand and fill it, but Briggs's open hand appeared.

"Let me," he said gently.

"Thank you," I said as I handed the cup to him. His eyes moved to Angela.

"Is tap water okay, or should I go get a bottle of water from the vending machine?"

Angela looked just as shocked at his question as I felt, but she managed to answer with a ragged, "Tap water is fine." She was even able to give him a weak smile.

"Should it be warm or cold?" Another question from Briggs that made my heart thump hard.

"Room temperature is great." Angela was now smiling in earnest, but only for a moment before the darkness took back over her expression.

"So, Briggs, what do you do?"

I watched as he held his fingers in the stream of water coming from the faucet at the sink in the room, adjusting the knobs to get the water to the perfect temperature. "I'm a web designer. I create webpages, do graphic design, computer stuff."

"That sounds interesting," my mom said in that obligatory motherly tone.

"I find it interesting," he replied, not unkindly. He finally found the water temperature to be just right and filled Raina's cup, turned the water off, and screwed the lid back on. I told myself it was completely normal for me to watch his forearms ripple as he twisted the cap. He walked back to where I sat on the floor with Raina and held the cup out to me. I took it, giving him a small smile, then tried not to follow him with my eyes as he settled against the wall behind me, leaning back and crossing his ankles. "I work for myself and there's freedom in that. I get to choose what projects to work on, who to take on as clients, and I get to be creative. I can take on as much as I want or need to, and I can arrange a schedule to meet my needs. There are worse jobs I could have."

"This seems like too small of a town for someone like you to make a good living in."

I shot my gaze over to my father, silently begging him to end the conversation, to not ask any more ridiculously personal questions thinly veiled as casual conversation.

"I only started living here full-time recently. I used to live in Portland. And I still travel there for business when I need to, but a large portion of my job can be done remotely."

My father nodded knowingly. "Portland seems like it would be a better fit for your vocation."

"Dad, stop it," I whispered sternly.

Briggs's hand came to my shoulder, kneading me there, then I heard his voice close to my ear where he whispered, "It's okay, firecracker."

Luckily, the entire conversation came to a halt when the doctor came back in. He did the same song and dance, checking over Beckett with detail and concentration, and finally he let out a sigh and gave Angela a smile.

"He's perfect. I don't think there will be any lasting effects. Continue the baby Tylenol as long as he seems uncomfortable, but if it's more than a couple days, make an appointment to see his pediatrician." The doctor placed a hand on Angela's shoulder and gave her a squeeze. "You did well, Mom. I know it's easier said than done, but try to relax. Beckett will feed off your energy, so he needs you to be calm and happy. He's going to be just fine."

"Thank you, Doctor," Brody said, reaching out again to shake his hand.

"The nurse will be by shortly with your paperwork." He gave one last look at Angela and she gave him a tearful smile, and then he left the room.

"Well, I don't know about anyone else, but I am looking forward to getting out of this place. I have all the fixings for a big spaghetti dinner just waiting at the house. I think we should all just try to finish the day on a good note." My mother's voice was full of forced cheerfulness, a weak smile spread across her face.

"Sounds like a good plan," my dad commented.

"Briggs," my mother said, stepping up beside him and placing a hand on his arm. "I hope you'll join us for dinner."

His eyes met mine quickly, but I didn't say anything. As much as I wanted him there, I didn't want to pressure him. This was already so far beyond our original arrangement of just spending time together. I kept my face as even as I could, but watched him as he said, "Thank you, but I've already overstepped my bounds."

My heart sank at his words, crashed into depths of my chest I hadn't even known were there. And I knew it was the right choice, that he'd made the right decision. If I was feeling this way after spending just a few days with him, clearly I wasn't handling a casual relationship the way I'd hoped. I couldn't handle looking in his eyes as I realized he was pulling away. So I turned back to Raina and put all my energy into loving on her.

Half an hour later we were all walking out of the hospital. Angela was still quiet, my parents were making normal conversation, and I was dreading having to say goodbye to Briggs in front of everyone. We walked through the sliding doors, all of us headed toward the parking lot, and I had no idea what to say or how to act.

We approached Angela and Brody's giant van we'd driven to the coast from Portland and I made myself look up at Briggs.

"Well," I said on a sigh. "Thank you for sticking around to make sure everything was okay. That was sweet of you."

"Let me drive you home," he said quietly.

"You don't have to," I told him, unable to keep looking at him, my gaze dropping to the ground.

"I want to," was his response.

"Let the man drive you home," my mother said from the backseat of the van and not too quietly either.

I didn't know which choice was worse: driving home with my family asking me a million questions about Briggs, or letting Briggs drive me home knowing it would probably be the last time I saw him. I looked back up at him and he was still watching me, eyes silently pleading with me, and I could no longer tell him no, even if I thought it was a mistake.

"Okay."

He nodded and then turned to the side, making room for me to walk past him, and with a hand at the small of my back, led me toward his truck.

We were silent as he opened the door for me. Quiet as he climbed into his seat and started the truck. And it continued as we made our way to the highway, heading back toward both our houses.

"Are you all right?" he finally asked.

I had no idea what he was referring to. Was I all right with what happened to Beckett? Was I okay with the distance I felt between us at that moment? I wasn't really okay with any of it, but that wasn't his problem and I didn't want to make it his concern.

"I'm fine," I said with a smile that I hoped looked genuine. I didn't want to punish him. Just the opposite, in fact. I wanted it to be easy for him, wanted whatever was going on between us to be something he looked back on with a smile, not with regret. "Listen, I know that was pretty heavy back there. I appreciate that you stayed, but I totally understand that it was a little much. My mom and dad mean well. They just want me to be happy. I'm sorry if they made you uncomfortable."

He was quiet for a moment, but then finally spoke.

"I don't want you to get hurt."

I sighed in relief. He was such a good guy.

"I know, Briggs. And I don't want you to feel like I'm manipulating you. I promise, I'm not. You don't have to come to dinner, you don't have to talk to my family, and you don't have to take care of me. I appreciate that you stayed, I do. But I'm not expecting anything from you."

"I know." The words sounded sadder than I would have expected, but I tried hard not to focus on that. I had never been in a casual relationship, especially not one that had an expiration date, and I was pretty sure this would be my last. I simply wasn't cut out for it.

He pulled up in front of my rental but left the engine running. He shifted to face me and placed his arm up on the back of the bench seat, his fingers brushing the back of my neck.

"Will you tell your mother I said thank you for the dinner invitation and give her my apology that I couldn't make it?"

"Yeah," I whispered, both loving and hating the way his fingers felt brushing against the skin of my neck, but I focused on it to keep my mind from thinking about what might be happening in that moment. I didn't want to wonder if whatever we had between us was over.

"Will you come see me later? After everyone's asleep?"

"Yes," I said, the word falling out on a sigh of relief. His fingers wrapped tightly around my neck and brought me across the bench until his lips were on mine. He kissed me deeply, our bodies pressing together, mouths fused. But it never moved past the kiss, and that was fine with me. My family would be pulling up soon, and we didn't need to be caught fooling around in his truck.

The kiss ended and we were both breathing heavily.

"Are we okay?" he whispered, his mouth still barely touching mine.

I couldn't help it. I reached up and slid my hand over his jaw, back into the hair at his nape, and pulled his mouth back to mine.

"Nothing's changed for me," I finally said after I'd kissed him silly. "I'll be over later, okay?"

"Yeah." His hand squeezed the back of my neck, but then he turned me loose.

The front door of the house was unlocked and I attributed that to the frantic way my family must have left. I was torn between being sorry I wasn't there for my family, but also glad I hadn't been there to witness what sounded like a terrifying experience.

I went upstairs and took a hot shower, trying to wash away all the tension of a crazy and stressful day. When I went back downstairs my mom was at the stove cooking dinner, and Angela and Brody were sitting at the table. Angela still held Beckett in her arms, and Raina was sleeping in her bouncy chair in the living room. The entire family was involved in a conversation that I'd arrived late to.

"I just can't be here anymore. I can't sit in this room without seeing him lying there, choking, and turning blue." Angela's words caught me off guard and I stopped as I entered the room, wary of the situation. It was more words than I'd heard her say all day, and they sounded angry.

"Babe, I hear you, and I understand. Trust me. But if we leave now we'll be driving in the dark and it will be late. That's not safe for anyone, especially after the exhausting day we've had. Let's sleep on it, okay? If you still feel like you want to leave tomorrow, then we'll leave. Promise."

My eyes snapped to my parents, who were exchanging glances in the kitchen.

"We're leaving?" I asked, my voice sounding anxious.

"Angela doesn't want to stay here, understandably," my mother explained.

And yeah, it was understandable. I probably wouldn't have wanted to return to the house if I'd been there that morning either. My heart hurt for her and it occurred to me that even though Beckett would be fine, Angela might not be. Not any time soon, anyway. Her injuries seemed to be a lot worse than little Beckett's.

"Of course," I offered softly.

"I just can't," she said, all anger gone, replaced by despondence.

"No one expects you to, baby," my brother said sweetly to her, kneeling at her side. "But it's not a good idea to drive tonight, all right?"

She nodded, but said nothing.

My mother and father whispered something to each other, having a private conversation, and I just stood there, taking everything in.

"Talia, would you please set the table for dinner?" my mother asked as my father headed up the stairs.

"Sure." I moved around the kitchen and the dining room putting plates, glasses, and silverware on the table. Angela was sitting at the table still, every once in a while a sniffle coming from her. Brody kissed her cheek and went upstairs, leaving us three women and the babies downstairs. I knew my mother's spaghetti routine by heart and moved around her in the kitchen, helping her prepare the meal.

"What time is Briggs coming for dinner? It'll be cold if he doesn't get here soon."

"He wanted me to thank you for inviting him, but he couldn't come," I said as I poured the pasta into a strainer in the sink.

"Well, that's a shame. I would have liked to talk a little more with him. Gotten to know him a little better."

169

Luckily, I didn't have to answer because my father came down the stairs already talking.

"I got a hold of the owner and explained the situation. He and his wife were very understanding and say if we choose to leave tomorrow they could have the place cleaned and try to rent it out for the weekend. If they can, they'll be happy to reimburse us for time we didn't use."

"That's very kind of them," my mother said. "Did you hear, Angela? If you still want to leave tomorrow, we'll do just that."

"I will. I do." Her words were curt.

My heart thudded in my chest and my mouth ran dry as I realized we would leave the next day. I immediately felt selfish for even thinking of myself after what Angela and Brody had been through, but I was. That would be my last night with Briggs. I hadn't been given very many to begin with, so the loss was devastating. I almost couldn't breathe thinking about losing nearly half my time with him.

Dinner was horrible. I'm sure it was fine, but it may as well have been cardboard for as much as I actually tasted it. I moved the food around on my plate and took only a few bites as not to draw attention to myself. Afterward, I helped my mom clean up and offered to help Angela with anything she needed, but she barely answered me, let alone asked me for help.

Finally, I went up to my room and threw on some yoga pants, a tank top, a hoodie, and my flip-flops, and waited for the rest of the house to go to bed. If I only had one more night with Briggs, I wanted as many minutes as I could etch out.

Close to ten o'clock I heard my parents make their way up the stairs and shut their bedroom door. I gave them another ten minutes to settle in and then made my escape. I felt ridiculous being a grown woman and sneaking out of a house, hiding from my parents, but I tried not to think about it. All I could think about was how it was almost over, and how much I hated that fact.

His door was unlocked, so I let myself in, locking it behind me. I crept up the stairs and saw his door cracked with soft light filtering through. I gently eased the door open and saw Briggs sitting on his bed, leaning against his headboard, his chest bare, and his lower half hidden by a blanket. He'd been looking at his phone, but he set in on the bedside table when he noticed me.

I didn't have any words for him yet, so I strode toward him, unzipping my hoodie and dropping it on the floor as I did. He swung his legs over the side of the bed and I easily stepped between them. Our contact was instantaneous. My hands were on his shoulders, his hands were on my ass, and our mouths were fused instantly.

His hands palmed my ass, gripping me hard, pulling me close, and my hands held on to his shoulders as my knees hit the bed on either side of his hips. Our mouths moved against one another's, tongues sliding, hands roaming. It took but one instant for his erection to press against my core, and more than any other time we'd been together, I needed him. The need was so strong, in fact, so dire, it had my arms trembling and my legs shaking. Perhaps it was the emotion of the day, or maybe the idea that it would be my last time, my last night, to be with Briggs, but I was taken over with the physical need to be close to him.

His mouth moved down my jaw and continued down my throat, and my mouth came to rest on his shoulder, my teeth biting into him gently there, using every part of me to hold on to him. His hands pulled my hips down and a moan escaped me as he thrust his erection against me, the friction too perfect. I rocked against him, trying desperately to find that oblivion he'd offered me before, to get to the place where all I could think about, the only thing I could feel, was him and me. The way we fit so effortlessly together, the way he could read me better than anyone had in my entire life, the way his hand simply felt right in mine, and I felt right in his arms. All of that boiled down to this: our connection. If I was losing him tomorrow, I wanted all of him tonight.

Without a warning, I pushed off him and sank down between his legs to the floor and pulled down the athletic shorts he wore, freeing him. I wrapped my hand around his cock, feeling the warmth and hardness of him, loving the way his breath caught at the first touch. There were so many things I wanted to say to him in that moment. I wanted to tell him he was perfect, beautiful even. I wanted to explain how much he meant to me and how much leaving him would hurt. But I didn't have the words, so I took him in my mouth instead.

He gasped and startled at the touch of my mouth, but I knew he was watching. I closed my eyes, not wanting to see his gaze on me. It felt all too intimate without the eye contact already. If I had to watch him while I made love to him with my mouth it would definitely push me over some proverbial cliff.

Using my mouth and my hand, I worked him up and down, making sure to stop and swallow when he was as far down my throat as I could handle. Every time he groaned, his fingers tangled in my wild hair. After just a few minutes he plucked me off the floor and stripped me of all my clothes, tossing them on the floor and pulling me onto the bed.

He lay back and said in a soft but strained voice, "Come here." He used both of his hands to tap his chest, so I crawled toward him, but as I tried to lie next to him, he shook his head. "Up, firecracker. I want you on my face."

Never had six words caused such a physical reaction to my body. He grabbed me by the hips and helped me straddle his chest, then slid lower, positioning his face at my opening. "Hang on to the headboard, Talia, and fuck my face."

Before I could say or do anything, his mouth was on me, his tongue taking a long glide from back to front, ending at my clit and focusing there.

I did as he said, reaching forward and holding on to the headboard because without it I wasn't sure I could hold myself upright.

"Oh, God," I moaned as his tongue worked me over.

His hands slid over the back of my thighs and nestled themselves in the crease between my sex and my legs, pulling down, creating an extraordinary white-hot burn of pleasure. The added friction, the intense intimacy of his face between my legs, and the magical way his mouth worked every part of me, all of those things combined caused me to lose a little bit of myself. His tongue touched me and the bolt of electric pleasure made my body jump away from him, but his hands pulled me back down, and the rhythm started. Soon I was shamelessly grinding my sex on his face, recklessly using his mouth to find my escape. He loved it, grunting against my clit, kneading my thighs with his strong fingers.

It didn't take long before I was panting and crying out, warning him of my impending orgasm.

"Briggs," I cried out as I bore down on his mouth. "I'm going to come." He moaned his approval and I teetered on the edge, only to be thrown over by the hard and swift smack of Briggs's hand on my ass. That was all it took for me to fall apart, breathlessly. I came, fantastically hard, and as tremors shook my entire body. Briggs slid out from under me, shucked his shorts, and reached for his drawer. "No, please," I begged, reaching one hand out for him as I leaned against the headboard. "I need you. Just you."

He crawled up on the bed and came behind me, his erection nestling at my backside, his hands smoothing around my waist. My knees were still on the mattress as I was unable to move enough to change position.

"Are you sure?" he asked, his mouth at the nape of my neck.

"Yes, please..." I begged.

He dipped behind me and I felt him position his cock at my entrance, then slowly slide into me.

"Fuck," he grunted, thrusting until he could go no farther, filling and stretching me. His mouth came to my neck and his hands found my breasts. He pulled out slowly, dragging the engorged head of his penis over every sensitive part of me, then pushed back in, so fucking slowly. I was still buzzing from the tremendous orgasm I'd had not a minute ago, and then, to have him bare and inside me, it was all too much. I held on to the headboard and dropped my head back onto his shoulder and let him use me, loving every moment of it.

He pushed in and dragged out, over and over again. It was the most magnificent torture. At some point I lost my strength and let my weight rest on my arms against the headboard, and the new angle just spurred him on. His hands gripped my hips and he pounded furiously into me, again and again, sending me on a downward spiral through another orgasm. I wouldn't have been able to pick myself up off the floor if I tried, but he grabbed me by the shoulders, hauling me back into his chest. One hand grabbed my chin, forcing me to look back at him, the other hand finding its way to my clit.

"I can't, Briggs."

"You can."

I cried out, both in frustration at how overwhelmed I was in that moment, but also because everything felt so terribly wonderful. I didn't think I could come again, but it wasn't up to me. I shouted my release just as his mouth came over mine. We weren't kissing, just connecting. Our open mouths were pressed together, but I didn't have the mental capacity to kiss him. I just wanted to make that contact. His breath panted heavier and heavier against my face and finally he thrust upward with such ferocity, I was caught off guard, yelping in surprise. But then he stilled and groaned, and when I felt the warmth of him coating me inside, I knew he'd come.

He held me for a moment. Perhaps he knew I needed the support, or maybe he liked having me in his arms, but he didn't let go. And I didn't want him to, if I was being honest. Who knew what would happen the next day when I left? I felt, deep down in my gut, that I'd never see him again. So if he wanted to hold me, I'd let him.

Finally, his entire body went lax. His arms fell away from me, as did his hips, and I gave a little gasp as he left me empty. He collapsed on the bed but tagged me on the way down, and I ended up lying next to him, still reeling from the intensity of being with him. We were both breathing hard, our slick, warm bodies sticky, and after a few moments I moved to sit up.

"No," he breathed, wrapping his arm around me, making it impossible for me to get up. "Not yet."

Not yet.

Two harmless words, but I felt them so deep inside of me. I'd only been with Briggs a few times, and not many men before him, but I knew it was different. Being with him was different. I knew as soon as our time together ended I'd miss him and what we shared and probably never find a connection as powerful as ours. So, *not yet* held a lot of weight. I didn't want to let go. Not yet. But there was little point in holding on.

I let him pull me back to his side, let myself enjoy the warmth of his arms holding me close, but only for a few moments. When I moved to get up again, his hold on me tightened.

"Hey, where are you going?"

"I need to clean up," I whispered, inwardly cringing.

"I'll take care of it. You stay here." Before he was done even saying the words he started to move, but I reached out to stop him.

"Briggs," I said, hand resting on his arm. "I need a minute. Alone."

He said nothing in response, but his arms did fall away, and he let me go.

I walked to his bathroom and turned on the light. I gripped the edge of the sink, trying to rein in all my emotions, but I could tell I was slipping over the edge of hysteria. When I looked up at the mirror, my reflection almost took my breath away. I looked beautiful. My skin was flushed and my hair was a mess, but if anyone else had seen me I knew they would have thought how pretty and happy I looked. Well, except for the tears welling in my eyes.

I turned on the faucet and splashed cold water on my face, hoping the shock of it would help curb the tears, but it didn't. So then I just prayed the sound of the running water would drown out my cries.

Chapter Fourteen

Briggs

When I woke up, the first thing I saw was Talia's red hair sprawled across her pillow. The sight instantly made me happy, but then, I had to remind myself that I couldn't get used to waking up with her. I definitely couldn't get used to turning to her in the middle of the night, waking her up by kissing down her body, then sliding inside of her as we sleepily made love. No, that I couldn't get used to. I'd made love to her two more times that night. After the first round, which was the most intense sexual experience of my life, I couldn't keep my hands to myself.

She couldn't either.

She was there with me, stroke for stroke, pant for pant, moan for moan.

Even though I couldn't get used to her being in my bed, I could take advantage of it. I slid over to her side, pressing my chest up against her back. We were both bare as we never saw the need to put clothes back on last night, and I loved the way her smooth warm skin felt like an extension of my own. When I touched her, even if it was a gentle hand on her hip, it felt like home.

She stirred, coming alive and realizing I was behind her, then relaxing into me.

"Good morning," I said against her shoulder.

"Mmmm," she groaned. "Is it morning? I feel like I could sleep forever."

"I'm down to stay in bed all day." I kissed down her arm, but could feel her tense beneath me. She stayed like that, still and tight, for just a moment more, and then she turned so she was suddenly facing me, her hands on my chest and lips meeting mine.

I kissed her back because I could. Because at that moment she was in my bed and she was mine. It was impossible not to kiss her back.

She pulled back, taking her lips from mine, and rested her forehead against my chest.

"We're leaving today."

She whispered the words, but she may as well have screamed them for the way they affected me. Like a punch straight to the stomach.

"Angela doesn't want to be in the house, understandably, so we're leaving." The last words were just a whisper.

I didn't know what to say, so I just pulled her closer and kissed her forehead. I knew we didn't have forever, but I thought we'd at least have a couple more days. After a few quiet moments, I said what I was thinking.

"That sucks."

She let out a soft laugh, but it only lasted a second or two before she was quiet again.

"Yeah, it does." She heaved a large sigh and I felt her try to pull away, but I wouldn't let her. I held her close.

"Stay." I said the word without thinking, but as soon as it was out, I knew I meant it. "Stay here with me. Finish the week with me."

She shook her head slightly. I felt her hair rub against my chest. "We all came in the same van. My car is in Portland. They're my ride back."

My mind was racing, along with my heart. I took her face in my hands and brought her eyes up to meet mine. "Is that the only reason you're going? Because they're your ride? Because I'll drive you anywhere you want to go at the end of the week. But if you want to leave, if you're ready to walk away, then I'll be happy for the last few days and I'll kiss you goodbye, but I'm not done with you yet."

"You want me to stay?" Her voice was shaky and practically silent, just air moving through her lips, and her eyes were darting back and forth between mine, asking more with her gaze than her words.

I didn't want to think about how she could ask me that question after last night. I didn't want to consider the idea that I was falling for her while she was keeping her distance. Even though that was what I needed her to do, keep her distance. But not until I got the time with her I was promised.

"Can you really ask me that after last night?" I fought the urge to tell her how much I wanted her, how much I wished things were different, but I didn't want to hurt her in the end by making her think I was ready for more. Ready and wanting were two very different beasts, and I seemed to be battling against them both.

Her eyes closed and her head shook, but I didn't let go. "I'm not ready to leave."

Her words opened a floodgate inside of me and all the air in my lungs rushed out as my arms wrapped even tighter around her. My lips found her neck and I breathed her in, relief surging through me. After a few long moments I pulled back and looked at her, happy to find a smile on her lips. "Are you sure? You don't want to be with your family?"

She lifted one shoulder in a shrug and said, "Angela just needs to go home. Beckett is fine. There's nothing I can do for them anyway."

"I'm selfishly very happy about all this."

"I'm not happy Beckett went through what he did, or that Angela is broken up over it"—she took in a breath and then continued—"but I'm happy I'll get to spend some more time with you." She smiled at me for a moment, but then it faded away. "I should probably go home and explain that I'm staying. I know they want to leave early. And they'll need help packing and cleaning up the house."

"Want me to come with?"

"Sure," she breathed, then kissed me quickly before climbing out of bed. She picked her clothes up off the floor and disappeared into the bathroom. I watched her the whole way.

Talia was right when she'd said her family wanted to leave early. The sun was barely up when we made our way back to their house, but everyone was inside bustling around. No one gave a second look at Talia coming home after sunrise, or seemed to care that I was with her. In fact, they seemed grateful for the extra set of hands.

I helped Brody load the van, the two of us making polite, friendly conversation as we did. Talia and her mother would come out whenever they had another item for us to load, and I never missed the way Talia's eyes met mine with a smile, or how she gave me an extra look over her shoulder before she went back inside.

We made quick work of everything and that was good because the owners had already scheduled a cleaning service to come through and there wasn't much time. Angela stayed in the bedroom upstairs with the babies and Brody mentioned she hadn't come downstairs at all that morning.

"It's probably good to get her home," I said as I stacked a suitcase in the back of the van.

"Yeah," he said thoughtfully. "She'll be okay, but she needs to go home. Being here is too stressful for her."

"I know Talia's really worried about her."

"What's really going on between you two?" Brody stood straight and propped both of his fists on his hips.

I just continued to load the van.

"I enjoy her company. She's a great girl. We're just spending time together."

"Does she know it's not serious?"

"She does. We've had extensive conversations about how we're both not ready for a relationship. For now, we're just friends."

"She's been hurt before, man. I like you and all, and you seem like a decent guy. But if you hurt her, I'll have to kick your ass."

I coughed back a laugh, swallowing it down, but then met his gaze. "Noted."

"I think this is the last of the big stuff."

Brody and I both turned at the sound of Talia's voice. She handed me a big duffle bag, but it was lighter than it looked. I found a spot for it and made it fit.

"Angela asked me to send you up so you can help her bring the babies down. I think she wants to wait out here or in the car until Mom and Dad are ready."

Brody gave me a sidelong glance, but then went inside, giving Talia's shoulder an affectionate squeeze as he passed by. Once he was inside the house, she stepped toward me.

"You're still sure you want to stay behind?" I wanted to give her every opportunity to back out, even though the idea of watching her drive away with her family made me grumpy. Her arms moved directly to my waist, sliding around all the way to my back, and her front pressed up against my chest. I tried not to focus on the feeling of her breasts against me because I knew that would only get me in trouble.

"I love my family, but that is not going to be a fun car ride. Plus, we had a deal—spend the week together."

My arms instinctively wrapped around her shoulders and I leaned down, brushing my mouth against hers.

"If you're sure," I said once I pulled away.

"I'm sure."

There was a commotion near the door and Brody and Angela appeared, both carrying a baby and a bag. Talia moved to my side, but I left one arm over her shoulder and kept her close. We stood by, watching as they loaded the babies up and turned the car on, keeping the cool air running. Finally, Angela came out of the van and pulled Talia into a hug, whispering something in her ear I couldn't make out. Brody held out his hand and I took it, shaking it firmly. When we finally released each other's hand, we were both smiling.

"It was nice to meet you," Angela said as she pulled me into a hug as well. It was short and unfamiliar, but as she pulled away she did say, "Take care of my Tally."

"I will. You take care of yourself." It might have been unsolicited advice, but she smiled graciously and made her way back to the van.

Talia and Brody were hugging and he was mumbling something to her. I was pretty sure he was telling her he could kick my ass if needed. She laughed and smiled up at him.

"Thanks, I'll keep that in mind." Her words came out on a laugh and I couldn't help but smile. That should have been an indication that I was a goner; her laughter made me happy. The thought settled in the pit of my stomach, but I couldn't keep the smile from my face. I'd deal with the consequences later. Brody pointed a finger at me as he backed up toward the car.

"I know where you live, man. Be good to her."

"Not a problem," I replied. I could deal with a protective brother, especially one like Brody. He wasn't trying to be a macho asshole—he legitimately wanted to protect his sister. And I couldn't blame him. If someone were trying to move in on my sister within a week, I'd probably be making threats too.

"Oh, wait," Talia cried out as her brother climbed in the van. "I didn't get to say goodbye to the babies." She disappeared around the van at the same time her parents came out of the house.

Her dad walked straight to me, offering his hand. "Thank you for all your help the last few days. We appreciate it more than you know."

"Anytime."

Talia's mother hugged me enthusiastically, but then pulled away and disappeared into the van without a word. That was okay with me.

I gave her dad a wave as he walked away and then Talia was back at my side. We stood in the driveway until the van disappeared. Only when they were out of sight did Talia let out a big sigh.

"As my mom got into the van she told me to have a good time and to leave with no regrets." She lifted her chin so she could look up at me. "My mom basically just told me to have a wild affair with you."

"I like her way of thinking."

184

"Me too."

Chapter Fifteen

Talia

Briggs had taken my bag and my hand and led me back to his house. He took me upstairs, watched me unpack as much as I could, then convinced me to take a nap with him. There really was no denying him that. Next to having sex with Briggs, sleeping next to him, with his arms wrapped around me, was my most favorite thing to do with him. Okay, and surfing. But napping was awesome. So we did.

I crawled under the covers to where he already lay, rested my head in that perfect nook of his arm, and fell asleep almost immediately.

When I woke, it felt as though I'd been asleep for days and I noticed I was alone in the bed. I looked around but didn't see Briggs. I listened, thinking perhaps he was in the bathroom, but I didn't hear anything in there either. I crawled out of his bed and walked down the stairs, wondering where he'd gone, and I spotted him through the sliding glass doors, sitting at his outdoor table with his laptop.

"Hey," I said, still sounding sleepy. "What are you doing out here?"

"I was working upstairs while you slept, but I got a video call from a client and I didn't want to wake you. So I came downstairs. Good nap?" He wore a knowing smile. I had probably drooled all over him.

"Yeah, I feel like I got hit by the nap truck."

"Not a bad way to go," he said, laughing. He closed his laptop, then reached out and wrapped an arm around my hips, pulling me to his side. For once he wasn't towering over me and I took the opportunity to thread my fingers through his soft, chocolate-colored hair. His eyes closed for a moment and it looked as though he was enjoying my touch. When his eyes opened again they looked sleepier. "I want to take you out tonight," he said, voice sexy and full of rasp.

"Hmmm, I think I can get on board with that plan. Where are we going?"

"Dinner. A nice place. Did you bring anything you could wear to a nice restaurant?"

I smiled down at him. "I think I can put something together."

"Good," he said, then slapped me on the ass. I yelped, surprised, but then laughed. "I've still got a little work I should get done here. Feel free to hang out with me, or inside. Whichever. I ran to the store and got some muffins and juice, in case you're hungry."

I threaded my fingers through his hair again. "Mind if I read out here? It's beautiful."

"It is," he said, his voice dreamy, as he ran his hand over the spot on my ass he'd just smacked. "Pull up a chair."

I leaned down and pressed a fast but sweet kiss against his mouth, then went inside and fished my Kindle out of my bag, grabbed a muffin, and rejoined him on the deck. It was beautiful outside—a perfect Oregon coast summer day. Not too hot, not a cloud in the sky, and the faint wind was warm. Luckily, Briggs's table had a big umbrella, so I didn't have to worry about getting sunburned. Instead, I propped my feet up on his lap, which made him smile, and I read.

We spent about two hours in relative, companionable silence. He worked, I read and nibbled on my muffin, only a few times stopping to ask him a question or say something that crossed my mind. Every once in a while his hand would drift to my foot, kneading my arches, rubbing my soles affectionately.

Eventually he closed his laptop again and let out a sigh.

"You feel like heading out in about an hour?" he asked, one hand running smoothly up my calf.

"Sounds good to me." And it did. The last few hours were so good. Lying with him. Relaxing with him. Just *being* with him was easy and wonderful. My family was likely all back in their respective homes, dealing with life, going back to normal, and all I could think of was that if I'd gone home, I would have been alone. I would have walked into an empty house. I might have sat quietly for a few hours reading, but the difference between the simple act of reading alone and reading while Briggs sat at a table with me was astounding. World-tilting. I let myself feel sad for just a moment, thinking about how I'd temporarily given up being all right by myself, given up being okay with being alone. But then I tried to focus on the fact that Briggs and I were still together and had a few days to make the most of our time together.

Upstairs I showered again, rinsing off my body but not washing my hair. I'd packed a black jersey dress. It wasn't exceptionally fancy, but it was black, which meant it could swing either way, and I could dress it up with jewelry and shoes. I slipped on my turquoise sandals and matching turquoise necklace and earrings. I also put a thin gold belt around my waist. I left my hair down, the red curls tamed by crème and a little bit of heat from my hair dryer. I left my makeup light, liking the natural look, just adding a little bit of mascara and lip gloss.

I'd monopolized the bathroom for a good thirty minutes, so I took one last look at myself in the mirror and decided I was pleased. I walked back into the bedroom to see Briggs standing in front of his dresser, buttoning up the cuff on his sleeve.

He looked divine.

He had on a dark pair of jeans and a white button-down shirt. His dark hair was mussed, but in a sexy way, and his lean muscles all along his shoulders and arms were barely contained by his shirt. It wasn't fancy, but it was sexy as hell.

"Wow," he said quietly, his eyes roaming up and down my body. "You look incredible."

I looked down at myself, blushing a little, not used to compliments of that nature.

"It'll do in a pinch," I said, trying to brush off his words. "You're not so bad yourself," I replied awkwardly. "I'm ready whenever you are."

"After you," he said, motioning toward the door.

Downstairs, he helped me up into his truck, his strong hands on my waist, hoisting me up. I couldn't even pretend to not like it. He climbed into his seat but wouldn't even start the truck until I slid to the middle, closing the distance between us. He drove with his hand on my thigh, the last two fingers on his hand resting right under the fabric of my dress. Just the visual had my heart rate elevated.

He drove down Highway 101 and I enjoyed the view. We were probably only about a half-hour away from sunset, so the sky was a beautiful orangey-red color. I felt the truck slow and watched as Briggs pulled into a parking lot on a hill. I looked around, but couldn't see a restaurant. He parked and then hopped out, then came around to open my door for me.

He took my hand and walked me back toward the highway, and it was only then I saw where we were headed. The restaurant sat on the other side of the road, nestled in the cliffside. It was a big white building that looked as though it was a hotel too.

I let Briggs lead the way, his warm hand enveloping mine. He walked us into the hotel and I followed him to the entrance of a restaurant.

"Good evening, welcome to Fathoms. Do you have a reservation?" The hostess was a younger brunette. She wore a friendly smile but was obviously all business.

"Yeah, party of two for Townsend."

She looked down at her iPad and then gave him a smile. "Right this way, Mr. Townsend." She led us around a corner and when we walked into the dining room of the restaurant I had to hold in a gasp. The entire wall of the building that faced the ocean was one continuous wall of windows. All you could see was beach and ocean.

The hostess led us to a table right next to the window and my eyes went wide. The view was absolutely breathtaking.

She laid menus in front of us, smiled, and told us our server would be with us shortly.

"Briggs," I whispered, leaning over the table. "This is amazing."

"It is," he said, smiling at me.

"I've never seen anything so beautiful."

"Me neither," he said, still looking right at me, his mouth holding that sexy smile. It made my lungs catch and heart sputter in my chest.

The waiter came and took our drink orders. I ordered a glass of white wine while Briggs ordered a rum and coke. I looked around at all the tables and was just in awe. There were candles lit, and each table had a small centerpiece with red roses in a low vase. The sun was setting over the ocean. It was so beautiful. Suddenly the thought occurred to me that Briggs might have taken his ex-wife to this restaurant, and the idea made me sick to my stomach.

"So, have you been here before?" I asked, trying to sound completely cool and uninterested in his answer.

"No. Actually, I've driven past it a million times but never been inside. I was telling Porter the other day I wanted to take you someplace nice and he recommended this restaurant. Said he took his wife here on their first date."

His response surprised me. Stunned me, even. It made me feel something a little too similar to feelings, to wanting, so I tried to push it away. Luckily, just then, the waiter delivered our drinks, so I took a small sip of my wine, thanking the wine gods for sparing me from having to respond to something so sweet and thoughtful.

"Actually," he said after taking a sip of his own drink, "Porter and Ella asked if we wanted to go over to their house for dinner tomorrow. What do you think?"

"It would be really fun to see them again before I go. Plus, I mean, no offense, but your kitchen isn't really up for cooking at the moment."

He laughed at my joke, which I was thankful for.

"True. I'll let him know we're in."

"Will your friend Patrick be there? With Megan?"

"No, they went back to Portland already."

"Darn. I really like Megan."

191

He only smiled at me as a response, but then the sunset caught his eye and his gaze moved to the horizon. I watched him for a few moments, loving the way the orange hues made his hair look a copper color, but then I pulled my eyes away and looked out toward the ocean. Pink, orange, purple, and even a little blue all played above the water. Wispy clouds accentuated the beautiful colors. The water right on the horizon was a deep blue, almost navy, while the water closer to the shore was almost the color of the turquoise I wore around my neck.

I jolted when I felt Briggs's hand close around mine, but when I looked over at him, he was still admiring the sunset.

Dinner was amazing—as I expected. Decadent and rich. Briggs convinced me to order dessert, but I made him split mine with me. It was the best piece of cheesecake I'd ever had and I vowed that one day I would go back there to have another. The bill came and when I moved even an inch to reach for my wallet, willing to pay my half, he practically growled at me and said it was his treat. I let him pay without a fight because, honestly, I liked that he wanted to so badly. It had been a long while since I'd felt taken care of, but Briggs seemed to be pulling out all the stops.

By the time we stood up to leave it was dark outside and I could no longer see the ocean. There were many other couples in the restaurant enjoying a romantic dinner by candlelight, and I knew I would remember this date for the rest of my life. He took my hand as we walked toward the exit, and I wrapped my free hand around his forearm, leaning against him.

The door was right in front of us, but Briggs turned to the right, pulling me to the desk at the front of the lobby.

"Hello," he said to the smiling young man behind the counter. "I have a reservation for Briggs Townsend."

"Wait, what?" I asked, stepping back.

"I see your reservation right here," the guy on the other side of the desk said, tapping away on his keyboard. "You've booked an ocean view room with a balcony and hot tub. I just need a credit card on file and I'll get you your keys."

"Briggs," I said as he reached into his back pocket and pulled out his wallet. "What did you do?"

"I got us a room."

I was at a loss for words, so I ended up just blinking in his direction for a few moments, but then I was able to speak. "But your house is just twenty minutes down the road."

"My house doesn't have a hot tub."

"I didn't bring a suit."

He leaned closer, his mouth just barely pressing against the shell of my ear. "I was counting on that." So that shut me up.

Briggs finished at the desk and the guy behind it was obviously smirking at us. My remarks had clued him in that we weren't tourists, so it was pretty clear why we were there.

This was a sex thing.

I wasn't complaining; I was just a little mortified.

I didn't say anything else as Briggs took instructions on how to get to the room, then took my hand and led us down the hall to the elevator. We were both quiet as we rode up to the fourth floor, but I gripped his bicep with my free hand and leaned my head against his shoulder, loving the way I fit so perfectly against him, as though the side of his body was made like a companion to mine.

The doors opened with a *ding*, and he led me down the hall, stopping at a door and inserting the key card. He let me enter first but didn't drop my hand.

"Briggs," I whispered, taking it all in. It was beautiful. Wide, enormous, picture windows showed off the indigo sky sprinkled with so many stars, they were countless. Along the edge of one of the windows was a hot tub so big, eight people could have sat comfortably in it—plenty of room for just two. The bedding was crisp white with two blue velvet club chairs tucked in the corner, perfect for reading. There was a balcony, but that would have to wait to explore, because no sooner had I taken in the gorgeous room, had Briggs wrapped his arms around my waist from behind me.

"You like?"

"Yes," I breathed. Then his lips feathered over my neck and it was suddenly difficult to stand. I turned and wrapped my arms around his neck, taking in the way his dark eyes were sparking. "This was very sweet of you. Incredibly romantic. It's too bad you don't date. You'd make an exceptional boyfriend." I'd said the words before I'd thought about how they'd sound out loud.

"Talia," he said, his voice full of apology, and that was the last thing I wanted. I didn't need him to apologize for being unavailable. He didn't owe me any apologies. I'd gone into this with eyes wide-open.

"Shhh," I said as I pressed a finger against his mouth. "That came out wrong. All I meant was this is wonderful. One day, when you're ready, you're going to make someone so happy. But right now, here with you, it's perfect and I'll look back on this night with so much warmth, Briggs, I promise." And I meant it. I knew it would probably hurt for a little while after we'd said our goodbyes, but I wasn't going to trade a little bit of sorrow for my time with Briggs. Not ever.

He was quiet for a moment, even after my finger fell away, but his eyes never left mine.

"If this were a year from now, Talia, you have to know—"

194

I kissed him then, but not because what he said made me happy, but because my heart couldn't hear it. I couldn't hear him say the words that I'd missed out on a future with him because I'd met him too early. That didn't seem fair—to him *or* me. Instead, I kissed him.

An hour later, after using my body to keep him from saying things my heart couldn't handle hearing, we sat in that incredible hot tub and looked out at the sky. Even though the tub could fit a ton of people, Briggs still kept me close, pulling my back into his chest, one arm wrapped around my waist to hold me there while the other hand lazily dipped in the water and then poured it down my arm.

There were two empty flutes on the windowsill that used to have champagne in them, along with a plate of half-eaten strawberries on the floor next to the hot tub. We'd made love and then as the tub filled with water, Briggs had called room service and ordered the decadent treat. He'd put on one of the hotel's fluffy robes when the knock had come at the door and I'd hidden in the bathroom, too embarrassed to be witnessed in our obvious sex den.

"I think it might be kind of fun and scandalous to work at a hotel like this."

"Scandalous?"

"Yeah, I mean, you would get to see people like us coming here just for sex and talk about them, make up their stories."

"Hmm," he said as he poured the hot water on my arm. "Maybe for a few weeks. I think eventually you'd start to see all the guests the same."

"Not possible. That guy down there at the check-in desk totally knew we were here just to do the nasty."

"The nasty?" he replied, his voice full of humor.

"Yeah, that was a bad descriptor." I turned my head and tilted it back so I could see his face. "It was incredible, like it always is with you."

He leaned down and kissed me, and I felt his smile against my lips.

"Next time try to use words like mind-blowing or off-the-charts."

I giggled as he pulled me closer, nuzzling into my neck. "I'll try to remember that."

"So," he said quietly, still letting warm water run down my skin, "your car is in Portland?"

"Yeah, my mom likes for all of us to drive together, and since Brody and Angela have the big van, we took their car."

He was quiet for a moment, but then said, "That's too bad. I kind of wanted to see where you live."

I thought about his words and couldn't quite decide if it was good he wouldn't come to Bend, or disappointing. I couldn't imagine, if he were taking me back to my house, he'd just drop me off at the doorstep. I'd invite him in, show him around, and we'd probably end up having goodbye sex. Then my house would be tainted. I'd have memories of him there. No, it was probably better we'd part ways far from my everyday life. I wondered if it bothered him that he'd have memories of me at his house. I supposed it was a good thing he was going to sell it in a few months.

"My place isn't anything special."

His body shook with laughter. "No, firecracker, *my* place isn't anything special."

"Well, I guess that's true. At least I have a refrigerator."

His lips came to rest on the top of my head and he spoke his next words into my hair. "But seriously, maybe some time I could come to Bend. See the town. See you. Visit."

196

My heart thudded to a complete stop and my lungs snagged on a breath. Surely he felt every single muscle in my body harden as my brain evaluated what he'd said. More than anything, my heart hurt. My eyes closed and I took a deep breath, trying to force my lungs to work again, and then I slid away from him—probably the hardest part—and sat on the opposite side of the hot tub. His face had changed and he looked concerned, confused as to why I would pull away.

"Briggs, this… it isn't what we talked about. Isn't part of the plan."

His hands came up and pushed through his wet hair. Tiny water droplets fell to his chest and ran back down into the pool of water around his abdomen. "I know we agreed this wouldn't be serious, and it still doesn't have to be. I'm just talking about visiting you. Is that not something you'd want? You're comfortable just walking away and never speaking again?"

"Are you?"

"No. That's what I'm trying to tell you."

"What is it that you want? I need you to be very clear." My heart, which had previously halted, was now thundering in my chest.

"I'm not one hundred percent sure," he said, exasperation clear in his tone. "All I know is that I don't want to drive away from you and never hear from you again, or never see you again."

Warmth spread through me at his words, followed closely by a wave of fear. I was so happy to hear I wasn't the only one feeling like this was more than we had intended, but I couldn't ignore the reasons we'd originally kept our relationship to just the one week to begin with.

"Before this started we both agreed neither one of us was ready for a relationship," I reminded him.

"I wasn't ready for anything, Talia. Especially not you."

"While I feel differently toward you than I did a week ago," I said slowly, trying to find the words one by one to accurately describe the whirling emotions coursing through me, "I don't really feel any differently about myself." I let out a breath, as though just saying the words took weight off me. "It would be so easy to just *be* with you, Briggs. You're incredible, and I feel incredible just being around you, but nothing would break my heart more than being with you for the wrong reason."

"It doesn't feel wrong," he said as he slowly moved to my side of the hot tub.

I knew being close to him would only make the conversation harder, but I'd be lying if I said I wasn't craving his touch. He sat on the bench next to me, but at the same time grabbed me by the hips and situated me on his lap, facing him, my legs straddling his thighs.

"You just got divorced," I whispered, pulling my arms in to cover myself, feeling more exposed than I ever had before.

"And you just got out of a really long-term relationship, but here we are, and it feels *right*, Talia." He pulled my arms away from my body, draping my hands over his shoulders, then dropping his hands to my waist again. I leaned into him because I wanted that contact, wanted to feel his body against mine.

"Think about it, though, just for a minute. This isn't real life, Briggs. I'm on vacation. You're in the middle of a mid-life crisis, remodeling a house so it doesn't remind you of your wife, and I'm having the no-strings-attached sex I never got to have in my early twenties. There's an attraction—yes. There are feelings—yes—because it would be impossible to be with you and not start to care for you, but maybe that's the point. I would rather have this one week with you, just one week of happiness, than risk ruining it all because we rushed into something."

He started to speak, to argue with me, but I cut him off.

"Do you have good memories of your wife? Or does the image of her with that other man pretty much fuck all that up? Because right now, if we said goodbye, I'd be sad, but I'd only have *good* memories. I would only remember the way you looked drowned in light from a campfire. Or the way your face lit up with laughter watching me learn to surf." I couldn't help but smile as I recalled the best week of my life. "I'd remember the way you made love to me and even though I knew it was all temporary, it felt like everything."

At my words, he pulled me closer, my sex lining up perfectly with his. He was hard, and I was high on champagne and simply his proximity. He slipped into me easily, both of us gasping at the contact.

"You can't tell me you want this to be over," he rasped, using his hands to move my hips in the way that had his cock moving in and out of me, using the water and its weightless capabilities to his—and my—advantage.

"No," I gasped. I didn't want it to be over. Ever. But that was exactly what I feared would happen if I let myself fall into something carelessly. Briggs deserved better than that. So did I.

I wasn't sure if he took my no as I meant it, or how he wanted to hear it, but either way, there was no more talking that night other than him urging me to come with him, and I did just that.

Chapter Sixteen

Talia

I woke up the next morning clinging to Briggs, and he was wrapped around me too. We slept late, neither one of us in a hurry to end the magical bubble we found ourselves in where we could speak freely about our feelings and wish for things we both knew couldn't ever be. When it was time to check out we put our clothes back on and walked to the truck, hand in hand. He opened my door for me, but before I could climb in, he brought his hand to my face, slid it back into my hair, and kissed me.

It was a soft kiss and torturously slow. It felt too much like a goodbye.

We drove through the same coffee stand we'd stopped at a few days prior, got some coffee and muffins, and then headed back to his house. We were practically silent the whole way, but I sat in the middle of the bench seat and kept his hand in mine.

When we pulled up to his house he turned off the engine, but made no move to open his door. After a few quiet moments, he turned toward me but kept his face down, looking at our hands intertwined.

"I want you to know I heard what you said last night. I listened and I understand where you're coming from. We have just one day left and I don't want to spend it trying to convince you to consider something more happening between us. So this is the last time I'll mention it." His eyes drifted up and caught my gaze. "Just know that when I drive away from you tomorrow, I'll be hoping to hear from you again."

He gave my hand a squeeze and then climbed out of the truck, leaving me there with a gaping hole in my heart. I'd never felt so torn before in my life. But eventually I pulled myself together and climbed out of the door he'd opened for me, ever the gentleman.

We ate our muffins and drank our coffees on his deck, exchanging mindless chatter about our plans for the day. The conversation was light, but I was thankful for it; to feel a little bit normal for a few minutes. Afterward, we decided to surf a little more. It was warm as afternoon approached, and surprisingly, the frigid ocean didn't seem too intimidating.

We suited up and headed out, spending a few hours laughing like we had the first time. I was able to stand on my board a little better, and I enjoyed watching Briggs flex his proverbial surfing muscles. It was a perfect activity to break the ice between us.

When the heat of the day started to wane, he tugged me from the ocean by my hand, took me back to his house, and led me right up the stairs and into his master bathroom. Laughing, we peeled each other out of our wetsuits, and then quietly made love under the hot water. It wasn't hurried or frenzied, though, it was lazy and thorough. Slow and deep. I thought he was trying to memorize every part of my body with his mouth and hands, and I did the same.

When I came, it was with my mouth open against his, but no sound. Just breaths and thumping of heartbeats. He followed a few moments later, but only with a quiet grunt. He kissed me then, the water trailing down our faces, but we didn't care.

After a few moments, he pulled out, leaving me empty in so many ways, and said, looking down at me with his hands on either side of my neck, "We've got to get ready to go if we're going to get to Porter and Ella's on time."

"Okay," I whispered in agreement.

An hour later we were pulling out of his driveway.

I'd managed to throw together a casual yet flattering outfit, but looked plain and frumpy standing next to Briggs in his tight-in-all-the-right-places jeans, green polo shirt, and boots. The man hardly tried to look attractive but managed to pull it off regardless. I wasn't complaining. Well, not really.

"Do you think we have five minutes to spare so I could pop into the store and grab something for Ella?" I asked, using the fold-down mirror in his truck to swipe some gloss across my lips.

"Like what?"

"I don't know. Flowers, maybe. Or wine if the flowers aren't great. Just something to give her to say thanks for having us over."

"That's a thing?"

"What?"

"You're supposed to bring something when you go over to someone's house for dinner? It's just a barbeque." He looked over at me for just a moment, laughing.

I shrugged. "It's nice to bring the hostess a gift. Plus, I want Ella to like me." I couldn't say the words out loud, but what I meant was, I wanted Ella to like me more than she'd liked his ex-wife. I knew Patrick was his best friend, but it definitely seemed like they'd all met his ex. I needed to leave some sort of lasting impression, wanted them to remember me as the nice woman he'd seen after the mess of his divorce. Plus, Ella was sweet and kind. I could totally see us being friends if our circumstances were different. If my relationship with Briggs was different.

"Ella would like you regardless of whether or not you brought her a gift."

"Okay, but that doesn't change my mind about wanting to bring one." I smiled sweetly at him, and it worked. Of course, I knew it would, so I wasn't surprised when he pulled into the parking lot of the only grocery store in town. He parked and I turned to him.

"You don't have to come in. I'm just going to run in real quick."

"You're going to pick out wine, and I'll pick out some flowers." He tried to sound as if he were irritated by the idea, but I knew better. Knew him better. He wanted to give Ella the flowers just as much as I did.

We were ten minutes late to Ella and Porter's house, but Briggs couldn't find a bouquet he liked enough, so I finally convinced him to go with the bundle of wildflowers. I thought it would suit her. I was right. She melted when he held them out to her, and I could have sworn I heard a quiet growl from Porter. She hadn't even finished smelling them before he'd taken them from her hands and found a vase to put them in. She laughed at Porter, but thanked Briggs warmly.

"You want a beer?" Porter asked Briggs, all signs of irritation gone. He didn't wait for an answer, just pulled two beers from the fridge and handed one to Briggs. "Let's go talk about something manly on the porch."

I couldn't hold in my laughter and neither could Ella, although hers was accompanied by a small eye roll. Porter passed Ella and kissed her right below her ear, making her squeal. My eyes shot to Briggs and caught him staring at me. Before he walked out of the door with Porter he winked at me. I blushed, but tried to keep my reaction under control. It apparently didn't get past Ella.

"So things with Briggs are still going well?" she asked, arranging the wild flowers in the vase Porter had filled with water for her. She kept her eyes on the flowers, but I knew she was absolutely interested in my answer to her question.

"Things are good." I didn't want to give away too much information. My relationship with Briggs was complicated enough, and honestly, I wanted it all for myself. Giving away a piece of what I felt for Briggs was almost painful. There was so little between us as it was; giving parts away tore at me.

"Momma! Andrew is awake!" This came from the dark-haired girl who came running into the kitchen, out of breath and jumping up and down.

"Thanks for telling me, Mattie. Want to help me get him ready for dinner?"

"Yeah!" The little girl continued jumping up and down in excitement.

"First, Mattie, I want to introduce you to my friend." Ella pointed in my direction and the little girl turned around, smiling widely, but calming considerably. "Talia, this is my daughter, Mattie."

"It's nice to meet you," the little girl said, walking toward me with her hand extended in the cutest little greeting ever.

I knelt down so we were at eye-level and took her hand in mine. "It's nice to meet you, Mattie. How old are you?"

"I'm four years old." She told me her age like it was the biggest accomplishment, as though being four were the most important job she'd ever had.

"Wow, you're so big and smart," I replied, smiling.

"Daddy says I'm too smart." Ella laughed behind her daughter.

"Daddy thinks you're too much of a lot of things."

"Andrew wants out," Mattie reminded her mother.

"Want to come meet Andrew?" Ella asked me.

"I'd love to."

I followed behind Ella, who followed behind Mattie, all the way up to the second floor of the tall beach house. As I neared the top of the stairs I could definitely hear a small child squealing from behind a closed door. Mattie pushed the door open and strode into the room without a care and I followed Ella in, pausing just inside the door.

The walls were painted a soft blue, like a cloudless sky, and the room was furnished with all white wood. Crib, chair, changing table, bookshelf—all white. Gray and dark blue accents adorned the room and it was adorable.

"Mama," I heard a voice call, and my eyes were drawn to the chubby-faced little boy bouncing in the crib.

"Hello, baby boy," Ella said in a sweet, mother-in-love voice I'd heard Angela use around her own children. She picked him up and pressed a loud kiss to his round cheek. He giggled and she smiled. "Talia, this is Andrew."

"He's almost two," Mattie supplied, already standing on a little white stool next to the changing table. I was beginning to realize this was a ritual.

Ella picked him up and carried him to the changing table, talking to him with sweet words as she peeled off his clothes and changed his diaper. Every step of the way Mattie was there, taking clothes from her mother and putting them in the hamper and handing her a clean diaper.

"You look like a good helper," I said to Mattie when I caught her eye.

"Mamma says I am going to be a good mommy one day."

"I think she's right."

"One day, twenty or twenty-five years in the future," Ella said with a laugh, giving me a smile.

"Are you a mommy?" Mattie asked me with the innocence only children can obtain.

"Nope, not yet. One day, though, maybe."

"Let's go see what Daddy needs," Ella said, giving Mattie's butt a light tap, urging her off the stool. She then hiked the hefty boy onto her hip, giving his cheek a squeeze. "I can't with these cheeks," she said when she caught me smiling.

"They look irresistible."

I followed them down the stairs, enamored by Mattie and how she seemed to rule the house. She walked right out the sliding door onto the porch and asked her father, "Daddy, do you need anything?"

"Just some love." He bent at the waist and pointed at his own cheek.

Mattie giggled and pressed a kiss to his cheek. His arm whipped out and snatched her around the waist, lifting her off the deck, and he pressed his face into her neck, kissing and tickling her all at the same time. She was giggling uncontrollably and it was impossible to not watch and smile. It was endearing, watching a father with his daughter, in a display of unabashed love and joy. Something squeezed around my heart and my eyes went to Briggs. He was also watching, but I could see a little bit of sadness in his eyes, just beneath the smile. I wanted to go to him, to thread my fingers through his, to show him I was there for him, but I didn't feel as though it was my place.

"Would you like some sangria?" Ella asked, pulling me from my trance.

"Oh, that sounds incredible."

"Here, take him and I'll be right back." She held Andrew out to me and my auntie instincts kicked in. I slid my hands under his arms and brought him to my chest, slipping one arm under his rump.

"Hey there, buddy," I said in my *talking to a baby* voice. I was a stranger to him and there was always the possibility that he would go into stranger danger mode, but all I got from him were big, drooly smiles. "You sure are a handsome boy," I said, bouncing him gently. He was *much* bigger than the twins. Obviously, he was an eater.

"Going to be a linebacker," Porter said from the grill.

Mattie had situated herself at the table, a coloring book and box of crayons all waiting and ready for her.

"I believe it," I said with a laugh. My eyes drifted to Briggs, but his gaze was already on me. Well, me and the baby in my arms. His eyes on me quite nearly knocked all the air from my lungs. It almost hurt, the way he was watching me hold a baby. I knew what he was thinking, because I was thinking the same thing. I was thinking about what it would be like to hold *our* baby. A baby we made because we loved each other and wanted to start a family, to tie ourselves together in a way that rose high above legal documents and verbal promises. Creating a life together would be the ultimate bond. And it was painful to realize that a part of me, and not a small part, wanted to hope for that with him.

"Talia, I'm going to color you a picture," Mattie said from the table. "Do you want a puppy or a butterfly?"

"Um, a butterfly sounds good."

"What's your favorite color?"

"Green," I replied.

She immediately set to sifting through the box of crayons, assumedly looking for the perfect shade of green.

"My favorite color is purple," she said as she continued to dig.

"Light purple or dark purple?"

"Dark. Like a violet. That's my grandma Tilly's favorite color too."

"Purple and green go well together. Can you add some purple to my butterfly?"

"Sure," she replied excitedly.

"Okay, here we go," Ella said, carefully stepping through the sliding glass door with two very full glasses of sangria. She set them both down on the table and then gently took Andrew from me and got him settled in a high chair at the end of the table. After tossing some cheerios on his tray she handed me my drink with a smile. "Cheers," she said, lifting her glass and tapping it against mine. "To summers at the beach."

I smiled and took a sip. It was damn good sangria.

"You got any free time tomorrow, Briggs? I have a few men who could spare a few hours at your house. We could get all the cabinets installed."

Briggs was in the middle of a pull on his beer when Porter asked the question, and I watched as his throat worked to swallow it down. His eyes fell to his feet at about the same time my heart plummeted to the bottom of my stomach.

"Tomorrow's no good. Driving Talia to Portland."

"You're leaving tomorrow?" Ella asked, surprise evident in her voice. "Already?"

"Yeah," I said, forcing a smile on my face. "I was only on vacation for the week. Time to get back to real life."

Briggs took another pull from his beer, but this time he looked angry.

"Oh," she said on a sigh. She sounded surprisingly upset. "When will you be back?" She asked me the question, but looked at Briggs for the answer.

"Ella," Porter said, his tone soft, but it was obviously a warning. "Baby, I need plates for these burgers."

"Okay," she said on a sigh, then stood up and went in the house.

"I'll help," I said quickly, shooting up from my seat, anxious to escape the awkwardness of the deck.

"I'm sorry about that. I wasn't trying to pry," Ella said as soon as we were alone in the kitchen.

"It's okay, there's nothing to pry into, really." I shrugged, trying to pretend like everything was fine. I wanted desperately for everything to be just that—fine. Perhaps if I lied to myself and everyone else enough, eventually it would all be okay.

"So, you and Briggs? You aren't going to keep seeing each other?" Her voice was so full of hope, it surprised me to realize how much Ella was rooting for Briggs and me to figure out our shit. All I could offer her was another shrug.

"It's complicated."

Her expression moved from hopeful to concerned.

"Talia, he's such a good man. I obviously don't know him as well as Megan and Patrick, but I know him well enough to know he'd lay down everything for the right woman." Her words were like alcohol poured on an open wound. There was already a sting buzzing underneath my skin, but her words ripped me open even more. "His ex is a nasty bitch, and he should be so bitter after what she did to him, but I know he's just waiting for someone to come along who'll be there for him."

"You're not saying anything I disagree with. He is a great man. The best I've ever met. But I've got my own issues, too. It's just bad timing, I think."

"Or, maybe, it's perfect timing," she practically whispered. She held my gaze for a moment, but then turned away when it was obvious I couldn't respond.

I helped Ella get what she needed for Porter and then we had a nice dinner. Mattie and Andrew proved to be entertaining and good ice breakers. There were no awkward silences because Mattie filled them all with her four-year-old chatter. And if she wasn't talking, Andrew was squealing, too excited about eating his dinner.

Eventually, the awkwardness melted away, and I shouldn't have doubted it. Ella and Porter were gracious hosts and there was something wonderful about being around them. It was interesting to watch them interact, to see how Porter would anticipate Ella's needs and provide her with whatever she needed before she, herself, even knew. And she was a constant source of comfort to him—that was obvious. She touched him whenever she got a chance. Nothing scandalous, but sweet, gentle, familiar touches. A hand on his forearm, or running her fingers through the hair at his nape. It was innocent but intimate all at the same time.

I found myself longing for that same familiarity with Briggs. I wanted to reach under the table and place my hand on his leg, but I knew it would be misleading. My need to touch him, to reach out and feel that physical connection with him, was overpowered by my head telling me no good could come from it. So we stayed painfully platonic while we spent the evening with Ella and Porter.

Even the ride home was a little uncomfortable. I was still holding back and I didn't know if it was for my benefit, or his, really. As he drove he reached out his hand and took mine, bringing it back to rest on his leg. That was nice, the connection, but what I wanted instead was to climb on his lap and bury my face in the crook of his neck and breathe him in. I wanted to taste him, feel his lips against mine. I wanted to be reminded, because I was afraid I'd already forgotten.

He parked his truck but didn't move right away to get out. Instead, he looked straight ahead, his fingers still laced through mine.

"I can feel you pulling back," he finally whispered. I wasn't brave enough to look at him, though. "We still have this one night and even if tomorrow you walk away and I never see you again, all I want for the next few hours is just to be with you."

I found enough strength to finally look him in the eye and say, "I want that too."

Chapter Seventeen

Briggs

I'd been clear with Talia about what I wanted; both long term and short. I wanted forever with her, but knew she wasn't ready for that. So, instead, I'd settle for one last night. But that didn't mean I wouldn't try my damnedest to show her what she meant to me, but we were beyond words at that point.

I shut my truck door after climbing down and crossed in front of the hood. I could feel her eyes on me as I walked toward her and the awareness of it made my blood run hot. It killed me thinking this would possibly—no, probably—be our last night together.

I opened her door and took her hand, guiding her down to the ground, then threading my fingers through hers, making every connection I could. She leaned into me, resting her cheek against my arm, and I was sure I heard her inhale, taking in my scent.

I unlocked the front door but didn't turn on any lights or even stop to take off my shoes. No, I went straight for the stairs and took her with me. I wasn't going to waste any more time with her. She didn't object and followed me up the stairs eagerly.

Once we were both in my bedroom, I closed the door and gently pushed her back up against it. She let out a surprised breath, but I captured it with my mouth when I closed my lips over hers. Her breath turned into a moan and her hands came up to cradle my face, while my hands grasped her hips and kept her pinned to the back of the door. I pulled back and braced my forehead against hers.

"I'm going to undress you, firecracker, and I'm going to take my time. I'm going to memorize every inch of you, taste every part of you, and I don't care if it takes all night, yeah?"

She nodded, almost frantically, but then said, "Yes," on a breath.

I kissed her again and my fingers slid under the hem of her shirt, just grazing the soft flesh of her stomach. She whimpered and I hardened at the sound. I would miss the noises she made when I touched her. My hands moved up her body and her top came with it. She lifted her arms above her head and allowed me to pull the shirt off, and I watched as her red hair cascaded back down to her shoulders.

My gaze slid lower to the swell of her perfect fucking breasts, watching as they moved up and down with her breaths, almost spilling out of the black lace bra she was wearing just to torture me. I palmed them both and licked the valley between, feeling her breath accelerate with my touch. I watched as her skin flooded with goosebumps and it made my cock strain, knowing I was having an effect on her, that her body responded to my touch that way. My mouth moved up her throat to her neck and when I captured her ear between my teeth she went from excited to frantic.

She gripped my shirt and tried tugging it off, so I pulled it off but then captured her mouth with mine. Her hands moved up from my waist and over my chest, then up to link behind my neck, pressing her body up against mine. Nothing in the world felt better than Talia's body, any part of it, touching me. She hitched one leg up, wrapping it around my hip, and I took the opportunity to press the bulge of my cock against her, hoping to show her exactly how much I wanted her. If she were any other woman, I'd fuck her against the door, but I couldn't give her sloppy and frantic tonight.

I pushed back and let my hands drop to her shorts, unbuttoning them, but never losing eye contact. I unzipped them and she pushed her pelvis forward a bit, giving me space to pull them down her legs, leaving her standing in matching black lace bra and underwear.

Wrapping my hands loosely around her ankles, I took my time sliding them up her calves, then the back of her thighs, stopping at the curve of her ass. When I stood, I lifted her and she wound all her limbs around me with a yelp.

I laid her gently on the bed, stripped off my pants, then crawled over her, letting my eyes take in every part of her. If that was the last time I would get to see her, all of her, I was going to take my time memorizing her.

I cupped one side of her face, trailing my thumb over her bottom lip. "How am I ever supposed to forget how perfect you are?"

She couldn't answer me, just took that bottom lip and pulled it between her teeth. Perhaps she was holding something back. Perhaps if I pressed her about it she'd tell me everything I wanted to hear. But I wouldn't pressure her into that, wouldn't force her into making the decision to be with me. Instead, I planned on using my body, and hers, to make sure she knew when the sun came up tomorrow what she'd be leaving behind.

I pulled the lip from her teeth, then kissed her. Her mouth opened on a moan and I slid my tongue inside, tasting her. I pulled away before I got lost in her mouth; I had other things in mind.

"Flip over," I said, my voice sounding gruffer than normal. Not questioning me at all, she rolled to her stomach and the sight made every last drop of blood in my body head straight for my cock. Her beautiful creamy skin, unmarred and perfect, dusted with freckles, clashed beautifully with the black lace of her underwear. It was the sexiest juxtaposition.

I was normally a breast man. But, Jesus, when she flipped over and I saw a strip of lace nestled between the globes of her ass, it was almost enough to make me lose control.

"Fuck, Talia," I said as I palmed both cheeks. "Give a man a warning next time."

"But then I wouldn't have gotten to hear your reaction."

A laugh rumbled through me at her words, and I realized I was feeling happy and content. Two things I hadn't felt in a while before that night she knocked on my door in a storm, and probably wouldn't feel for quite some time after tomorrow.

My hands slid up and I hooked the thong, pulling it down slowly, groaning as I watched it peel off her ass and down her legs. I tossed it on the floor and then moved to unclasp her bra, kissing her at the nape of her neck as I did. She writhed on the bed, and I knew she wanted to touch me. I wanted that too.

I placed my lips at the small of her back and kissed all the way up her spine, loving the way she moved under me, as though she couldn't get enough of my touch. When I placed a kiss on her shoulder she rolled, her mouth finding mine, and then it was as if we'd ignited. Her hands smoothed over my biceps, then up my waist and around to my back, only to move lower, her fingertips finding their way under the waistband of my boxer briefs. She pushed them as far down as she could reach and then I took over, using my legs and feet to kick them off, never breaking our kiss.

Without words, with nothing between us except longing, need, and perhaps a little bit of hope, she drew her knees up around my waist and I slipped into her.

She was ready for me, wet and perfect, and in the back of my mind I wondered if it would always be this easy with her, this effortless. It had never been that way with anyone else, and I was scared to death it wouldn't be that way with anyone after her either.

I couldn't stop kissing her. The fear that I would open my mouth and say things I shouldn't kept my lips pressed firmly against hers. If I couldn't say the words, I'd show her with my body. So, I did. I made love to her, hoping with every breath and every kiss, she'd realize what she meant to me. She'd hear what I wasn't allowing myself to say and tell me she felt it too.

215

Each time I pushed into her, she'd whimper against me, her hands always touching some part of my body. When I dragged out, inevitably hitting the spot inside her that would make her tremble, she gasped, urging me on with her body.

When I finally found the perfect rhythm to make her splinter and fall to pieces, watching her come undone sent me right into oblivion with her.

Chapter Eighteen

Talia

When the morning came, when the sun beamed through the window of Briggs's bedroom like it had every other morning I'd been there, I was instantly sad. There weren't even a few moments of ignorant bliss or sleepy morning amnesia. Nope. The instant my eyes opened my heart hurt.

Briggs's arm was slung over my waist, his front to my back, and I was securely nestled against him. His breaths puffed out against my shoulder, and he *held* me. He wasn't just sleeping next to me, he was grasping onto me.

I squeezed my eyes shut again, trying to block out reality.

I was leaving today. Leaving this house. Leaving the beach.

Leaving Briggs.

I pushed my face into the pillow, hoping to stave off the inevitable. If I could fall back asleep, I could have a few more hours with him. He must have felt me stir because his arm pulled me even closer and he groaned, the air from his lungs tickling the skin of my neck.

We were both silent for a moment, and I tried to imagine what he was thinking. Was he happy morning had come and I would finally be leaving? Did he still want me to stay? Did he still want something more from me than I could offer? Either way, no matter which direction I went, I would be letting down half of myself. The smart thing to do would be to protect myself, protect my heart, and make sure I wasn't putting myself in jeopardy, even if it was only emotional distress.

But I knew that would be impossible.

Leaving Briggs would break me.

As if he could hear my thoughts his arm lifted from me, freeing me, and I was instantly cold. Instantly empty. Irrevocably sad. The hardest part, though? Knowing I couldn't tell him any of that. He'd try to convince me to stay if I did, try to talk me into moving forward with him. Today it would be hard to resist him.

"Morning," I managed to squeak out.

He groaned again and I could hear what sounded like his hands rubbing his eyes. "Morning," he finally responded after a few quiet moments. "I'm going to hop in the shower real quick so we can head out. Coffee and muffins good for you for breakfast?"

"Um, yeah. Sure." I practically stumbled over the words, his nonchalance at our situation taking me by complete surprise. I wasn't sure what to expect, but normal, absolutely-nothing-wrong Briggs was not it.

"Great. I'll be fast in the bathroom so you can get a shower in too. If we leave early enough we can beat the traffic in the city."

If we leave early enough?

Had I been completely imagining the night before? How tender he was with me? How every movement of his body seemed to be a plea, asking me to reconsider?

That was how the next hour went. Briggs was quiet but polite, and I was going crazy wondering why I was the only one dreading our separation. I packed my duffle bag, trying to remember everything, all the while thinking about how, after everything, he was going to just do a drive by my parents' house and slow down just enough so I could jump out of his truck without getting seriously injured.

218

He carried my bag downstairs, tucking it behind the bench seat of his truck, and helped me climb in even though I was fully capable at that point. He settled into his own seat, buckled up, and let out a big sigh.

"Ready?" he asked, looking over at me.

"As I'll ever be," I replied with a forced smile as my stomach turned.

He drove us silently to the coffee hut and ordered my coffee with familiarity, not even bothering to ask what I wanted. It was what I wanted, though, and that only irritated me more. He handed me my coffee and muffin and I took it silently, not even thanking him. He didn't seem to notice, though.

This was a new feeling for me, especially around Briggs. I wasn't usually petulant, but the idea that my leaving wasn't affecting him at all drove me crazy. I was considering giving him the silent treatment for the entire two-and-a-half-hour drive. But then it occurred to me that it was our last hours together and my irritation with him was overpowered by the realization that our time was up.

We'd been on the highway for about thirty minutes before I finally broke down. Sighing, I turned toward him and spoke.

"Can I be honest with you for a minute?"

Without taking his eyes off the road, he responded, "I hope you'll be honest with me always."

"It's just, well, I'm a little upset that you don't seem to care that this is over," I said, motioning between us. "I know this is what we both knew was coming, but you're being very aloof about the whole thing."

"Aloof?" he said, and I could have sworn I heard him try to hold back a laugh.

I narrowed my eyes at him.

"You're not upset at all? That this is over?"

"Are you?"

"Of course I am!"

"Listen, firecracker, I'm trying to give you exactly what you asked for. You know I don't want to lose you, but I'm willing to give you the space you asked me for. So, yeah, I'm acting like I'm not upset because I thought it would be easier for you that way. But this," he said, waving his hand around in front of him, motioning toward the road, "this is the last thing I want to be doing."

"Well," I said harshly, crossing my arms over my chest. "You could have been a little less chipper about it."

He let out an exasperated breath and out of the corner of my eye I watched him run one hand down his face.

"Come here," he said, finally, after a few minutes of silence.

"What?"

"Come here." He reached out and grabbed my hand, practically dragging me across the bench until I was sitting right next to him. "We've got two hours left and I want you right next to me."

"I'm sorry I snapped at you," I whispered as I let myself relax into him. The difference in how it felt to be just a few feet from him to being in his arms was staggering.

"It's okay, Talia. I'm just as upset as you are." He rubbed his hand up and down my arm, holding me close. It was ridiculous how much better I felt knowing I wasn't the only one anxious about being apart.

"I've had a really great time with you this past week," I said softly, running my hand over his knee, trying to touch him as much as I could.

"Same here, baby," he said against the side of my head.

220

Eventually we slipped into normal conversation, the kind that seemed to only take place during car rides. He told me about his brother and a few stories about his childhood. I regaled him with the tale of my junior prom where my brother punched my date when he caught him groping me on the dance floor.

"It's a brother's duty to stick up for his sister. I would've done the same thing if I ever caught someone's hands on my sister. You know, if I had a sister."

"Hmmm. Macho chivalry isn't dead after all."

He laughed. "It's not chivalry when it's your own sister. It's just, I don't know, instinct. Protect the women in your life. Punch bastards who touch them. Simple." He shrugged as though his statement was common law.

"Okay," I said, trying to change the subject from punching people. We still had another hour left in our drive and I was desperately trying to distract myself from counting down the miles as they passed. "Let's play two truths and a lie."

"I've never played that one."

"It's easy. You list two things that are true and one that's a lie, then the other person has to guess which one is the lie."

"Sounds easy enough. You go first."

"All right, let's see." I tapped my pointer finger on my chin, contemplating what to share. "I'm afraid of spiders, I've never been out of the country, and I'm allergic to mangos."

"Okay, so one of those is a lie?"

"Correct. You have to guess which."

"Well, I think you're probably telling the truth about the spiders—haven't ever met a woman who didn't scream at the sight of a spider. And mango is kind of a weird thing to be allergic to, right? I mean, that's an odd allergy. So, I'm going to guess you're lying about never leaving the country."

221

"I've never had a mango in my life, so I wouldn't know if I'm allergic to them," I say with a smile. "And it's true, I've never been out of the US. Hawaii is the closest I've ever come."

"Not even Mexico? Or Canada?"

"Not even."

"And you're afraid of spiders?"

I shivered involuntarily in my seat. "I loathe spiders."

"Interesting, but not surprising."

"All right, your turn," I said as I pulled one leg up under me, turning to face him. He was smiling and I wanted to remember what he looked like when he was happy.

"Hmm," he said thoughtfully, resting his hand on my thigh and giving it a gently squeeze. "Okay, I hate camping, my nickname when I was a kid was Moo, and my thumbs are double jointed."

I narrowed my eyes at him as I contemplated my options. "I don't want to jump to any conclusions here, but I'm pretty sure if any of your digits were double jointed, I would have figured that out in the last week." His face was like stone and he gave nothing away, just kept driving, eyes on the road. "But, I secretly hope you're telling the truth about camping because, I too, hate to camp." I watched his face for any kind of tell, but there was no reaction at all. "Moo seems like a reasonable nickname." Not even a twitch of his face. "So, I think you're lying about the joints."

His response was to hold up his hand and I watched in horror as he brought the tip of his thumb up and over the back of his hand without the aid of his other hand at all. Then he looked over at me and with a straight face said, "I love to camp."

"Oh my God," I said through laughter. "First of all, don't ever show off that trick with your thumb. It's creepy. Second, I should have known you liked to camp, what with the fires on the beach." I let out a sigh. "So, what's with Moo then?"

He shrugged, putting his hand back down on my thigh, spreading his fingers wide as though he was trying to touch as much of me as possible. "I guess my parents worked really hard on the whole barnyard animal thing when I was a baby and all I said for a few weeks was moo." A smile crept across my face picturing a tiny Briggs toddling around imitating a cow.

Suddenly, I realized we'd only spoken about his parents a little, and he hadn't mentioned much about them. "Where are your parents now?"

"Camping," he said, no fluctuation in his voice at all, face emotionless.

"Seriously, Briggs."

"Seriously. They camp for a living."

"Shut up," I said, laughing and smacking him on the arm.

"When they retired they sold their house and bought a camper. They hop around from campsite to campsite as hosts. I'm not kidding."

"Oh," I said, waving a hand in the air. "I can do a camper."

He laughed and it made something inside my chest open up. I loved hearing him laugh. It was the best sound. That and the way he said my name.

"What did they do before they retired? And if you say camp, I'll kick your ass."

He laughed again and my heart sputtered.

"Mom was a secretary at a high school and my dad was the foreman at a mill in town. The mill shut down, forcing my dad into early retirement, but he and my mom had always been ridiculously frugal. So, they both retired, and now they run campsites together."

"That's really interesting. I didn't even know that was a job people could do."

"It is a little unorthodox."

"But still pretty cool. How long have they been married?"

"Almost forty years now. They met in high school and married right after. Mom was only seventeen."

"Wow." It seemed as though both Briggs and I had been products of couples with good marriages. My whole life I'd wanted what my parents had. Sure, they fought and argued, but they always made up. I watched my father dote on my mother, and I watched my mother go out of her way to make my father happy. I'd always wanted someone I could love like that and someone who cared for me the same way. Perhaps that was what made me complacent. Maybe I wanted what my parents had so badly, I couldn't admit to myself when it became obvious we were lacking something real. "Can I ask you a question that might come across as insensitive or rude?"

"Shoot," he said, eyes still on the road.

"Did you feel like you'd failed at your marriage? I mean, with your parents' marriage as an example, were you disappointed when you realized yours was over?"

"Well," he said at first, but then was quiet for a few moments. Finally, he continued, "Regardless of how long or successful my parents' marriage is, mine failed. I played my part in that, but I definitely don't take all the blame. Do I feel like a failure? Sometimes. But I'd rather end a bad relationship than stay simply because of other people's notions of success. Who's to say divorce isn't a success? I'd feel more like a failure if I stayed with Cecily after everything that happened."

"Were your parents disappointed?"

He let out a sharp laugh. "That Cecily and I divorced? Fuck no. They hated her."

"Really?" I gasped, the drama of it all drawing me in. "Why?"

"Because they could see from the beginning that she didn't love me the way I loved her."

Those words hurt, even though I knew it was completely irrational. Not only did just the idea of Briggs loving someone make my stomach turn, the anger knowing he loved someone so much and that she hurt him, well, it had me feeling a little homicidal.

I let out a breath, trying to push the tension out of my body. "I regret this line of questioning," I said with a sad laugh, trying to lighten the mood in the truck.

"Did your parents like the guy you were with for so long?"

"Yeah," I replied, my tone wavering, "but in their defense, I kept a lot of stuff from them."

"Like?"

"I only told them the good parts. I always made it seem like everything was great. I think normal people complain about their partners on occasion. I never did. Everyone was shocked when it ended. I was too, but as time passed, I understood."

"What were some of the bad parts you kept to yourself?"

"Just that I never felt that all-encompassing love for him, that toward the end he seemed to dislike more about me than he enjoyed, or that we weren't connecting on any level for a long, long time."

He gripped my thigh tighter at my words and I had to look away from him to keep my composure. We'd both been through a lot, and a very large part of my brain was telling my heart to realize that not enough time had passed. The threat of being hurt by Briggs, even if he didn't intend on inflicting, was very real and probable.

A silly get-to-know-you game was making it very clear to me that ending whatever I had with Briggs was the right decision. Even if it made me incredibly sad.

We were both quiet for a while after my depressing statement, but neither one of us moved to disconnect from each other physically. I wanted his touch as long as I could get it, so I never moved out of his reach.

"You're going to want to take the next exit." My voice was low and threatening to break, and my heart started thundering in my chest as our inevitable separation grew closer. He followed my directions and then my parents' house was coming into view. "It's the blue house up there on the right," I said, my voice practically a whisper.

He pulled his truck right up behind my car, put it in park, and killed the engine. Neither one of us moved. In fact, we sat there in silence for a minute or two. Finally, Briggs's hand cupped my cheek and he pulled my face to look at him.

"Hey," he said as his thumb swept over my cheek. "This was the best week of my life, I'm going to miss you like crazy, and I can't wait to drive away from here."

I laughed, but only to keep myself from crying. "I'm guessing that last one is a lie?"

"Your turn," he said, inching closer.

"I wish things were different, I'm going to miss you like crazy, and I definitely could never fall in love with you."

His mouth closed over mine in the softest, most tentative kiss. It was not hurried or even sexy. It was slow. He was kissing me as though he was trying to memorize exactly how it felt to have his lips against mine. It was a new kind of kiss from him. He'd never kissed me goodbye before.

"Have lunch with me," he rasped as he pulled away. "Coffee, anything, just... don't go yet." His pleading voice almost broke me, almost made me stay.

"It's not a good idea, Briggs." It wasn't a good idea because if I stayed with him for even just one more afternoon, I didn't know if I'd have the strength to ever leave. And we both needed that. As much as I wanted him, I knew it wasn't right.

He let out a breath, still holding me to him, then he kissed me one last time. "All right," he said. He broke away from me and opened his door, shutting it behind him. The sound made me jump and the stinging behind my eyes was coupled with the tightening in my throat. I knew I was close to losing my composure. I took a deep breath as he walked around the front of his truck, but when he opened my door I wasn't any farther from a breakdown. He reached his hand out to help me down, but as soon as my feet were on the ground, he let me go. I watched as he grabbed my bag, then closed the door, holding the bag out to me as he leaned back against his truck.

"Well," I said as I took the bag from him, the awkwardness of not knowing how to say goodbye to that man taking over.

"You have my number." His voice was curt, his words short.

227

"Yeah." I rocked back on my heels, trying to delay the inevitable, but then I found some inkling of courage way deep down inside and took a step toward him, letting one of my hands rest on his chest. My eyes found his and I said softly, "It really was the best week."

He didn't respond, just kept looking right into my eyes. I got the message. He wasn't backing down.

I rose up on my toes and pressed my lips to his cheek. I came back down to my feet, but stayed close, wanting so badly to just crawl against him, to nestle into his chest and have him hold me one more time. But he didn't touch me.

"You gotta be the one to walk away, firecracker."

I'd never heard words that hurt as much as those did.

"Okay," I breathed. I didn't need to be told twice. I backed away from him, my hand falling away from his chest, and I looked up again to see his beautiful brown eyes, but he was looking at the ground, avoiding my gaze. Stepping back, I gripped my bag in my hand and made my way to my car, every step pounding up my body from the pavement. No one was home at my parents' house and for that I was grateful. I didn't need an audience, but I did need to get away.

I unlocked my car and climbed in, started the engine, took one last look at Briggs in my rearview mirror, and drove away.

He watched me go until I was out of sight.

Chapter Nineteen

Talia

"What kind of ice cream did you decide on?" Angela's voice was loud through the speaker on my phone, which was sitting on the counter as I ran my ice cream scoop under hot water—a little trick I used to make it easier to dish up ice cream. A girl needed an entire arsenal of tricks to get through a breakup. If there was a way to make scooping ice cream easier, heck, that would save me time every single day. Sometimes twice, depending.

Granted, I wasn't really dealing with a breakup. A breakup required a relationship. Briggs and I hadn't ever been in a relationship. We'd just had sex. Lots of sex. And maybe I caught some feelings for him, but I was trying my damnedest to forget about them. And him.

"I went with chocolate chip cookie dough."

"Ah," she said. "Solid choice."

"Are you partaking in this ritualistic drowning of sorrows in ice cream?" I asked, licking my spoon clean.

"I've got my Neapolitan all dished up, just waiting for the show to start."

"That's just gross, Angela. Neapolitan is the black sheep cousin of the ice cream world. Plus, it's boring."

"It's my favorite," she said indignantly. "Your brother likes it," she added snidely.

"Well, then it's obvious you're a match made in boring heaven." I was joking and she knew me well enough to tell. But I told myself to back off. Angela had been a huge support to me for the last week since I'd seen Briggs. I had gotten in my car and planned to drive all the way home to Bend, but I was only five minutes from my parent's house when I'd finally had a total breakdown. I drove to Angela and Brody's house and luckily they were both home.

They let me in, Brody made a few obligatory brotherly comments about kicking Briggs's ass for hurting me, but then he'd been the perfect brother and husband and taken the babies on a nice long walk so Angela and I could talk. Or, rather, so I could cry and Angela could tell me how everything was going to be okay and how I'd made the right decision.

I ended up sleeping on their couch that night and driving home the next day after stopping to have breakfast with my parents. They didn't ask about Briggs, and I didn't offer any information, but I was sure they could tell by the bags under my eyes that I'd been upset.

I made it home before sunset that day and walked into my empty house and a new wave of sadness rolled over me. All I'd done for the previous twenty-four hours was question my own judgement, worrying about whether or not I'd made the wrong choice.

"Oh, it's starting," she said with excitement.

I grabbed my bowl and my phone and wandered into my living room, plopping down on the couch and pulling a throw blanket over my lap.

"I swear to you, Angela, if that douchebag gives that skank who had sex with him in the hot tub a rose, I'm going to boycott this show altogether."

"You know he will," she said with a laugh.

"I know," I groaned right before shoving a spoonful of ice cream in my mouth.

That was how we spent the next hour of our lives—watching crappy reality television and making our own snarky commentary. And to be completely honest, that was how the last week had gone. I'd go through my day, trying my best to keep my mind occupied, and then at night Angela would call and we'd watch a movie together, or a show, and we'd wallow. Well, I'd wallow and she'd keep me company. We never spoke about Briggs after that first day when he'd dropped me off. She never asked and I never offered up information.

I looked forward to our conversations, but knew she was probably getting tired of checking up on me. She had her own life to deal with.

The show ended, and the douchebag had totally given a rose to the skank he'd banged in the hot tub.

"Why do guys always pick the ones who are the worst for them?"

"Hmmm," she replied, sounding as though her mouth was full, probably with ice cream. "I think men sometimes need women to make decisions for them. Like, they can have all the right feelings and know the best choices, but can't take the reins, you know? So, in that particular scenario, I think he likes that she's forward. He doesn't have to guess with her."

"Men are dumb." I didn't mean that. Not all men were dumb, just some of them.

"This is true. But women can be pretty silly too."

"You mean, like, riding a practical stranger in a hot tub while a major cable channel is filming? That kind of silly?" I hopped up from the couch and made my way to the kitchen to throw away my empty ice cream carton.

Angela laughed. "No, I mean, like, being afraid of happiness. Or, running from a good thing. Leaving a great man behind because a dumb man made bad choices. Punishing themselves for things that weren't in their control. Stuff like that."

I saw right through her words. They weren't veiled very well, anyway.

"Anyone in particular you have in mind?"

"Nope. Just generally speaking."

"Angela..."

"I think I hear the babies fussing. I better go check on them. Talk to you tomorrow."

She hung up before I could say anything more, and that was probably best. I tossed the carton in the garbage and then leaned up against the counter, staring at the screen of my phone.

It had been one week and there hadn't been one tiny peep from Briggs. No phone call, no text, no smoke signals, nothing. Not that I'd been expecting to hear from him, but I couldn't ignore the fact that with every day that passed without word from him, the sadder it made me. He'd been very clear about his feelings and I'd been transparent too. And at the end of the day, I knew the ball was left in my court. I just wasn't sure which game we were playing anymore.

I tapped open my text screen and started typing, but then erased it and started again. I erased that too, and then clicked the light off on my screen and let out a frustrated sigh. I had no idea what to say to him and, furthermore, I didn't know how he'd react if I said anything at all.

I flipped off the lights as I left the kitchen and walked to my bedroom and then continued into my bathroom. I did my nightly bedtime routine and then climbed into bed. My body was ready for sleep, but my brain was still buzzing about Briggs.

I grabbed my phone off my nightstand and brought up another text.

Did I make a huge mistake?

That time I hit send without a second thought and then waited for the response that came just a minute later.

No, I don't think so. You needed time to figure out what you wanted. Did you figure it out yet?

Angela was always the best at giving advice and leading me along. She helped me see the answer to my issues without forcing me to get there.

I sighed and thought about her question.

I think I knew what I wanted before we even left the beach. I'm just really scared. What if I get lost again? What if it doesn't work out and I've molded my life to another man who is just going to leave me broken?

Her response to that took more than a minute, but I wasn't even close to falling asleep, so I didn't mind waiting.

I obviously didn't get to know him as well as you did, but Briggs didn't strike me as the kind of man who'd leave anyone he cared about, let alone allow you to get lost. It seemed to me like he wanted to help you find yourself.

She was right. She was so fucking right.

I think I made a huge mistake.

No, you made the right choice. Now you know for sure.

How'd you get so smart?

Who knows? Maybe it's just a good day. Tomorrow I'll be crazy again. Lucky you.

I am lucky. You're the best sister I could have asked for.

Ditto. Now I don't want to gross you out, but your brother is looking at me like he's going to eat me alive.

Oh, gross. Good night.

I didn't hear back from her, but that was good because it would have been weird. Instead, I lay in my bed, tossing and turning, thinking about Briggs and trying to imagine what he might have been doing. Was he on the beach, sitting around a campfire? Was he working late installing some cabinets in his kitchen? Could he have gone to Tilly's and was currently fighting off women? Or worse, not fighting them off? Taking them home?

I eventually fell asleep, but it was to the images of Briggs with a faceless, busty, blond woman draped all over him.

The next morning, I woke up and my brain gave me about five seconds of peace before more images of faceless women seducing Briggs were tormenting me. I brought my arm up to cover my eyes and tried to talk some sense into my imagination.

Briggs wanted to be with me just a week ago. Surely he hadn't moved on so quickly.

I knew I needed to talk to him, but I wanted a few hours to try and figure out exactly what I expected out of him. I desperately wanted to call him and just hear his voice—I knew it would go a long way to soothe me—but I also knew I couldn't just call him to say hi. He deserved more than that. He deserved an explanation or answers.

I got out of bed and dug my hiking boots out of the closet. Bend was famous for its hiking trails, and it had been a long time since I used any of them. But fresh air and wide-open spaces would do my head and my heart a lot of good. I geared up with boots, a water bottle, granola bar, and sunblock, and drove to my favorite spot along the Metolius River.

There were lots of mountains in Bend, but I preferred hiking along the river—also there was less chances of running into rattle snakes near the water. It was an easier, two-mile hike in with beautiful scenery. The sound of the rushing water was soothing, and after a few minutes I could feel myself start to relax and my mind begin to settle.

I started thinking about the week I'd spent with Briggs and how effortless it was to be with him. I'd only ever been with one man, but it had never been as easy as it was with Briggs. I wasn't naïve enough to believe it would always be so simple, that there wouldn't be bumps along the way, but something told me working at a relationship with Briggs would be rewarding in a way spending my whole life with someone else couldn't compare to.

I wanted to love Briggs. To be with him. Fight with him. Play with him. Laugh with him. Argue, joke, and live with him. Life. I wanted a life with him.

And I'd driven away. Not only that, but driven him away too, in a sense.

I sat down by the river and pulled my phone from my pocket, cursing the wilderness for not providing a cell signal. It would be a little while yet until I could talk to him, it seemed. At least until I got out of the forest and away from this river, closer to civilization. It was a hot day, but the canopy of the trees shaded me well, and there were so many birds singing. It was the most peaceful environment I'd been in since the beach with Briggs. Suddenly I desperately wanted him to see this trail, to hike it with me, to experience my home the way I did.

I stood up, took a drink from my water bottle, and then headed back the way I came, making excellent time back to my car.

Once I was out of the protection of the trees, the sun beat down on me, immediately warming my skin and reminding me how hot a summer in Bend can be. I'd been spoiled with cool beach temperatures and was now reminded of why I bought deodorant in multipacks.

I made it to my car and turned the engine over, cranking up the air conditioner. I plugged my phone into the charger and stared at the screen. My hands were trembling with nerves. I knew I had to call Briggs. It was my turn to go out on a limb for him. Before I could talk myself out of it, or even convince myself I could drive home first, I pulled up his number in my contacts and hit the Send button.

The phone rang a few times and I was torn between hoping it would go to voicemail so I could lob the ball right back into his court, and wanting him to pick it up so I could get it all over with.

The phone clicked and I heard his gorgeous voice say tentatively, "Talia?"

I'd forgotten to breathe, so my lungs were burning, and I finally exhaled and a word flowed out. "Briggs," I breathed.

"How are you? Is everything all right?" Of course his first instinct was to make sure I was okay. He wasn't angry, he wasn't irritated, he was concerned.

"Yeah, everything is fine. I just wanted to, uh, I don't know, call. And say hi." I was a single woman in my early thirties and I couldn't talk to a man on the phone without making an idiot of myself.

"Listen," he said, his voice soft and soothing. "I'm glad you called. I was hoping you would. And there's a lot to talk about, but right now—"

He never got to finish his sentence because he was interrupted by a woman.

"Briggs," I very clearly heard a woman call his name through the phone. "I'm waiting. You said you'd be just a minute." She was whiney and insistent, and I instantly felt ill.

I wished I could have come up with something clever to say, but the truth was I was stunned into silence. I heard a muffled sound, as if he was trying to cover the mouthpiece, but then I heard him answer her.

"I said I'd be there in a minute, Cecily."

"Cecily?" My question came out as the most pathetic squeak and tears I wasn't prepared for spilled down my cheeks.

"Listen, Talia, it's not—"

I didn't hear what he said next because I ended the call.

Chapter Twenty

Briggs

"God dammit, Cecily," I growled, turning on her. She was standing in the doorway of the beach house with an innocent look on her face.

"What?" Her eyebrows bunched and I knew that meant she was irritated with me. I didn't fucking care.

"Get what you need and leave." I grabbed my keys off the counter and started toward her. Smartly, she moved out of my way, stepping backward out of the house and then to the side. I marched past her and made my way to my truck.

As I opened my door to climb in, she cried, "But you said you'd help me load this up!"

I looked at her, trying not to call her every dirty name I'd thought about her in the past year, and simply said, "Get your husband to help you." I started the engine and roared out of the driveway, pointing my truck in the direction of Talia.

As soon as I hit the highway I was dialing her number again and again. The phone rang and rang, then eventually, I was being sent directly to her voicemail, so I knew she'd turned her phone off. No matter. I was going to get to her one way or another. Even if she'd answered her phone and I was allowed to explain, I'd still drive all night just to get to her. She called me, which meant she was ready to talk, and I needed to see her. I needed to touch her and feel her in my arms.

Typical of Talia, my firecracker, she was going to make me work for it.

She didn't want to answer her phone. That was fine with me. I'd find a way to her.

Two hours later, after shaving thirty minutes of the travel time, I pulled up in front of Talia's parents' house. The sun was just setting, so it wasn't too late, but I was still nervous walking up to their door. They could very easily turn me away and tell me to get lost. It was very possible they weren't going to be too keen on giving me their daughter's address, especially if they knew she hadn't given it to me to begin with. But I had to try.

I knocked and then took a step back, shoving my hands in my pockets. The door opened and I was relieved to see Talia's mother. I knew she had a soft spot for me.

"Hello, Mrs. Lennick. I hope I'm not interrupting or disturbing you."

Her eyes went wide with recognition. "Briggs? Is everything okay? Is Talia all right?"

"I'm sure she's fine, but she's not exactly communicating with me right now. Is there any chance I could talk to you for a minute?"

"Of course," she said, still a little confused. She stepped back and opened her door to allow me in and I gave her a small smile, hoping I would eventually win her over. "Let's sit at the table." I followed her into the dining room and she pulled out a chair for me. "Here, you sit. I'll be right back."

I did as she asked and looked around the room. It was bright and cheery with yellow walls and white chair rails. I wondered for a moment if this was the dining room of Talia's childhood. We hadn't really covered childhood homes yet, so I had no idea, but I could picture her sitting at that table doing her homework.

A moment later Lillian came back into the dining room with an enormous tray of cookies and a tall glass of milk.

"Here we go," she said, putting the platter in front of me like it was a snack. She then placed the milk near me and took the seat right next to mine. "So, to what do I owe the pleasure of your handsome face?"

I tried not to blush, so instead I just dove right in.

"There's been a misunderstanding with Talia. She heard something, but she doesn't know what, and I'm afraid she's jumped to conclusions."

"Oh, dear. That Talia, always making trouble where there never was to begin with."

"It's not her fault, really. I would have probably thought the same thing, had the situation been reversed."

"Well, what did she hear?"

I really didn't want to explain this to Talia's mom, but I knew there was only one path to her, and that was it.

"I dropped her off here last week and we left things a little, uh, open-ended. I told her I wanted more and she explained that she needed more time. So I left and told her to call me when she was ready."

"Sounds reasonable."

"Yes, well, she finally called me about two hours ago, and unfortunately, she heard my ex-wife in the background."

"Oh, dear. Yes, I can see why she wouldn't want to talk to you right now."

Damn.

"I just need a chance to explain to her that it wasn't what she's imagining."

"Well, what was it then?" She tilted her head to the side and gave me a withering look.

I swallowed, but my mouth was dry, so I reached out and took a drink of the milk she'd placed in front of me. Then, hoping for the best, I gave her my answer. "With all due respect, Mrs. Lennick, I'd really like to explain it to Talia first."

She stared at me for what felt like forever, but in reality was only a few long moments. Then she sighed and relaxed into her chair. "Talia is her own worst enemy lately," she said as she waved her hand in the air dismissively. "She's so worried about being nothing with somebody, she never took the time to realize that she could be everything with the right someone." She leaned forward and looked in my eyes. "I think you could be good for her, Briggs. So I'm going to help you. What do you need?"

A wave of relief washed over me and my whole body seemed to slump forward. "I just need her address."

"Oh," she cried out in surprise, smiling widely at me. "Is that all?"

"That's all. I'm going to drive to her house tonight and straighten this all out."

"Tonight? It's a three-and-a-half-hour drive to Bend from here."

"That'll give me a lot of extra time to think of exactly the right thing to say to her."

She reached her hand out and covered mine, giving me a motherly pat. "Just make sure you tell her the truth, Briggs."

"Always," I replied with a nod.

Chapter Twenty-One

Talia

I'd spent hours crying. Hours. Even as I sobbed, I tried to convince myself it was dumb to cry over Briggs. It was one week. One week spent with a guy shouldn't make me this emotional when he turned out to be a dick. I was proud of myself when I finally dried up. But the dwindling sadness only made more room for anger.

And I was angry.

Infuriated, even.

I'd cleaned my whole house in an angry rage, scrubbing and swearing, cursing myself for even allowing feelings for him to take root.

By the time I lay in bed, I was stuck somewhere between angry, sad, numb, and disappointed. Disappointed in him for not being who and what he said he was, but also disappointed in myself for even entertaining the idea of a relationship with him.

Who the hell did he think he was? He was asking me to change everything for him, to make room for him in my life, to *change* for him, and then he went back to his ex-wife after one week? *One week?* Suddenly, the rage was back, but I knew stomping around my house and cleaning it again wouldn't satiate it. I needed to yell at him. There was an enormous need to yell every single thought I had at his face. I knew he probably didn't care what I thought or said, but I *needed* to tell him all the terrible things I was thinking about him.

I picked up my phone and was one second away from calling him, but I realized yelling at a phone wouldn't be nearly as therapeutic. Plus, there was a juvenile need to make a scene. And yelling at him in front of Cecily, explaining what had happened between us, well, there was some sort of beautiful redemption in that.

So, I slid my feet into my flip-flops, pulled on a hoodie, grabbed my purse, and opened my front door. Before the door had even closed behind me I was running into a thick, hard, wall of a person.

"Ooofff," I groaned as my hands reached out to balance myself. Arms wrapped around my waist, pulling me up, and I was pulled into a familiar embrace. My body betrayed me for a moment, smelling him, enjoying the feeling of his arms around me, but then my heart stopped, only to thump back to life with anger.

"Steady," he said, his voice familiar and caressing my skin as though he were actually touching me. As soon as I was steady, I pushed myself back from him. He stumbled backward, which gave me a tiny bit of satisfaction, but I kept my steel expression.

"What are you doing here?" I practically spat the words at him.

"I needed to talk to you." He looked exhausted. Terrible, even. Well, good. He deserved to be tired and miserable. "Where are you headed at eleven at night?" His eyes roamed over my body from head to toe, then back up to meet my eyes. "And in your pajamas?"

"Actually," I said, cocking my hip out to the side and crossing my arms over my chest, "I was on my way to see you. I was going to give you a piece of my mind, but seems you saved me the drive." I looked past him at his truck. Everything was bathed in darkness, not even the moon offering a lot of light, but I could tell the truck was empty. "Where's Cecily? I had a list of things I wanted to tell her too. Did you leave her back at the beach house? Is she enjoying the new kitchen?"

"Talia," he said softly, his voice full of pain. He took a step toward me, but I retreated equally.

243

"No," I snapped, holding up my hand. "You don't get to come close to me or say my name." The anger that had been coursing through me just moments ago was melting away and I could feel the sadness coming back. Damn him. "How could you?" I whispered, the tears making their return. "You could only wait six days? Seven was too many? What the hell, Briggs?"

"It wasn't what you think. Let me explain."

"Explain what? Go ahead, tell me what your ex-wife was doing in your house. Tell me why, when I called to tell you that I missed you and wanted to make our relationship work, she was there asking you to come back to bed?"

My words seemed to affect him, but it wasn't anger or hurt I saw in his eyes, it was regret.

"She wasn't asking me to come back to bed. She wanted me to go out to the garage with her. She was never upstairs or anywhere near the bedroom. I swear. Please." He stepped toward me again, but when I stepped back I was pressed up against the door. I had nowhere else to go. "Weeks ago, she'd called and asked if she could stop by to get a storage container she'd accidentally left in the garage. I didn't want any of her shit, didn't even know it was out there, but I wasn't going to keep her from it. She said she was going away for a bit, on her honeymoon, and that she'd stop by when she was back in the States. I told her fine, and I hadn't spoken to her since. She showed up just before you called, without warning, and I just wanted her to get her shit and be gone."

He took another step toward me, closing the distance between us, and my breath caught in my throat. He looked so sad and upset, and there was something deep inside me that was screaming at me, reminding me how much he despised Cecily. Even I had a hard time believing he'd take her back.

"I would've waited forever, Talia," he whispered, stepping even closer, his hand coming up to cup my cheek. I didn't have the strength to stop him. The opposite, actually. I craved his touch, even if half of me was still fighting it. "I didn't invite her in, I didn't ask her to come back to me, and I don't want her. I want you."

My eyes closed at his words, tears streaking down my cheeks.

"Just when I thought I could open up and let you in, I called and heard her voice. It almost killed me, Briggs. I was going to drive to your house and yell at you until, I don't know, you both spontaneously combusted." It wasn't funny, but I laughed a little anyway. Laughed, then cried again.

He stepped closer, closing the rest of the space between us, and I had to look up to meet his gaze. His other hand came up to my other cheek and he used both his thumbs to wipe away my tears.

"I'm so glad you called, but I'm not glad you heard what you did. I'm sorry."

"Is she gone?" I asked, my voice a whisper.

He shrugged. "I'm not sure. I mean, I assume she left. I ran out the door as soon as you hung up on me."

"You did?"

"Yeah," he said, smiling a little. His hands moved down from my face and rested on either side of my neck. "I left her standing in the kitchen."

Suddenly it dawned on me that he was standing outside of my house. "How did you know where I lived?"

"I went to your parents' house first. Your mom says hi. I've got a bag of cookies in the truck."

Then I really did laugh. His eyes bore into me. They were intense and dark, and they still held a question. I brought my hands up to rest on his waist.

"I want to believe you, Briggs. And I do, really. I should have let you explain and I shouldn't have overreacted, but when I heard you say her name..."

"Hey," he said, tilting my head back up and bringing me so close our chests were touching. "I'm here, with you. It's you I want. I can't remember ever wanting anything more than I want you to be with me."

"I'm scared," I admitted in a raspy whisper.

"I know, but I won't let anything happen to you."

"Aren't you scared? Even a little? After everything?"

He shook his head.

"No, I'm not. I'm only afraid that you're going to tell me to leave and that this will be over."

As soon as he said the words, I realized I was afraid of that too.

"Do you want to come inside?"

"More than you know," he rumbled, his voice low and deep. His face dipped low, his lips lining up with mine, and I took in a sharp breath, bracing for his kiss. "Is this all right, firecracker?"

"Yes," I breathed, and then his lips were on mine. He kissed me slowly, but deeply. His tongue pushed through my lips and I moaned in the back of my throat, letting him take my mouth, loving the way it felt so damn familiar and safe. I could have stood there all night kissing him on my porch, but his words broke into my fuzzy reality.

"Let me take you to bed," he said, his mouth still against my lips.

I pulled away and reached behind me, opening the door, then laced my fingers through his and led him to the bedroom.

"I'll give you the tour later," I said just before his lips hit mine again. He walked me backward until my legs hit the bed, and then we were both tumbling down. As soon as his weight was on me, my legs immediately wrapped around his waist, bringing him as close to me as possible. He groaned as his erection met my core, and I gasped along with him.

He was unzipping my hoodie and pulling my shirt up and over my head in a flash. I kicked off my flip-flops and watched as he pulled his shirt over his head in one fluid motion. I shimmied my cotton shorts over my thighs, taking my panties with them. He stood up, unbuttoning his jeans and pushing them down, his eyes locked on mine the whole time. Perhaps it was the fact that five minutes earlier I wasn't sure if I'd ever be with Briggs like that again, but I couldn't get naked quick enough. Even though we both disrobed in record time—me throwing my bra onto the floor and him crawling over me with that sexy and determined look in his eyes—I still needed more.

Without even as much as a word, I let my legs fall open and he closed the distance between us. He came to me and I opened my arms to him, wrapping my ankles around his back as he sank into me. He filled me and let out a groan while my breath shuddered in my chest.

How could I have ever questioned it?

"Fuck," he whispered, his voice raspy and strained. "I missed you so fucking much, firecracker."

"I'm sorry I drove away. I didn't trust myself."

"It's okay, Talia," he said as he pulled out and pushed back in, igniting every nerve in my body, sending shockwaves through my limbs. "Everything's going to be all right, but right now, I need to feel you." Then he silenced me with his mouth.

Chapter Twenty-two

Talia

I registered the arms wrapping around my waist before I even knew I was awake. I thought it was a wonderful dream. Briggs's arms holding me close, nothing but the day ahead of us; surely this wasn't my reality. But when his lips kissed the sensitive area between my neck and shoulder, I started to realize my best dreams might have come true.

"Morning," he said against me.

"Morning." I stretched, my ass hitting his erection, making me smile and him groan simultaneously. I rolled to face him, threading my arms around his waist, curling into him, loving the warmth he offered. Empty beds were dumb. Waking up with Briggs was the best feeling in the world.

"What are your plans for the day?" he asked, pushing my crazy red hair out of my face.

I shrugged with one shoulder. "I don't have any plans. What about you? When do you have to leave?"

"My schedule is pretty flexible." He nudged his nose against my ear, breathing against it, making goosebumps flood the surface of my skin.

"How flexible?" My body arched toward him, seeking contact.

"It just so happens, all my work was in my truck when I left, so if you've got a few hours today to spend grabbing me some basics—a pair of jeans, a few shirts, toothbrush, stuff like that—I think I'd like to stick around and spend some time in Bend."

"You're staying?" I pulled back to look him in the eyes.

"If you'll have me." I let his words sink in, let my heart take them in. He was staying. "I'll need to go home eventually, but I figure I could spend a few days here with you, maybe a week. Unless that's a problem for you?"

"No," I said in a breathy voice. "That's not a problem for me." Then a thought occurred to me. "What about your house? What if Cecily didn't lock it up, or lit it on fire or something?"

He chuckled against my neck, which did wonderful things down below. "I'll call Patrick in a little while and ask him to go check on the house. He's got a key and he's with Megan at the beach." He ended the sentence with a kiss and a lick, dragging his scruffy face along my throat.

"Okay," I squeaked, grasping at him.

Suddenly, much to my dismay, he pulled his face from me and put some distance between us. "Before we get carried away, I want to talk. There wasn't much talking last night after we came inside."

I blushed at his words. "All right. What are we talking about?" I smoothed my hands up his bare chest, hoping to distract him.

"Well, I just want to make sure we're on the same page."

"Which page are you on?" I smiled, knowing I was being a brat.

"I'm on the page where this"—he paused and pointed a finger between the two of us—"is serious and exclusive. Where you're mine and I'm yours and we work at it, all the time."

"You want a long-distance relationship?" I would do anything to be with him, but long distance was hard, and I needed to hear him say he was up for it.

"I want us to be together. There's nothing tying me to the beach house except time. I figure we spend as much time together as we can, get to know each other, start building a life with each other in it, and then when the time comes to sell my house, well, we can decide where to go from there together."

"That sounds serious," I murmured, moving close to him again, feeling as though I was done talking.

"I am serious, firecracker. It could never be casual, never with you. Besides," he said, running his hand into the hair at my nape, "I'm ready for serious. I know you think it's too soon for both of us, but you wanna know what I say to that?"

"What?" I asked, a smile blooming on my face, knowing I was going to like what he had to say.

"I say fuck all that. We get to be happy too."

Epilogue

One Year Later

Briggs

"These kiddos are about ready for bed," Angela said, brushing her hand over Beckett's hair.

"This one's already gone," Brody said, Raina fast asleep in his lap.

"Aw, I'm kind of sad this is their last campfire here," Talia said, the light from the fire casting an orange glow over her freckled skin. Her crazy hair was pulled up into a messy bun and she looked absolutely beautiful—like always.

"There'll be more campfires, babe."

"Not here, though. This was the place they had a lot of firsts."

It was true. Talia's family had spent a lot of time at my beach house over the last year. Sometimes all of them would come down for a weekend, or just a few of them, but Talia was here the most. When it was cold out we'd stay in the house and light a fire in the living room and watch movies curled up on the couch. In the spring, she helped me clean the house from top to bottom and then made decisions about drapes and area rugs, helping me stage the house for the market. During the last month I'd taken her surfing a few times, but we both enjoyed just lazing around on the sand, especially when she wore that red bikini. In June I officially put the house on the market and it only took a few weeks to find a buyer, and now I had exactly one month to find a new place to live.

Talia was excited about the sale, knowing it was what I'd wanted all along, but I could tell the change worried her. As our relationship sailed along we'd hit important milestone just like any other normal relationship: she'd met my parents, we'd gone away for a weekend, we'd had our first big fight, we'd made up more than once, we exchanged keys, and we'd talked about our future together in vague and sometimes not so vague terms.

I knew, from listening to what she'd said and also listening to things she hadn't said, that she wanted to live together. She was hoping that the sale of my house meant we'd move in together and start the next phase of our relationship. I wanted that too, but I also wanted much more.

"Let's get the babies to bed," Angela said.

George and Lillian had headed back to the house an hour before, so when Angela and Brody took the babies back, it left just Talia and me sitting in the sand. I had one knee up and she was sitting in the space between my legs, snuggled in with her head leaning back against me.

"I'm gonna miss this," she said with a sigh.

"The beach isn't going anywhere."

"No, but I'm still going to miss this beach and this house. I know you don't love it like I do, but there've been a lot of good memories at this house."

She was right. I'd told her I loved her for the first time on this beach, sitting around a campfire just like the one we sat around then. It had been a few months after we met and we'd just ended a particularly long spell between visits. Absence had definitely made the heart grow fonder in our case, and being without her only made me realize what I'd already known on some level—that I loved her. She'd cried when I said the words, then kissed me, whispering the words against my lips, making me incredibly happy.

I ran my hand up her arm, trying to soothe her a little. "I know. And you're right. But we can make more memories at other houses."

She titled her head a little to the side and back, her eyes meeting mine. "Yeah?"

"Yeah. I was sort of hoping I could move all my stuff to Bend and then maybe we can look for a house. A new one, where we can get a clean slate and get a fresh start." I watched as her eyes went wide and her mouth dropped open a bit.

"Wait," she said, sounding a little breathless. "Are you saying you want to live together?"

Laughing, I replied, "Yeah, firecracker. What did you think was going to happen when I sold this place?"

"I don't know," she said as she turned around on her knees and wrapped her arms around my neck. "I wanted this so badly, but I didn't know if you were ready or if you even wanted that." She squeezed her arms around me and my hands ran up her back, holding her to me.

"Of course I want it. I want everything with you," I said softly against her ear. I felt her tremble and I knew she was close to tears. That was pretty typical for Talia. Any time I did something sweet she cried about it. And I loved that about her. She never took my affection for her for granted. She was always soaking up the love I gave her, and she returned it tenfold. "So, you're cool with me coming to Bend?"

"Yeah," she squeaked, her head trying to nod against my shoulder, making me laugh.

"Okay, good. 'Cause I was doing it whether you liked it or not."

That made her laugh, so all was good. She pulled back and kissed me hard, and it was difficult to not wrap her legs around my waist and take her one last time by the fire. That had happened once, and once was enough. Sandy sex was checked off my bucket list, but it was not something either of us wanted to relive.

"I've got one more surprise, babe, but you've got to turn back around to get it."

She sat back on her heels and wiped her fingers under her eyes. "Another surprise?" She let out a sigh that sounded a lot like the ones she had after an orgasm. If I hadn't already been hard, that would have done the trick. She smiled at me, then turned around and settled herself between my legs again. "Do I need to cover my eyes?" she asked, laughing.

"Not this time," I said as I tossed a bag of marshmallows, two chocolate bars, and a box of graham crackers in her lap.

"S'mores!"

"I didn't want to break out the good stuff while the kids were here, 'cause I knew Angela wouldn't let them have any."

"Good call," she said, laughing even harder.

I could listen to her laugh for the rest of my life. In fact, that was exactly what I was hoping for.

"Here, hand me a marshmallow."

She opened the bag and popped one in her mouth before handing one back to me. I loaded it onto a skewer and then handed it to her, knowing I only had about thirty seconds to get the rest of it ready because my girl fucking burnt the crap out of marshmallows until they were a black piece of sugary charcoal and that was how she liked her s'mores. And true to form she shoved that fucker right in the flames until it was bubbling and brown, then pulled it out and watched it burn. After a few moments she blew out the flames, then held her hand out like a surgeon and said, "Cracker."

Over the last year we'd nailed our s'mores routine, so it didn't surprise her when I held out a graham cracker for her marshmallow, but the platinum diamond engagement ring sitting atop did make her halt. I held that cracker out, heart absolutely stopped, waiting for her to say something. Or do something. Give me any indication that she wanted to be mine forever. My lungs weren't working and everything had fallen silent. Even the fire stopped crackling. Every bit of my future rested on her shoulders and I wanted more than anything for her to just say yes.

"Briggs," she finally said, her voice so soft I almost couldn't hear her. "What is that?"

"It's a ring, firecracker."

"Okay, but what is it for?"

"It's for your finger."

"Briggs, I'm a woman dangling on the edge here hoping the man she loves is asking her to marry him, so it'd be in your best interest, if that's indeed what you want, to tell me exactly what's going on so we can get to the part where I say yes." She turned, her eyes begging me to do exactly what I'd planned, so I gave her what we both wanted.

"Talia, I've never met anyone who makes me feel as good as you do, who loves me as much as you do, or who makes me want to be worthy of her love like you do. We started on this beach and I wanted to be on this beach when I ask you to be my wife. So, will you marry me and let me love you forever?"

"Yes," she said immediately, eyes shining, mouth smiling. Then she laughed a little and held out her left hand, letting me slide the ring down her finger. It was not two seconds later that she launched herself at me, s'more forgotten, lips crashing into mine. She kissed me deep, giving back to me everything I'd just laid out for her, exactly like I knew she would. "I love you," she whispered onto my lips a few minutes later. "There's nothing on this earth I love more than you." She pulled back and rested her forehead against mine. A few moments later she pulled back farther, her hands framing my face, but her eyebrows drawn together. "That was a dirty trick, Briggs Townsend."

"What was?" I asked with a laugh, loving the way she said my last name and anxious to hear her take it as her own.

"Asking me to live with you as a diversion. You were trying to throw me off."

"Worked like a charm," I said, smiling wide, my hands on her ass.

A slow smile spread across her face. "Yeah, it did."

"You ready for forever with me?" I asked, reaching forward and kissing her softly.

"Yeah." She sighed again, making me want her enough to almost forget we were in the sand.

"I promise I'll spend forever learning who you are, changing with you, and loving every part of you."

"And I'll work every day to give you everything you've ever wanted."

"I know you will, firecracker."

Books by Anie Michaels

The Never Series

Never Close Enough

Never Far Away

Never Giving Up

Never Standing Still

Never Tied Down

Never With You

*The Private Serials*_

The Love and Loss Series

The Absence of Olivia

The Presence of Grace

The With A Kiss Series

Kiss Cam

Riled Up

Stand Alone Novels

The Space Between Us

Instead of You

Acknowledgements

Lesley, Andrea, Danielle, Kelly, Beeca, and Ali – thank you for reading the book early and giving me your valuable input. Betas are so important to the publishing process and I couldn't have done it without you guys. Thank you for loving Briggs.

Andrea and Stefanie – Thank you both for your help with the book in its final stage. I rely on very few special people to help me polish my books and I am so lucky and fortunate to have found help in both of you. I appreciate the time and effort you give up for me and my books and I never want you to think it is taken for granted. Thank you so very much.

I would also like to thank my grandfather who passed away while I was writing this book. I didn't have many reliable or consistent male role models in my life, but you were *always* there for me and everyone else in our family. You were one of the most supportive people and I'll never forget the impact you made on my life.

Lastly, I want to thank all the readers who love the Never series and took a chance on this book and these knew characters. Talia and Briggs were loud from the moment they entered my imagination and even though they're fictional, they're important and needed their story told. Furthermore, Ella, Porter, Megan, Patrick, Kalli, and Riot needed them, too. I had thought the Never gang was complete, but I was wrong. So, if you've been around since the beginning, or are just now starting the series, thank you so much for reading this book.

www.ingramcontent.com/pod-product-compliance
Lightning Source LLC
Chambersburg PA
CBHW020555180626
46810CB00007B/2512